STAKEOUT
ON PAGE STREET
and other DKA files

JOE GORES
(Photograph by Dori Gores)

STAKEOUT

ON PAGE STREET

and other DKA files

JOE GORES

Crippen & Landru Publishers
Norfolk, Virginia
2000

Cover painting by Carol Heyer

Cover design by Deborah Miller

Crippen & Landru logo by Eric D. Greene

ISBN (limited edition): 1-885941-43-9
ISBN (trade edition): 1-885941-44-7

FIRST EDITION

10 9 8 7 6 5 4 3 2 1

*Printed in the United States of America
on recycled acid-free paper*

Crippen & Landru Publishers
P. O. Box 9315
Norfolk, VA 23505
USA

Email: CrippenL@Pilot.Infi.Net
Web: www.crippenlandru.com

For DORI

The Love of My Life

Forever

TABLE OF CONTENTS

INTRODUCTION

I started as an investigator with the L.A. Walker Company in 1955, a few months after I had finished my course work for an M.A. in English lit at Stanford. I was living over Floyd Page's Weightlifting Gym in Palo Alto, California, teaching body building in return for my rent. I knew I wanted to be a writer, but I wasn't good enough to sell anything and I needed money to live on. Teaching was out—your creativity rightly would go to your students. So I was looking for something exciting . . .

An L.A. Walker field agent named Gene Matthews who worked out at Floyd's used to tell wondrous tales of his nighttime adventures thugging cars. I asked if I could ride around with him, and fell in love with the repoman's life. On your own, work all hours, adventure, excitement, even danger—what more could a 23-year-old wanna-be writer hungry for real-life ask for?

Head office for L.A. Walker was in Los Angeles, but David Kikkert ran things in San Francisco out of a second-floor walkup at 1610 Bush Street. I went up to the City to ask him for a job. He said, "No." He said, "College kids don't work out." When I wouldn't go away, he finally took a chance on me, at $275 a month. To his surprise, I worked out.

For a few years, everything was swell: I was having the time of my life and writing on the side. But in 1960, old man Walker died. His sons, who had never been in the repo game, showed up in San Francisco to run things themselves. It was a disaster. Clients were dropping like flies.

In desperation, Dave found rent money for an old Victorian at 760 Golden Gate Avenue that could be converted into an office. It had been an upscale whorehouse in the early years of the 20th century, and was just a block from the apartment house where Hammett's "The Whoozis Kid" takes place. Then Dave got everybody together and said he wanted to form his own repo/P.I. firm, and also had to warn any of us who went with him that David Kikkert and Associates might go belly-up in the first month. Some stayed with Walker, some went with Dave, but DKA was in business.

Meanwhile, a funny thing had happened: I had started to sell my stories. I even joined the Northern California Chapter of Mystery Writers of America. Writing reports of my field work (we carried 50-75 cases at all times, most of them requiring written reports every three days) had taught me how to put the basic who, what, where, when, why and how into my writing that made it compelling to clients and salable to editors. But I sure couldn't make a living on short story sales at $75 or $100 a pop. And I was hooked on the repoman's life.

So I scraped up $1,100 and went partners with Dave. Not just as one of the associates—also as his partner. The other associates were office manager Hiroko Ono, her assistant Ronile Lahti, field men M. J. O'Brien, Floyd Ryan, Isidore "Izzy" Martinez, myself, and Ken Warner. We were the nucleus of the firm. The guts of DKA. Within a year, L.A. Walker had folded and DKA was thriving.

× × ×

In May 1966, Tony Boucher urged me to give a talk about the repo game to the monthly meeting of MWA's Nor-Cal Chapter. I called it "My Gun is Quick But My Aim is Lousy" and I was so nervous I almost threw up in the men's john ahead of time. But it went well: Tony even suggested I pitch Fred Dannay to do a series of procedural stories about a fictionalized DKA for *Ellery Queen's Mystery Magazine*. Fred agreed and I got busy on the first story.

× × ×

Since this would be maybe the first private eye procedural series (Hammett's Op stories had been written before the term "procedural" had been coined), I wanted to make my DKA tales ring true. So I stuck as close to reality as I could.

The real DKA specialized in repossessions, skip-tracing, fraud and embezzlement investigations for financial institutions, auto dealerships, loan outfits, and insurance companies. During the intervening five years, DKA had become the biggest repo agency in the state. We had a staff of skip-tracers, collectors, clerks, typists, a receptionist, a bookkeeper, a shifting number of field men, some 15 field offices (usually one-man) scattered around California, and affiliation with dozens of repo agencies all over the country.

Naturally, that's what the fictional DKA became, too.

In other words, David Kikkert and Associates of 760 Golden Gate became Daniel Kearny Associates of 760 Golden Gate.

Dave became Dan (not literally, but you get the idea).

Hiroko Ono became Kathy Onoda. When Hiro died of a CVA at age 26, so did Kathy (in the DKA File novel *Gone, No Forwarding*).

Ronile Lahti, who succeeded Hiro as office manager, became Giselle Marc —who succeeded Kathy Onoda as office manager.

Ronile started out typing after-school skip-letters for DKA while getting a Masters Degree in history from SF State. Once she decided to forego teaching for DKA, she got her own P.I. license. My fictional Giselle Marc did the same.

Maurice James O'Brien—the best field man in the firm after Kikkert himself, and always just known as O'B—became Patrick Michael O'Bannon, ditto and ditto.

Ex-fighter Floyd Ryan became ex-fighter Bart Heslip.

Sly and tricky Isidore "Izzy" Martinez became sly and tricky Trinidad "Trin" Morales.

Stan Croner, once a VP of Crocker-Anglo Bank, became Stan Groner of Cal-Cit Bank, a regular fixture of the DKA novels.

Ken Warner became Ken Warren, but he came later. He does not appear in these stories at all. Ken had a serious speech defect, and, until *32 Cadillacs*, I couldn't figure out how to use him as a character without seeming to make fun of his impediment. Since that novel, Ken will be always with us.

Larry Ballard became... Well, there was no Larry Ballard with the real DKA. I guess Larry is kind of me. In File #1, he's been with DKA a month, as I had been while working the case that formed the basis of that story. Larry, tall, lean, blond, blue-eyed and hawk-nosed, is certainly not me physically, but from the beginning he has thought like me, reacted like me to the things he does, sees, hears, experiences and learns as a repoman.

Even the most fanciful of these dozen DKA File Stories is based at least loosely on a case I worked, featuring people I worked with or met on investigations. I add a great many fictional twists, I make the characters larger than life at times, but by and large these stories reflect my years at DKA.

File #1 appeared in the December 1967 issue of *EQMM*, File #12 in the March 1989 issue. In between those two stories there were the ten other tales in this book, plus three DKA File Novels: *Dead Skip* (1972), *Final Notice* (1973), and *Gone, No Forwarding* (1976). Since 1989 there have been two more novels, *32 Cadillacs* (1992) and *Contract Null & Void* (1996); a sixth, *Cons, Scams & Grifts*, will be out from Mysterious Press in 2001.

Larry Ballard and Bart Heslip have walk-ons in the non-DKA novelette "Smart Guys Don't Snore" that is reprinted in my collection *Speak of the Devil* (Unity, Maine: Five Star 1999).

And the DKA office at 340 11th Street appears as a disused laundry in my "Dance of the Dead" (*The Armchair Detective*, Vol. 24, No. 2).

× × ×

When I started writing the series in 1966, most of my characters were in their mid-20s. Kearny and O'B were in their early 40s. In the File novel I am working on now, set in our current year of 2000, most of these same characters are in their mid-30s. Kearny and O'B are in their early 50s. To be realistic, everybody should be in their 60s and 70s, because 34 years of real time have passed.

What the hell goes on?

What goes on is a problem faced by every mystery writer who creates a long-term series. Time keeps passing, we as writers keep getting older (if we're lucky) and keep developing and changing (if we're even luckier). But what about our characters? Who wants a 60-something ingenue flashing a less-than-dazzling smile and too much skinny leg? Who wants a dashing hero who has to pop Viagra to hang on to his bubbling blonde bimbos?

Most of us, too, not realizing what we faced down the road, recklessly sprinkled references to well-known world events in our early stories. Wars are really tough to get around later. I made Dan Kearny and O'B World War Two vets—as were Dave Kikkert and the real O'B. Hiroko Ono had grown up in a California Japanese relocation camp during that same war, so of course Kathy Onoda had to, also.

You will find no such time-fixing references in later DKA stories and novels. But not I alone have painted myself into such corners:

The Nero Wolfe stories start in 1934 and end in 1975. In the early ones he refers to a wife in Egypt. In *Over My Dead Body* (1940), a woman in her 20s suspected of murder claims to be Wolfe's daughter. Do the math on *those* factoids.

Travis McGee is a WWII vet and fought at the Bay of Pigs.

Robert B. Parker's Spencer is a Korean war vet.

Ross Thomas' Mac and Padillo started their adventures in post-WWII Germany. Artie Woo and Quincy Durant appear in 1978.

Kinsey Milhone had her first case over a dozen years ago.

Other problems face the series-writer. First, as you get older yourself, your attitudes and interests and physical capabilities change, grow, alter, narrow and fade. It is harder to trigger your readers' willing suspension of disbelief. And unless you are eternally vigilant, the past begins to coat your material with its soft warm patina of nostalgia.

Second, society itself keeps changing (never with such dizzying speed as nowadays). Its structure, its mores, cars, banking hours, salaries, entertainments, communications, the racial makeup of neighborhoods . . . The list is of course endless.

How did these other writers I mentioned deal with these three interwoven streams of time—your own age, society's age, and your characters' ages?

Rex Stout keeps Nero and Archie ageless, while making society contemporary. Archie goes off to war against the Nazis, the Commie menace comes and goes, J. Edgar Hoover becomes one of the bad buys . . . But they remain unchanged. Stout's greatest legerdemain begins with *Too Many Cooks* (1938) and ends with *A Right to Die* (1964). In the first, Paul Whipple is a 20-year old black waiter at a summer spa in the mountains. In the second, he is a successful businessman pushing 50, with a son the age he was in the first. In both books, Nero and Archie are the same age.

In John D. MacDonald's first Travis McGee novel, *The Deep Blue Goodbye* (1964), Trav is a burly beach bum taking his retirement in segments aboard a Florida houseboat. By *The Green Ripper* (1979), while bumming his way around California on a case, he is called "Pops" by the young people he meets. He ages *almost* in real time—but even for the great John D., the Bay of Pigs and WWII had to disappear from the later books.

Robert B. Parker's Spencer is still around, making out with Susan and wise-cracking and beating people up and occasionally killing them. He has aged some since his debut in *The Godwulf Manuscript* (1973), but we hear no more about Korea. And Parker has started two newer series with much younger protagonists.

Most of Ross Thomas's protagonists are a sort of soft-edged 38 when they first appear, then just sort of drift around without being too well-defined. He did three Mac and Padillo novels, then dropped them, did three Artie Woo and Quincy Durant novels, and played games with them. In *Chinaman's Chance* (1978), Artie's twin boys are infants; in *Voodoo, Ltd.* (1992), they are poised to enter Harvard in the fall. Artie and Quincy haven't aged a bit.

Sue Grafton set her Kinsey Milhone character to conquering the alphabet in *"A" Is for Alibi* in 1985; now, 15 years later, Kinsey is still at it but has never gotten out of the late 80s. Kinsey lives in real time, but Sue herself has pointed out that she is now writing what are in essence 1980s period pieces.

I haven't even touched on those master tricksters, Don Westlake and Larry Block. Suffice it that Don, writing under his Richard Stark pseudonym, started the Parker series in 1962 with *The Hunter*, ended it in 1972 with *Plunder Squad*, and restarted it in 1997 with *Comeback*. Throughout, Parker remains the same cold, dark, hard, mean thief we know and love. In *Comeback*, nothing had changed, really not even society, and to hell with all of us.

Larry brought back the burglar, Bernie Rhodenbarr, after a many-year hiatus, but nothing has changed for him, either. Bernie and Carolyn exist in a magic bubble, selling books and washing dogs and burgling away. Larry saved his greatest sleight-of-hand, however, for the Evan Tanner series. Tanner fell off the radar screen in the 1960s. When Larry felt the urge to bring him back in the late 1990s, he cheerfully tells us that Tanner has been cryogenically frozen for 30-some years, and now has been thawed out. Somehow, Larry makes this all work.

✕ ✕ ✕

When I realized (much too late) that the problem existed, I decided to set each new DKA story or novel squarely in the time it was written. The cases my detectives handle, the people they pursue, willy-nilly move against the backdrop of what is going on as I write. Against this ever-shifting backdrop, the DKA crew ages, but *slo-o-o-o-wly*. In the course of 34 calendar years, they have collectively grown some eight to ten years older.

But they do develop and mellow, in their own sloth-slow way. Wives and girlfriends are featured, drop back into the shadows, re-emerge. Dan Kearny's marriage almost collapses, his kids grow up. Giselle takes an occasional lover but eventually dumps him. O'B is finally trying to do something about his boozing. Bart is still an ex-fighter with wins in 39 out of 40 fights (37 by knockout), and Morales is still a son-of-a-bitch. Ken Warren is bulking ever larger in my mind, taking on some sort of mythic quality like the golem of Jewish legend.

And Larry Ballard has developed from a rather lanky even though athletic kid into an expert scuba diver and a black belt in karate. The romantic youth who moons over a lost girl in File #1 is still seeking love in the latest novel, but serially—he moves from lover to lover with restless abandon.

None of this is by *my* design. It just sort of happens. All of my protagonists are very different people than they were back in 1966. They have become more complex characters all by themselves; I can only go where the DKA crew wants to take me.

Come with us.

> Joe Gores
> San Anselmo, CA
> June 2000

FILE #1: FIND THE GIRL

Preface

*When I sent my proposal for this series to Fred Dannay, the half of the
Ellery Queen writing team who was Editor-in-Chief of* Ellery Queen's Mystery
Magazine, *I stressed true-to-life and procedural. Which meant no murders,
because repomen, like other real private eyes, seldom run across murder. It
also meant no guns. During my years in the field, I never carried one. In tight
situations, guns tend to go off, and repos are by definition tight situations. I
sure didn't want to shoot someone over a car. Or get shot by someone. So, no
murder, no guns. Not in the short stories.*

*Since these were procedurals, I thought I had to make them quasi-
documentary in tone. So I conceived the idea of a time-line to run across the
top of each scene in the story. The first words of "Find the Girl" are: Tuesday,
May 23rd; 8:15 a.m.*

*The time-lines are missing from the second story, "Stakeout on Page
Street," have a brief encore in the third, "The Three Halves," and then disappear forever. By then I had realized that they added little and interfered with
the flow of the narrative.*

"Find the Girl" is the most procedural of all the stories, as Dead Skip, *the
first File Novel, is the most procedural of the long forms. And for the same
reason: up to a point, both are true, based on single real cases, because I
needed the crutch of the familiar. I felt that if I could write them as if I were
reporting on fieldwork actually done on a real case, I would be all right.*

*The only totally fictional element I introduced into "Find the Girl" was
Larry Ballard, the central investigator in the case and truly a "green pea"—he
has been with DKA a month when the story opens. Larry has no real-life
counterpart among the real DKA crew. Except me, of course.*

*Thus, "Find the Girl" unfolds just about as it did in real life, even to
Ballard's confrontation with Kearny at the end. Because I had only been with
DKA's predecessor, the L.A. Walker Company, for a month at the time I was
handed the file, I had a like confrontation with Dave Kikkert at the end of the
real case.*

With the same results.

FILE #1: FIND THE GIRL

Tuesday, May 23rd: 8:15 a.m.

Larry Ballard was halfway to the Daniel Kearny Associates office before he remembered to switch on his radio. After a whine and a blast of static, O'Bannon's voice came on loudly in mid-transmission.

". . . Bay Bridge yet, Oakland 3?"

"Coming up to the toll plaza now. The subject is three cars ahead of me. I'll need a front tail once he's off the bridge, over."

"Stand by. KDM 366 Control calling any San Francisco unit."

Ballard unclipped his mike and pressed the red TRANSMIT button. "This is SF-6. My location is Oak and Buchanan, moving east, over."

"Oakland 3 is tailing a red Comet convertible across Bay Bridge, license Charlie, X-ray, Kenneth, 8-8-1. The legal owner, California Citizens Bank on Polk Street, wants car only—contact outlawed."

Oakland 3 cut in: "Wait by the Ninth and Bryant off-ramp, SF-6."

"Control standing by," said O'Bannon. "KDM 366 clear."

O'Bannon set down the hand mike on Giselle Marc's desk, leaving it flipped to MONITOR. He was a wiry red-haired man about 40, with twinkling blue eyes, freckles, and a hard-bitten drinker's face.

"Who's SF-6? The new kid?"

"Right. Larry Ballard. With us a month yesterday." Giselle was a tall lean blonde who had started with DKA as a part-time file girl while in college; after graduation two years before, she had taken over the Cal-Cit Bank desk. "He's a green pea but he's eager and maybe—just maybe—he can think. Kathy's putting him on his own this week."

O'Bannon grunted. "The Great White Father around?"

"Down in his cubbyhole—in a vile mood."

O'Bannon grimaced and laid his expense-account itemization on her desk with great reverence. Giselle regarded it without enthusiasm.

"Why don't you do your own dirty work, O'B?" she demanded.

Same day: 10:00 a.m.

Ballard was lanky, well-knit, in his early twenties, with blue eyes already hardened by his month with DKA. He was stopped, by Dan Kearny himself, at the top of the narrow stairs leading to the second floor of the old Victorian building that housed the company offices.

"That Comet in the barn?"

"Yes, sir," said Ballard.

"Terrif. Any static?" Kearny was compact and powerful, with a square pugnacious face, massive jaw, and cold grey eyes which invariably regarded the world through a wisp of cigarette smoke.

"I front-tailed him from the freeway. When he parked on Howard Street, Oakland 3 and I just wired up the Comet and drove it away."

Kearny clapped Ballard's shoulder and went on. Ballard entered the front office, which overlooked Golden Gate Avenue through unwashed bay windows. Three assignments were in his basket on the desk of Jane Goldson, the phone receptionist with the Liverpool accent: through her were channeled all assignments, memos, and field reports.

Carrying the case sheets, Ballard descended to the garage under the building. Along the right wall were banks of lockers for personal property; along the left, small partitioned offices used by the seven San Francisco field men. He paused to review his new cases before leaving.

The most puzzling one involved a new Continental, financed through Cal-Cit bank, which had been purchased by a Jocelyn Mayfield, age 23. She and her roommate, Victoria Goodrich, lived at 31 Edith Alley and were case workers for San Francisco Social Services. What startled Ballard was the size of the delinquent payments—$198.67 each—and the contract balance of over $7000. On a welfare worker's salary? Even though her parents lived in the exclusive St. Francis Woods area, they were not cosigners on the contract.

From his small soundproofed office at the rear of the garage Dan Kearny watched Ballard leave. Kearny had been in the game for over half of his 43 years, and still hadn't figured out the qualities which made a good investigator; only time would tell if Ballard had them. Kearny jabbed an intercom button with a blunt finger.

"Giselle? Send O'Bannon down here, will you?"

He lit a Lucky, leaned back to blow smoke at the ceiling. O'B had come with him six years before, when Kearny had resigned from Walter's Auto Detectives to start DKA with one car and this old Victorian building which had been a bawdy house in the '90s; and reviewing O'B's expense accounts still furnished Kearny with his chief catharsis.

He smeared out the cigarette; through the one-way glass he could see O'Bannon approaching the office, whistling, his hands in pockets, his blue eyes innocent of guile. When he came in Kearny shook out a cigarette for himself and offered the pack. "How's Bella, O'B?"

"She asks when you're bring the kids for cioppino again."

Kearny indicated the littered desk. "I'm two weeks behind in my billing. Oh . . . this expense account, O'B." Without warning his fist smashed down in sudden fury. "Dammit, if you think . . ."

O'Bannon remained strangely tranquil during the storm. When Kearny finally ran down, the red-headed man cleared his throat and spoke.

"Giants leading three-two, bottom of the third. Marichal—"

"What do you mean?" Kearny looked stunned. "What the—"

O'Bannon fished a tiny transistor radio from his pocket, then apologetically removed miniature speakers from both his ears. Kearny gaped.

"You mean—while I—you were listening to the ball game?"

O'Bannon nodded dolorously. Speechless with rage, Kearny jerked out the expense-account checkbook; but then his shoulders began shaking with silent laughter.

Same day: 9:30 p.m.

Larry Ballard parked on upper Grant; above him, on Telegraph Hill, loomed the concrete cone of Coit Tower, like a giant artillery piece about to be fired. Edith Alley ran half a block downhill toward Stockton; Jocelyn Mayfield and her roommate, Victoria Goodrich, had the lower apartment in a two-story frame building.

The girl who answered the bell wore jeans and sweatshirt over a chunky figure; her short hair was tinted almost white. Wide cheekbones gave her a Slavic look.

"Is Jocelyn here?" Ballard asked.

"Are you a friend of hers?" Her voice was harshly attractive.

Ballard took a flier. "I was in one of her sociology classes."

"At Stanford?" She stepped back. "Sorry if I sounded antisocial. Sometimes male clients get ideas, y'know?"

He followed her into the apartment. "You must be Vikki—Josie has mentioned you. You don't act like a social worker."

" 'Say something to me in psychology'? Actually, I was a waitress down in North Beach before I started with Social Services."

There were cheap shades at the windows of the rather barren living room, a grass mat on the floor, a wicker chair and a couch, and an ugly black coffee table. The walls were a depressing brown. It was not a room in keeping with monthly automobile payments of $200.

"We're going to repaint eventually," Vikki said. "I guess."

Ballard nodded. "Has Josie mentioned selling the Continental?"

"The Continental?" She frowned. "That belongs to Hank—we both use my Triumph. I don't think he wants to sell it; he just got it."

"Hank, huh? Say what's his name and address? I can—"

Just then a key grated in the front door. Damn! Two minutes more would have done it. Now the subject was in the room, talking breathlessly. "Did Hank call? He wasn't at his apartment, and—"

"Here's an old friend of yours," Vikki cut in brightly.

Ballard was staring. Jocelyn Mayfield was the loveliest girl he had ever seen, her fawn-like beauty accented by shimmering jet hair. Her mouth was small but full-lipped, her brows slightly heavy for a girl, her brown liquid eyes full-lashed. She had one of those supple patrician figures maintained by tennis on chilly mornings.

"Old friend?" Her voice was low. "But I don't even know him!"

That tore it. Ballard blurted, "I'm—uh—representing California Citizens Bank. We've been employed to investigate your six-hundred dollar delinquency on the 1967 Continental. We—"

"You dirty—" The rest of Vikki's remark was not that of a welfare worker. "I bet you practice lying to yourself in front of a mirror. I bet—"

"Vikki, hush." Jocelyn was blushing, deeply embarrassed. Vikki stopped and her eyes popped open wide.

"You mean you did make the down payment on that car? It's registered in your name? You fool! He couldn't make a monthly payment on a free lunch, and you—" She stopped, turned on Ballard. "Okay, buster. Out."

"Vikki, please." Then Jocelyn said to Ballard, "I thought—I had no idea the payments—By Friday I can have all the money."

"I said out, buster," Vikki snapped. "You hear her—you'll get your pound of flesh. And that's all you'll get—unless I tear Josie's dress and run out into that alley yelling rape."

Ballard retreated; he had no experience in handling a Vikki Goodrich. And there was something about Jocelyn Mayfield—private stock, O'Bannon would have called her. She'd been so obviously let down by this Hank character; and she had promised to pay by Friday.

Monday, May 29th: 3:30 p.m.

Jane Goldson winked and pointed toward the office manager's half-closed door. "She's in a proper pet, she is, Larry."

He went in. Kathy Onoda waved him to a chair without removing the phone from her ear. She was an angular girl in her late twenties, with classical Japanese features. Speaking into the phone her voice was hesitant, nearly unintelligible with sibilants.

"I jus' rittre Joponee girr in your country verry littre time." She winked at Ballard. "So sorry too, preese. I roose job I . . . ah . . . ah so. Sank you verry much. Buddha shower bressings."

She hung up and exclaimed jubilantly, "Why do those stupid S.O.B.'s always fall for that phony Buddha-head accent?" All trace of it had disappeared. "You, hotshot, you sleeping with this Mayfield chick? One report, dated last Tuesday, car in hands of a third party, three payments down —and you take a promise. Which isn't kept."

"Well, you see, Kathy, I thought—"

"You want me to come along and hold your hand?" Her black eyes glittered and her lips thinned with scorn. "Go to Welfare and hint that she's sleeping around; tell her mother that our investigation is going to hit the society pages; get a line on this Hank no-goodnik." She jabbed a finger at him. "Go gettem bears!"

Ballard fled, slightly dazed as always after a session with Kathy. Driving toward Twin Peaks, he wondered why Jocelyn had broken her promise. Just another deadbeat? He hated to believe that; apart from the Mayfield case he was doing a good job. He still carried a light case load, but he knew that eventually he would be responsible for as many as 75 files simultaneously, with reports due every three days on each of them except skips, holds, and contingents.

The Mayfield home was on Darien Way in St. Francis Woods; it was a huge pseudo-colonial with square columns and a closely trimmed lawn like a gigantic golf green. Inside the double garage was a new Mercedes. A maid with iron-grey hair took his card, returned with Jocelyn's mother—an erect, pleasant-faced woman in her fifties.

"I'm afraid I'm not familiar with Daniel Kearny Associates."

"We represent California Citizens Bank," said Ballard. "We've been engaged to investigate certain aspects of your daughter's finances."

"Jocelyn's finances?" Her eyes were lighter than her daughter's, with none of their melting quality. "Whatever in the world for?"

"She's six hundred dollars delinquent on a 1967 Continental."

"Indeed?" Her voice was frigid. "Perhaps you had better come in."

The living room had a red brick fireplace and was made strangely tranquil by the measured ticking of an old-fashioned grandfather's clock. There was a grand piano and a magnificent Oriental rug.

"Now. Why would my daughter supposedly do such a thing?"

"She bought it for a"—his voice gave the word emphasis—"man."

She stiffened. "You cannot be intimating that my daughter's personal life is anything but exemplary! When Mr. Mayfield hears this—this infamous gossip, he— He is most important in local financial circles."

"So is California Citizens Bank."

"Oh!" She stood up abruptly. "I suggest you leave this house."

Driving back, Ballard knew he had made the right move to bring parental pressure on Jocelyn Mayfield, but the knowledge gave him scant pleasure. There had been a framed picture of her on the piano; somehow his own thoughts, coupled with the picture, had made his memory of their brief meeting sharper, almost poignant.

Same day: 5:15 p.m.

Dan Kearny lit a Lucky. "I think you know why I had you come back in, Ballard. The Mayfield case. Are you proud of that file?"

"No, sir." He tried to meet Kearny's gaze. "But I think she broke her promise to pay because this deadbeat talked her into it."

"You took a week to find that out?" Kearny demanded. "Giselle found out that the subject walked off her job at Welfare last Friday night—took an indefinite leave without bothering to leave any forwarding address."

Kearny paused to form a smoke ring. He could blast this kid right out of the tank, but he didn't want to do that. "I started in this game in high school, Ballard, during the Depression. Night-hawking cars for Old Man Walters down in L.A. at five bucks per repo—cover your own expenses, investigate on your own time. Some of those Oakies would have made you weep, but I couldn't afford to feel sorry for them. This Mayfield dame's in a mess. Is that our fault? Or the bank's?"

"No, sir. But there are special circumstances—"

"Circumstances be damned! We're hired to investigate people who have defaulted, defrauded, or embezzled—money or goods—to find them if they've skipped out, and to return the property to the legal owner. Mayfield's contract is three months delinquent and you spin your wheels for a whole week. Right now the bank is looking at a seven-thousand dollar loss." He ground out his cigarette and stood up. "Let's take a ride."

Later, ringing the bell at 31 Edith Alley, Ballard warned, "This Victoria Goodrich is tough. I know she won't tell us anything."

Vikki opened the door and glared at him. "You again?"

Kearny moved past Ballard so smoothly that the girl had to step back to avoid being walked on, and they were inside. "My name is Turk," he said. "I'm with the legal department of the bank."

She had recovered. "You should be ashamed, hiring this person to stir up trouble for Josie with her folks. Okay, so she's two lousy payments behind.

I'll make one of them now, and next week she can—"

"Three payments. And since the vehicle is in the hands of a third party, the contract is void." He shot a single encompassing look around the living room, then brought his cold grey eyes back to her face. "We know Miss Mayfield has moved out. Where is she living now?"

"I don't know." She met his gaze stubbornly.

Kearny nodded. "Fraudulent contract; flight to avoid prosecution. We'll get a grand-theft warrant for her seven-thousand dollar embezzle—"

"Good God!" Vikki's face crumpled with dismay. "Really, I don't know Hank's addr—I mean I don't know where she's gone. I—" Under his unwinking stare, tears suddenly came into her voice. "His wife's on welfare; he's no damn good. Once when he'd been drinking he—he put his hands on me. I guess she's with him, but I don't know where."

"Then what's Hank's last name?"

She sank down on the couch with her face in her hands and merely shook her head. Ignoring her, Kearny turned to Ballard. "Sweet kid, this Mayfield. She steals the woman's husband, then a car, then—"

"No!" Vikki was sobbing openly. "It isn't like that! They were separated—"

Kearny's voice lashed out. "What's his last name?"

"I won't—"

"Hank what?"

"You've no right to—"

"—to throw your trashy roommate in jail? We can and we will."

She raised a tear-ravaged face. "If you find the car will Josie stay out of prison?"

"I can't make promises of immunity on behalf of the bank."

"His name is Stuber. Harold Stuber." She wailed suddenly to Ballard. "Make him stop! I've told everything I know—everything."

Kearny grunted. "You've been most helpful," he said, then strode out. Ballard took a hesitant step toward the hunched, sobbing girl, hesitated, and then ran after Kearny.

"Why did you do that to her?" he raged. "Now she's crying—"

"And we've got the information we came after," Kearny said.

"But you said to her—"

"But, hell." He called Control on the radio. When Giselle answered, he said, "Mayfield unit reportedly in the hands of a Harold Stuber—S-t-u-b-e-r. Check him through the Polk Directory." He lit a cigarette and puffed placidly at it, the mike lying in his lap.

"The only listing under Harold Stuber shows a residence at 1597

Eighteenth Street; employment, bartender; wife, Edith."

"Thanks, Giselle. SF-6 clear."

"KDM 366 Control clear."

Driving out to Eighteenth Street, Ballard was glad it had been Vikki, not Jocelyn Mayfield, who had been put through the meat grinder. Vikki wasn't soft, yet Kearny had reduced her to tears in just a few vicious minutes.

The address on Eighteenth Street was a dirty, weathered stucco building above the heavy industrial area fringing Potrero Hill. It was a neighborhood losing its identity in its battle against the wrecker's ball. Inside the apartment house, the first-floor hall wore an ancient threadbare carpet with a design like spilled animal intestines.

"Some of this rubbed off on your true love," remarked Kearny.

Ballard gritted his teeth. Their knock was answered by a man two inches over six feet, wide as the doorway. His rolled-up sleeves showed hairy, muscle-knotted arms; his eyes were red-rimmed and he carried a glass of whiskey. He looked as predictable as a run-away truck.

Kearny was unimpressed. "Harold Stuber?"

"He don't live here no more." The door began to close.

"How about Edith Stuber?"

The hand on the door hesitated. "Who's askin'?"

"Welfare." When Kearny went forward the huge man wavered, lost his inner battle, and stepped back. The apartment smelled of chili and unwashed diapers; somewhere in one of the rooms a baby was screaming.

"Edie," yelled the big man, "coupla guys from Welfare."

She was a boldly handsome woman in her thirties, with dark hair and flashing black eyes. Under a black sweater and black slacks her body was full-breasted, wide-hipped, heavily sensual.

"Welfare?" Her voice became a whine. "D'ya have my check?"

"Your check?" Kearny's eyes flicked to the big man with simulated contempt. He whirled to Ballard. "Johnson, note that the recipient is living common-law with a Caucasian male, height six-two, weight two-twenty, estimated age thirty-nine. Recipient should—"

"Hey!" yelled the woman, turning furiously on the big man, "if I lose my welfare check—"

Kearny cut in brusquely, "We're only interested in your legal spouse, Mrs. Stuber."

Her yells stopped like a knife slash. "You come about Hank? He ain't lived here in five months. When he abandoned me an' the kid—"

"But the Bureau knows he gets in touch with you."

"You could call it that." She gave a coarse laugh. "Last Wednesday he come over in a big Continental, woke us—woke me up an' made a row 'bout Mr. Kleist here slee—bein' my acquaintance. Then the p'lice come an' Hank, he slugged one of 'em. So they took him off."

Kearny said sharply, "What about the Continental?"

"It set here to the weekend, then it was gone."

"What's your husband's current residence address?"

She waved a vague arm. "He never said." Her eyes widened. "He give me a phone number, but I never did call it; knew it wouldn't do no good." Behind her the baby began crying; the big man went away. Her eyes were round with the effort of remembering. "Yeah. 860-4645."

Back in the agency car, Kearny lit a cigarette. "If it's any consolation, there's the reason for her broken promise. He gets busted Wednesday night, gets word to Mayfield Thursday, on Friday she quits her job. Saturday she sees him at the county jail, finds out where he left the car, drops it into dead storage somewhere near his apartment, and holes up there to wait until he gets out. Find her, you find the car."

"Can't we trace the phone number this one gave us?"

Kearny gestured impatiently. "That'll just be some gin mill."

The next day the Mayfield folder went into the SKIP tub and a request went to the client for a copy of the subject's credit application. Skip-tracing began on the case. The phone number proved to be that of a tough Valencia Street bar. DKA's Peninsula agent found that Stuber had drawn a thirty-to-ninety-day rap in the county jail, the heavy sentence resulting from a prior arrest on the same charge. Stuber said he still lived at Eighteenth Street and denied knowing the subject. A stakeout of the jail's parking lot during visiting hours was negative.

Police contacts reported that the Continental had not been impounded, nor was it picking up parking tags anywhere in San Francisco. Stuber had no current utilities service, no phone listing. The time involved in checking dead-storage garages would have been excessive. By phone Giselle covered Welfare, neighbors around the Edith Alley and Eighteenth Street addresses, the subject's former contacts at Stanford, Bartender's Local Number 41, all the references on the credit application. Ballard supplemented with field contact of postmen, gas station attendants. newsboys, and small store owners.

None of it did any good.

Thursday, June 9th: 7:15 p.m.

Ballard was typing reports at home when his phone rang. He had worked thirteen cases that day, including two skips besides Mayfield; it took him a few moments to realize that it was her voice.

"What have I done to make you hate me so?" she asked.

"I'm all for you personally, Josie, but I've got a job to do. Anyway, if I let up it just would mean that someone else would keep looking."

"I love him." She said it without emotion—a fact by which she lived. "I love him and he said he would leave me if I let them take his car while he's—away. I couldn't stand that. It's the first thing of beauty he's ever possessed, and he can't give it up."

Ballard was swept by a sudden wave of sympathy, almost of desire for her; he could picture her, wearing something soft, probably cashmere, her face serious, her mouth a pink bud. How could Stuber have such a woman bestowed on him, yet keep thinking of a damned automobile? How could he make Jocelyn see Stuber as he really was?

"Josie, the bank objects so strongly to Stuber that they've declared the contract void; as long as he had possession, they'd hold the account in jeopardy. Surrender it. Get him something you can afford."

"I couldn't do that," she said gravely, and hung up.

Ballard got a beer from the refrigerator and sat down at the kitchen table to drink it. After only one meeting and a single phone conversation, was he falling for Jocelyn Mayfield? He felt a deep physical attraction, sure; but it wasn't un-satisfied desire which was oppressing him now. It was the knowledge that he was going to keep looking for the car, that there was no way to close the case without Jocelyn being badly hurt emotionally.

Friday, June 17th: 10:15 a.m.

"If I see her mother once more, she'll call the cops," Ballard objected. "Stuber gets out June twenty-ninth. We could tail him—"

"The bank's deadline is next Tuesday—the twenty-first," said Kearny. "Then their dealer recourse expires and they have to eat their loss—whatever it is. Find the girl, Ballard, and get the car."

The intercom buzzed and Jane Goldson said, "Larry's got a funny sort of call on 1504, Mr. Kearny. She sounds drunk or something."

Kearny gestured and stayed on as Ballard picked up. The voice, which Ballard recognized as Jocelyn's, was overflowing with hysteria.

"I can't stand it any more and I want you to know you're to blame!" she cried. "My parentsh hate me—can't see Hank on weekends 'cause I know you'll be waiting, like vultures—sho—I did it." She gave a sleepy giggle. "I killed myself."

"You're a lively sounding corpse," said Kearny in a syrupy voice.

"I know who you are!" Surprisingly, she giggled again. "You made Vikki cry. Poor Vikki'll be all sad. I took all the pillsh."

Kearny, who appeared to have been doodling on a sheet of scratch paper, held up a crudely printed note: Have Kathy trace call. Ballard switched off, jabbed Kathy's intercom button. Please God, he thought, let her be all right. What had brought her to this extremity?

"I'll trace it," rapped Kathy. "Keep that connection open."

He punched back into 1504. "—Ballard's shoul when I die—lose car, lose Hank, sho—" Her singsong trailed off with a tired sigh; there was a sudden heavy jar. After a moment a light tapping began, as if the receiver were swinging at the end of the cord and striking a table leg. They stared at one another across the empty line.

The intercom buzzed, making Ballard jump. Kathy said, "469 Eddy Street, Apartment 206, listed under Harold Stein—that'll be Stuber. The phone company'll get an ambulance and oxygen over there. Good hunting."

Ballard was already out of his chair. "It's a place on Eddy Street—we've got to get to her!"

As they rocketed up Franklin for the turn into Eddy Street, Ballard said, "We shouldn't have hounded her that way. Do you think she'll be all right?"

"Depends on how many of what she took. That address—between Jones and Leavenworth in the Tenderloin—crummy neighborhood. The nearest dead-storage garage is around the corner on Jones Street. We can—hey! What the hell are you doing?"

Ballard had slammed the car to a stop in front of a rundown apartment building. "I've got to get to her!" he cried. He was halfway out the car door when Kearny's thick fingers closed around Ballard's tie and yanked him bodily back inside.

"You're a repo man, Ballard," he growled. "That might not mean much to you but it does to me, a hell of a lot. First we get the car." Ballard, suddenly desperate, drew back a threatening fist. Kearny's slaty eyes didn't flicker; he said, "Don't let my grey hairs make a coward of you, sonny."

Ballard slumped back on the seat. He nodded. "Okay. Drive on, damn you."

As they turned into Jones Street, a boxy white Public Health ambulance wheeled into Eddy and smoked to a stop on the wrong side of the street. At the garage half a block down, Kearny went in while Ballard waited in the car. Why had he almost slugged Kearny? For that matter, why had he backed down?

Kearny stuck his head in the window. "It's easy when you know where to look." He laid a hand on Ballard's arm. "On your way up there call Giselle and have her send me a Hold Harmless letter."

Ballard circled the block and parked behind the ambulance. On the second floor he saw three tenants gaping by the open door of Apartment 206. A uniformed cop put a hand on Ballard's chest.

"I was on the phone with her when she—fainted."

"Okay. The sergeant'll wanna talk with you anyway."

She was on the floor by the phone stand, her head back and her mouth open. Her skin was very pale; the beautifully luminous eyes were shut. A tracheal tube was down her throat so that she could breathe. The skirt had ridden high up one sprawled thigh, and Ballard pulled it down.

"Is she—will she—"

The intern was barely older than Ballard, but his hair already was thinning. "We'll give her oxygen in the ambulance." He opened his hand to display a bottle. "Unless she had something in here besides what's on the label, she should be okay."

Ballard glanced around the tiny two-roomer. There was a rumpled wall bed with a careless pile of paperbacks on the floor beside it; he could picture her cooped up there day after day, while her depression deepened. Above the flaked-silver radiator was a large brown water stain from the apartment upstairs; it was a room where dreams would die without a whimper.

Ballard backed off; instead of talking to the detective in charge he would call her folks so that their own doctor could be at the hospital to prevent its being listed as an attempted suicide.

That afternoon DKA closed the file on the Mayfield case. She was released from the hospital a few days later and returned to 31 Edith Alley. Without really knowing why, Ballard went over there one Tuesday evening to see her; she refused to come out of the bedroom, and he ended up in the living room, drinking tea with Vikki Goodrich.

"She's grateful for what you did, Larry. But, as far as anything further—" She paused delicately. "Hank Stuber will be out tomorrow." She paused again, her face suddenly troubled. "She's going to surprise him and pick him up in my Triumph; he doesn't know about the Continental. After that I guess she'll be—well, sort of busy."

Leaving the apartment, Ballard told himself that ended it. Yet he sat behind the wheel of his car for a long time without turning the ignition key. Damn it, that didn't end it! Too much raw emotion had been bared . . .

Thursday, June 30th; 8:15 a.m.

Each short journalistic phrase in the *Chronicle*, read over his forgotten restaurant eggs, deepened his sense of loss, his realization that something bright in his life had been permanently darkened.

Police officers, answering a call late last night to 31 Edith Alley, were greeted by Miss Victoria Goodrich, 24, a case worker with San Francisco Social Services. The hysterical Miss Goodrich said that her roommate, Jocelyn Mayfield, 23, and Harold P. Stuber, 38, had entered the apartment at eight p.m. Stuber had been drinking, she said; by ten p.m. he had become so abusive that he struck Miss Mayfield. According to Miss Goodrich he then departed, and Miss Mayfield locked herself in the bathroom.

At eleven p.m. Miss Goodrich called for police assistance. They broke down the locked door to find Miss Mayfield on the tile floor in a pool of blood. Both wrists had been slashed with a razor blade. The girl was D.O.A. at San Francisco General Hospital. Stuber, an unemployed bartender who was released only yesterday afternoon from the county jail, is being sought on an assault charge.

Ballard thought, I've never even seen the son-of-a—I could pass him on the street and not even know it. He felt a sudden revulsion, almost a nausea, at his own role in the destruction of Jocelyn Mayfield. Half an hour later he slammed the *Chronicle* down on Kearny's desk.

"Stuber said he'd leave her if we took the Continental while he was in jail. He left her, all right."

Kearny looked at him blandly. "I've already seen it."

"If we hadn't taken the car—"

"—she would have killed herself next month or next year over some other deadbeat. She was an emotional loser, Ballard, a picker of wrong men." He paused, then continued drily, "It's the end of the month, Ballard. I'd like to review your case file."

Ballard dropped his briefcase on the littered desk. "You know what you can do with your case file, Kearny? You can take it and—"

Kearny listened without heat, then reached for his cigarettes. He lit one and sneered, through the new smoke, "What will you do now, Ballard—go home and cry into your pillow? She's going to be dead for a long long time."

Ballard stared at him, speechless, as if at a new species of animal—the square pugnacious face, the hard eyes which had seen too much, the heavy cleft chin, the nose slightly askew from some old argument which had gone beyond words. A long slow shudder ran through the younger man's frame. Work—that was Kearny's answer to everything. Work, while Jocelyn Mayfield lay with a morgue tag on her toe. Work, while scar tissue began its slow accretion over the wound.

All right, then—work. Very slowly he drew his assignments from the briefcase. "Let's get at it then," he said in a choked voice.

Dan Kearny nodded to himself. A girl had died; a man had had his first bitter taste of reality. And in the process DKA bought themselves an investigator. Maybe, with a few more rough edges knocked off, a damned good investigator.

FILE #2: STAKEOUT ON PAGE STREET

Preface

In "Stakeout on Page Street" I was trying to fictionally combine three real elements: staking out a parked car; the tensions between black and white in our nation at the time; and The Haight-Ashbury District during San Francisco's Summer of Love—flowers in the hair, and all that. The Haight, then, was a colorful and outré scene that was still relatively unknown outside San Francisco.

In real life, I had spotted the car off the hot-sheet after learning it had been picking up parking tickets on Clement Street. I had also learned that the cops were after this dude as a child molester—in the parlance of the day, a "dicky-jerker." This guy liked 'em young, eight, ten years old. (I had to make the boy into a girl and increase her age to 15 to keep Fred Dannay from having a heart attack when he read the story.)

We knew where the car was, but we didn't know where the subject was. And we couldn't ask around about him for fear it would get back to him. We wanted to help the cops, but if they grabbed him in the car, they would impound it and we would miss our repo. If we grabbed the car, on his return he would know something was wrong and would rabbit.

So I staked out the car for 27 hours straight. If he came back to it, I had to finger him for the cops in such a way that they would grab him on the street while I was grabbing the car.

This stake-out did not occur in The Haight-Ashbury in the late '60s, but a decade earlier in the Richmond District near Golden Gate Park (his favorite kid-hunting grounds). Neither of the real cops was a racist: I created Mac-Lashlin as a foil for Bart Heslip. And I made the subject black so Bart would have to deal with a racist cop at the same time he had to deal with a black man gone bad enough to give the cop an excuse to hold on to his racism.

Benny Nicoletti, the good-guy cop, went on to appear in a couple of the DKA novels as an old friend of Dan Kearny's; indeed, he plays a pivotal role in Gone, No Forwarding.

The title is an obvious homage *to Raymond Chandler's "Pickup on Noon Street."*

FILE #2: STAKEOUT ON PAGE STREET

Barton Heslip carried their drinks over to his rather broken-down couch and switched off the floor lamp; the streetlight outside, filtered through ancient lace curtains, was kinder to the apartment. Lou Rawls was soulin' from the record player.

"What you put in these drinks, honey?" Corinne's black eyes gleamed suspiciously from her heart-shaped face, less black than his. She was strikingly pretty, with high cheekbones and a wide warm mouth. Heslip could feel her body heat through the knobbly weave of her suit.

"Bourbon, baby. Just bourbon."

"It tastes more like kerosene."

"I didn't notice you offering to kick in for the bottle, baby."

She giggled and burrowed into the crook of his arm. "Bart, how come you to ever quit fighting?"

"I looked in the mirror one morning and heard those angel wings flapping. Ears getting thick, scar tissue forming around the mouth." He shrugged. "I decided that was all she wrote."

He tightened his arm around her shoulders and she came to him urgently, face raised, lips parted, eyes burning hungrily.

The phone shrilled.

After the fourth ring Heslip groaned and padded on stockinged feet across the room, moving with the easy grace of the trained athlete. His exaggerated breadth of shoulder and depth of chest made him seem much bigger than his 158 pounds. He was almost plum-black, with kinky hair and the inevitable thin mustache. His tight-clipped head seemed too small for the muscular column of his neck.

"Yeah?" he growled into the phone.

"Bart? Larry Ballard. Listen—"

"You listen, cat; it's past two thirty in the Sunday ayem."

"Bart, I spotted this car from the skip list and tailed it until the guy parked. 1965 Dodge Dart, green, license Baker, X-ray, Eddy, 1-9-9. But you see, my skip list is a month old, and I thought—"

Heslip's face was that of a boxer just before the bell. His voice was thin with excitement. "Was a Negro cat driving it? Young stud about our age, maybe with a chick who has long black hair?"

"Yeah. He was a Negro. She went into an address on Page Street, in The Haight-Ashbury, and he took off walking."

"You cut back to that car and take out the coil wire so it won't start—but *don't* move the car. It's registered to a Gloria Jensen, and the cat is Floyd Matthews. Wanted by the cops for statutory rape. If he knew we'd caught up with the car, he'd think the cops had, too, and he'd cut out. Oh, and you'd better call Mr. Kearny at home on the radio.

"Two thirty in the morning?"

"He'll know how to contact the cops handling the case. I'll be in my car in five minutes; radio your location." He started to hang up, then added, "You should have taken out the coil wire *before* you called me."

He padded into the bedroom, unmindful of the girl on the couch. If the car was gone—Larry had been a Daniel Kearny Associates' field agent for only three months; Heslip had been with DKA three years. Larry had ridden with him as a trainee, and a close friendship had developed between them.

Heslip riffled through his SKIP folder, found the Gloria Jensen assignment. Delinquent seven months, now being handled on a contingent basis; they would be paid for their investigation and their expenses only if the vehicle was recovered. A voice brought him up short.

"Hey, lover boy, you disremember something?"

"Huh?" Then he laughed and crossed to the couch and switched on the floor lamp. Corinne Jones slammed her highball glass down on the coffee table bitterly.

"I didn't mean no damned floor lamp, lover. I meant *me*."

Heslip, flipping through the mass of reports and memo carbons stapled face-out to the back of the assignment sheet, spoke without looking up. "Sorry, honey, but this is a hot one and—"

"Lover, you got a hot one right here." Then she also laughed; it was deep rich laughter which lit up her whole face. "I swear, Barton Heslip, once we're married you're gonna get yourself a new job."

"I like this one, honey."

He sat down on the couch to lace his shoes. It was an old argument between them, but O'Bannon assured him it was one carried on as a running dialogue between every married field investigator and his wife. Something had chased the laughter from Corinne's face.

"And I s'pose here goes our picnic tomorrow—today, rather."

Heslip was pulling on his dark windbreaker. "This'll just take a couple of hours. You get some sleep, I'll be right back."

She grunted and uttered a very distinct Anglo-Saxon noun as he waggled his fingers at her and slid through the front door, out into the chill San Francisco morning, just three minutes after hanging up the phone. The narrow, high-shouldered old Victorian houses seemed drawn up against the cold Pacific mist. Down in the Bay the foghorns were bawling at one another. He coaxed his company Plymouth into life, flicked on the radio, and drove toward The Haight-Ashbury.

The radio blared unintelligibly. He adjusted the squelch and Ballard's voice came in: "SF-6 calling SF-3. Come in, Bart."

Heslip depressed his mike's red TRANSMIT button. "Go ahead."

"Affirmative on that coil wire; my 10-20 is Page and Cole. I have instructions from Mr. Kearny, over."

"Tell me when I get there," said Heslip. "SF-3 clear."

It was nearly three a.m., but The Drug Store coffeehouse on Haight and Masonic was jammed with teens and post-teens, juveniles up to forty years old; white, black, and brown; bearded, long-haired, miniskirted, ponchoed; acid-heads, pot-blowers, freak-outs; the tuned-in, turned-on, dropped-out, unwashed hippies of The Haight-Ashbury. Psychedelphia.

Two years before, the district had been scheduled for a bisecting freeway; the hippie head-count had risen as the rents had fallen. Heslip didn't know what the subject and Matthews were doing there, since he had turned up their liaison only this past Friday; the cops didn't have it yet. This put DKA in the enviable position of being able to do a favor for the police, which never hurt.

He identified Ballard's Ford on the corner of Page and Cole by its tall whippet aerial. A spark glowed carelessly from the front seat as he drove by, parked on Cole, and walked back.

When he opened the door, Ballard said, "The Dart's two up from the corner, across Page—in front of that VW bus painted all those screwy colors. She's in 1718 Page, at the far end of the block."

Heslip punched him lightly on the arm. "I could see your cigarette when I came up the street."

"Not from that apartment—I've kept it cupped in my hand."

Ballard was a lean man, conditioned like a basketball player, his hard blue eyes oddly at variance with his mid-twenties face. He was dressed in slacks and a white shirt and a windbreaker. Heslip went into his detachable accent, which was useful in getting information from newly arrived southern Negroes who would mistrust a well-spoken black man nearly as much as they would a white one.

"What if de *boss* man come up de street *be*hin' de car an' see dat cigarette like Ah done, huh?"

Ballard shrugged and grinned. "What do you expect at three in the morning? Saul Panzer? Dan says an Inspector Benny Nicoletti will be here to stake out the apartment, and you're supposed to stake out the car. Apparently Matthews is a travel agent for the hippies."

"A pusher, huh? Visit heaven on a sugar cube." "Which would explain their presence in The Haight-Ashbury; this was obviously his market area. "You gonna hang around for the fun?"

"Can't. I was leaving for Eureka when I spotted the Dart; I've got to be there at noon to pick up that black '67 T-Bird for Cal-Cit."

"Better split, cat; you got close to six hundred miles, half of 'em dragging a tow. You did a damned good job of spotting on this Dart." He opened the door as Ballard started the engine. The street was totally deserted. "What does the subject look like?"

"Black hair worn long and pressed flat. Miniskirt and white stockings with knit designs. Heavy three-color sweater. Wild figure, but I didn't get a look at the face."

"Where's the coil wire?"

Ballard brought it out from under the seat and Heslip stuck it in his jacket pocket, and watched Ballard out of sight. Then he sauntered across Page and past the green Dodge Dart. Man! He'd wanted this car for five months, and here it was.

He kept right on, past 1718 Page—a tiny frame building with an empty store on the ground floor, a single apartment above. Its pale green paint was flaking. Next to the building was an alleyway stuffed with boxes of trash and super-market bags full of garbage. None of the windows in the twin bays had drapes or shades. No lights showed anywhere.

A black Mercury stopped on the corner of Clayton and a heavily built man in his early forties got out to block Heslip's way. He wore slacks and sports shirt with a screaming herringbone jacket that would have made him look like a Fillmore Street pimp, except he was white.

"Benny Nicoletti," he introduced himself. He had a surprisingly high, squeaky voice, and his face missed meekness only by the eyes. They were cop's eyes. He stuck out a hand and Heslip took it. "I met you at Dan Kearny's."

"Sure," said Heslip. "Good to see you again."

A sandy-haired giant, a full head taller than Heslip, came around the back of the car. His jaw jutted, his eyes were muddy and utterly flat, like twin pools of stagnant water.

"This is my partner, Sandy MacLashlin," said Nicoletti. "Bart Heslip, Mac. Dan Kearny's man."

MacLashlin nodded without removing his hands from his pockets. He was chewing on a toothpick. Heslip drew back his own hand quickly, annoyed with his own slight anger at MacLashlin's snub.

"I hear this Matthews got a white chick with him." MacLashlin had a flat-planed, savage face. "Any white girl shacks with a boog . . ." His eyes were intense on Heslip's face; he spat noisily into the gutter.

"You sure she's still living with Matthews?" said Nicoletti.

"She was Friday, when I got the lead." Heslip's voice was sullen.

Nicoletti nodded. "We'll try to take him on the street, Bart, so we don't have to impound the car. You got an eyeball of him?"

"No, just of the girl, from the guy who spotted the car."

Walking away, Heslip found that his hands were fisted at his sides like rocks gathered for a stoning. Remember, baby, he's just a little old hater. Maintain cool. But in the car he slammed his fist into the dashboard several times. Oh, how he wanted to open up the side of that MacLashlin's jaw like a can of tomato sauce and spread those big white Mr. Charlie teeth around.

Time passed without a person moving on Page Street, not anyone at all. Twice a prowl car went by. It was getting light. At six thirty MacLashlin appeared, walking down Cole. Even giving him fifty pounds, Heslip decided, he could take the big man. He'd won 39 out of 40 fights, 37 by K.O.; in the service he'd fought all the way up to heavy just to find opponents, and he still worked out three times a week. MacLashlin opened the door to hike in his solid backside, tossing away a chewed toothpick.

"Little bar up the street here, The Alpine, opens at six a.m." He belched. "I gotta spend my Sunday waiting for some boog to show up, may as well enjoy myself, huh, Heslip?"

"Whatever you say, Inspector." Heslip stared straight ahead.

"You sure this Matthews isn't a friend of yours?" When Heslip didn't respond, he leaned closer; his grin was sour with cheap bar whiskey. "Bet you make it with the white chicks, huh?" His tone harshened. "Matthews made it with some runaway fifteen-year-old while she was high on pot. White girl from Piedmont. Rich folks. They signed the complaint."

Heslip met the muddy eyes. "Maybe you plan on having him resist arrest a little bit if he shows up?"

MacLashlin nodded judiciously. "Maybe something like that."

"I'm here to repossess a car, Inspector."

"*Keep* it that way."

Heslip watched him out of sight. He slid lower in his seat and breathed deeply to relax, to thrust MacLashlin from his mind. When would Matthews be back? Larry had done a damned good job spotting that car. Good man, Larry. Had almost quit over the Mayfield case two months ago, but Mr. Kearny—

His door was wrenched open, nearly spilling him into the street. Dan Kearny's cold gray eyes were regarding him from a yard away.

"Nice nap, Heslip? Eight o'clock. They shoot sentries for that."

"Just dozed off this second, Dan." He shot a surreptitious look at the Dart. "The girl's still in 1718 Page, and the car is right—"

"I saw it." Kearny had climbed in; he leaned forward to punch the dash lighter. He was a stocky, compact man with a flattened nose, thinning curly hair, and a jaw to crack gravel. As he'd done for three years, he offered a cigarette; Heslip refused it as he'd done for three years. Pungent smoke filled the car.

"Nicoletti's partner is riding me, Dan. Hard."

Kearny looked up sharply. His face was square and pugnacious and his eyes were chipped from flint.

"If you're going to start something, do it on your own time."

"Nothing like that." But Heslip knew he wasn't sure. He went into his dialect routine. "Boss, Ah sure as hebbin thought this yere *was* ma own time. Ah mean, it bein' de *Lawd's* day an' all dat."

Kearny started to grin. "Quit clowning. Do you think this stakeout will nail Matthews?"

"I think I should just ask her when he's coming back. Hell, if he's pushing pot and acid in The Haight-Ashbury, Dan, she's used to spade cats coming around to make buys."

Kearny drew thoughtfully on his cigarette, then nodded and stubbed it out in the ashtray. "Right. I'll go talk to Benny about it."

Heslip waited. You had to hand it to Kearny. Seven years before, at 36, he'd founded DKA with one car, a field man named O'Bannon, an old Victorian building on Golden Gate Avenue which once had been a bawdy house, and a Japanese secretary named Kathy Onoda who now was office manager. By specializing in frauds, defalcations, and embezzlements—and in the recovery of the chattels or money involved—Daniel Kearny Associates blanketed the state of California.

Page Street was waking up. A Spanish woman went by with a small girl, obviously going to Mass. Three hippies went by, just as obviously not going anywhere. Their steps were languid, their violently unconventional dress merely another sort of conformity. Long greasy hair and unkempt beards; an ancient poncho, a red-lined evening cape, a serape; dirty ski cord trousers; two pairs of boots, one set of thonged leggings; tiny jingling bells on one ankle and golden hoops in pierced ears. Heslip was invisible to them: he was with it, cool, he dug, because black cats always were with it, cool, and dug.

Kearny returned. "Benny says wait until ten o'clock, and see him afterwards so he knows what happens. MacLashlin didn't like it."

"He's afraid I'll tip off the Jensen chick to the stakeout."

Kearny nodded and went away.

Foot traffic increased; a few cars went by Sunday-slow. His rearview mirror was twisted so he could see the Dart without turning. Two old duffers appeared in it, standing on the corner in the sun with their arms folded on their chests. One of them gestured at a group of passing hippies.

"Look at 'em," he said aggrievedly. "They don't do nothing. All day they don't do nothing. They walk up and down the street." He thought for a moment. "They don't do as much as *I* do, and I don't do nothing."

Heslip rolled up his window, locked the car, and crossed Page Street. The VW bus behind the Dart had Idaho license plates and was a sunburst of red, yellow, tan, brown, orange, blue (two shades), black, and green rectangles of varying sizes. On the back was an ornate red and gold sign, *Make Love Not War*, and on the side was painted the single purple word, *Rejoice*. A pilgrim newly arrived in Mecca. They descended on The Haight-Ashbury in droves, seeking free love, symbiotic relationships, acid, pot, and the ultimate turn-on that would congeal mankind into a quivering jelly of love.

Heslip lifted a lip unconsciously. You made it on your own, baby, or you didn't make it.

Four small Negro kids were sprawled across the sidewalk like the spokes of a wheel, their hub an open comic book. A middle-aged white woman emerged from a well-kept apartment house to glare at Heslip, sniff at the children, and flounce down the street. On the next stoop three Negro women exclaimed over a box of candy; behind them a white man in bedroom slippers cursed some electric doorbell wires he was twisting with a linesman's pliers.

The stairwell to 1718 Page was smeared with small dirty handprints. Heslip knocked firmly on the door at the head of the stairs. A white girl opened it. Gloria Jensen. Her file said 26 but she looked 35. Her eyes were pouched, her black hair filmed and lifeless; the broken-bottle scar on her cheek was recent enough to have been a gift from Floyd Matthews.

Three years before she would have been truly striking; now only the full, ripe body thrusting out against her striped sailor's jersey and hip-huggers made any pretense at youth. Her bare feet were gray with ancient dirt.

"You want who, dad?" Her intonation and voice-timbre were an unconscious copying of Negro speech patterns.

"Floyd here?" He broadened his vowels into, "Flauid heayh?"

She moved back from the door, conned. "Like what's the gig?"

"I'm *Re*joice." He accented the first syllable of the word he'd borrowed from the VW bus. "*Re*joice Jackson. My—" He checked suddenly, suspiciously. "Okay to talk?"

"Like sure. Come on in, man, but Floyd's not here, y'know?"

There were no rugs, no curtains, no stove, no refrigerator, no furniture apart from a wooden table and two chairs, one leaning up against a wall at a disconsolate angle. Two mattresses were side by side under a dirty swirl of sheets like old mashed potatoes. For decoration there were several bright, mildly pornographic "psychedelic" posters in the hippie style of Wes Wilson and The Family Dog.

Heslip took the sturdier-looking chair, the girl the other. On the table stood a typewriter with manuscript paper piled beside it.

"Word is that Floyd's a cat with good acid," he said cautiously.

"Like he'll be back in an hour. We gotta be cool, the fuzz want bust him on a 226B." Her face became indignant. "Bum rap, y'know? She like begged him. We've got some speed, and some real gone grass at ten dollars a lid, but acid—" She shook her head.

Speed: dexedrine, benzedrine, methedrine. Grass: marijuana. Favored "head" drugs of the hippies, who scorned heroin, opium, barbiturates, alcohol, and tranquilizers as "body" drugs which were depressants, turning the user off rather than on.

"I need acid, man, like twenty tabs at least." Two thousand milligrams of lysergic acid diethylamide, eighty bucks' worth; plenty to interest a small-time retail pusher like Matthews. He added, "Say, Floyd doesn't have a connection for the Big H, does he?"

"He wouldn't *touch* the Heavy, Rejoice. He just wants to help people turn on." She gestured proudly at the typewriter. "He turned me on to acid because I'm a writer, y'know?" Her nervous fingers were weaving febrile air pictures. "He gave me a tab right in this room. I started freaking freely, I could hear him talking but my mind was going out and coming back between his syllables, like fly casting, y'know? I'd read Huxley, I wanted it to be the *writing* experience, like an experiment sort of thing, y'know?"

Her face and voice had become agitated; she hugged herself abruptly, as if she were cold. "But I just wasn't capable, y'know? I mean Floyd said I was coming out with these great things, these great insights, but it just wasn't *me*." She was silent for a long moment, then she shuddered. "It was a bad trip. Since then I just blow pot."

Heslip stood up abruptly, filled with pity. "Yeah. Like, ah, gotta trip around a little, dig? Maybe I run into Floyd, I dig him by what he's wearing y'know?"

"Sure. Ah—Kelly green ski cords and a like olive-green velour shirt with short sleeves. I mean very distinctive."

Emerging into bright sunshine was like leaving the smells of a sickroom: the slightly fermented sweetness of pot, ill-disguised with incense; the sharp urinous reek of a toilet carelessly unflushed for a week; the acrid chalkiness of spilled milk, soured on cabinet tops. As he often did after catching up with a bad skip, Heslip had a sense of unreality: he knew more about Gloria Jensen than her mother, probably more than the wig-picker she'd consulted in 1966 . . . whom she'd sat behind in eleventh-grade English; her graduate sociology grades at Berkeley; the doctor who'd been supplying her with birth-control pills since her Tijuana abortion the year before; which garage had an unsatisfied $42.38 repair lien on the Dodge Dart.

He sat down on the steps of an old Victorian, out of sight of the apartment, and waited until Inspector Nicoletti walked up to join him.

"Matthews is expected back by noon. Wearing green ski cords and a short-sleeved olive-green velour shirt. Whatever the hell that is."

"My wife was talking one day, said it looks like a cheap velvet," said Nicoletti in his deceptive squeak. "Think she burned you?"

"No chance. I know the type—civil rights, pot, social protest."

"I just bet you do." MacLashlin had left the stakeout car; his eyes were bloodshot and his breath reeked of stale whiskey. "Why'd you take so long up there, Heslip?"

Heslip let it pass.

MacLashlin belched suddenly, explosively. "This boy a pusher like we heard?"

"I wouldn't know about that, Inspector."

MacLashlin turned to his partner. "I think he burned the stakeout to her, Benny. I think I'd better go up there and sniff around."

"She'd make you as fuzz in ten seconds," said Heslip flatly.

Nicoletti said mildly, "She doesn't have to let you in, Mac. Officially we don't know she exists. Anything you found in a search would be inadmissible as evidence anyway."

Heslip left them still discussing it, and went back down Page Street to a stoop just three cars away from the Dart. Sitting in the sun he clenched and un-clenched his fists.

A hippie came to roost like a chunky stork on the white fire hydrant on the corner and opened a paperback book titled *Leisure—the Basis of Culture.* He wore his hair in long yellow unkempt curls; he had a sleeping bag slung on a leather strap over his right shoulder.

Twenty minutes later Heslip saw MacLashlin cross Page toward 1718. He started up with an audible curse, then settled back. He knew that to the girl, MacLashlin would have FUZZ emblazoned across his chest in letters three feet high. To hell with him. His concern was the "repo"—the car. The blond hippie on the fire hydrant threw him a puzzled look and returned to his reading. After eight minutes MacLashlin left again.

A black man clacked by in pointy narrow shoes which flashed in the sunlight like knife blades. He was tall and meaty, slightly stooped, wearing a full mustache that drooped over the corners of his mouth. Heslip glanced up casually, then did a double-take. Kelly green ski cords. Olive green short-sleeved shirt that looked like velvet. Heslip stood up. Good old Floyd Matthews had come home.

Matthews had the car key in his hand, but continued on past the Dart toward 1718. Good. Ten paces beyond it. Fifteen. The car was out of it.

At the far end of the block Inspector Nicoletti's screaming jacket was crossing Page. MacLashlin's bulk was just rounding the corner on the odd-numbered side of Page. Both men moved casually, so the intercept would be just before Matthews reached the apartment.

Then the window facing Matthews on the near-side bay was thrown up. Gloria Jensen's face appeared, white and tense.

"Fuzz!" she shrieked. *"Split!"*

The big Negro spun like a halfback and raced toward Heslip, almost before the second word had left the girl's mouth. MacLashlin was clearing the parked cars across Page, his revolver dwarfed in his huge paw, but he was half a block behind. Nicoletti, sprinting, his pistol out, was even farther away. Neither man could shoot. Matthews would be around the corner and away before they could catch him.

Not Heslip's business.

So he jammed a foot between the running man's legs.

Matthews went down, skidded, came up snarling. Heslip was between him and the corner. Face contorted, Matthews whipped out a switchblade and lunged, all in a single movement, so fast it was a blur.

Heslip, on his toes like a bullfighter, saw the blade flash by an inch from his belly, and chopped a short hard left into the big man's unprotected midsection. His face went gray, he faltered: and then the leather strap of the blond hippie's sleeping bag was flipped over Heslip's shoulders from behind. He was jerked off his feet by a vicious snap of the leather.

Heslip's body was momentarily supported by the strap. His knees pumped to his chin, then shot straight out like pistons. His heels caught Matthews above the heart with a force that smashed the big man against the apartment building like a swatted fly. The switchblade went flying.

As it did, Heslip heaved his weight forward against the strap. He went down, hard, and the blond hippie was flipped clumsily over his head, right into MacLashlin's arms. The big hands fielded him expertly, whirled him, and slammed him up against the side of a parked car. Heslip darted forward, pumped fists into Matthews until the man's eyes rolled up and he sagged down the wall. Heslip danced back waiting for the count.

Inspector Nicoletti trotted up, panting. Heslip's head ached. It wasn't good to let go like that, to lose control; but the first blow had transferred all his frustrated rage at MacLashlin to the luckless Matthews.

MacLashlin had frisked and cuffed his blond prisoner. He said disgustedly, "Hell, he don't even *know* Matthews. Just heard someone yell that we were fuzz, so he decided to help out against us."

Heslip realized there hadn't been sight or sound of Gloria Jensen since her Paul Revere act. She probably was very busy flushing her ex-lover's pharmacopoeia down the toilet. Maybe now she'd go visit her family in Carmel for a while. She'd have to walk.

Nicoletti snapped the cuffs on Matthews and jerked him ungently to his feet, ignoring his moans, and they trundled the two cuffed men to their car and thrust them into the rear seat.

"I guess that's it," said MacLashlin in a satisfied voice. Nicoletti was radioing for a cruiser to take the prisoners in for booking.

"Not quite." Heslip's voice was soft. "You an' me got a li'l frien'ly sparrin' to do. No badge. No gun. No uniform, baby."

"*Fight* you? You crazy, boy?" MacLashlin had an odd look in his eyes. "I'm a policeman on duty. Benny and me—"

Nicoletti said abruptly, "You're on your own till the squad car comes, Mac."

Crimson shot into MacLashlin's face. Heslip put a hand in the middle of the big man's chest and pushed, almost contemptuously. The muscles whitened along MacLashlin's jaw as his eyes darted from one to the other. Suddenly the tension left him.

"Can I walk on the ceiling?" He shrugged and turned away.

Heslip had never had a finer compliment. MacLashlin didn't want to fight, not because he feared a beating, but because he might be humiliated by a black man. Then Nicoletti's voice jerked at his partner like a bullwhip wrapped around his neck.

"Mac! You still owe him an apology."

"What the hell goes on?" MacLashlin's face was chalk; he backed away uneasily, looking from one to the other, hand on holster.

Heslip realized that Nicoletti was going to push it. And MacLashlin would have to give in, because Nicoletti was the harder. Two officers, partners in an unmarked car, had to depend on each other's judgment, intuition, and guts to stay alive. To Nicoletti it really had nothing to do with Heslip, or the color of his skin.

Heslip cleared his throat. "Thanks, Benny," he said levelly. "But don't bother. It would break his teeth to say it."

Turning away, he caught amazement on MacLashlin's brutal features. It was enough.

He could feel their eyes on his back, burning like sunlight through a glass as he walked away; then a black-and-white cruiser swung into Clayton from Oak, and the feeling was gone. Suddenly he felt fine.

He pulled the coil wire from his pocket. Yeah! Dodge Dart, delinquent seven months. In twenty minutes more he'd have it in the barn. Tomorrow the Jensen file at DKA would go into the CLOSED file.

He flipped up the hood of the car; then a thought sagged his jaw. Corinne! He hadn't even called her! How was he going to square last night? And the missed picnic today? He slowly replaced the coil wire. You in some mighty deep stuff, baby. But then he grinned. He began singing.

His tune was: *A Good Man Is Hard To Find*. His lyric was: *A Hard Man Is Good To Find*.

Hell, man, all he had to do was convince Corinne of that.

FILE #3: THE THREE HALVES

Preface

Ronile Lahti, the real-life Giselle Marc, had bought a copy of EQMM the day it hit the newsstands with this story in it. She invariably bought anything of mine that turned up in print—at that time, she was probably my most loyal reader after my folks. Before she could read it, O'B came into the office.

Giselle said to him, "Joe's got a new story out."

"Lemme see it," said O'B.

He got his bottle out of the desk drawer as he often did at the close of a long day, and poured himself a drink. Then, freckles magnificent, red hair blazing, blue eyes bubbling, he propped his feet on the edge of Dave Kikkert's desk and started to read the story. But after only a few moments, he leaped to his feet and hurled the magazine across the room.

"That goddamn Gores!" he yelled.

"What's wrong?" cried Ronile in alarm.

He picked up the magazine and tossed it to her. "Read the first paragraph."

The first paragraph notes that "O'Bannon . . . was reminiscing, his feet propped on the edge of Kearny's desk, a glass of bourbon in hand, his freckles magnificent, hair blazing, blue eyes bubbling . . ."

I had watched O'B do it a hundred times.

In real life, I was after a car, not an embezzler; but I did track down the subject in Santa Rosa much as O'B does in the story. The carny background came from back in 1955. After finishing my course work at Stanford in the spring of that year, I went to Minnesota to visit my folks, then spent part of the summer with a travelling tent show. I worked the midway, running the Tilt-a-Whirl through a series of small Midwestern towns.

Soon after I left the carnival and returned to California, I got my first job as a private eye with L.A. Walker Company. A decade later, when I needed a carny background for this story, I drew on my memories of that long-ago summer making the rounds of county fairs across the middle of America.

FILE #3: THE THREE HALVES

Friday, February 28, 6:06 p.m.

Field agents at Daniel Kearny Associates of San Francisco, who had been working fifteen-hour days as they did at the end of every month, could now begin to relax. Patrick Michael O'Bannon had come with Kearny from Walters Auto Detectives seven years before; now he was reminiscing, his feet propped on the edge of Kearny's desk, a glass of bourbon in hand, his freckles magnificent, hair blazing, blue eyes bubbling.

"Dan, remember that time we spotted that Lincoln Continen—"

Kearny's intercom buzzed; he winked at O'B and picked up. Even relaxed over a drink he looked aggressively tough, a little older than O'Bannon's 41, with a slightly flattened nose, a massive jaw, and gray eyes cold enough to chill bone marrow. In a fair imitation of O'Bannon's voice he said, "Kearny left five minutes ago."

Kathy Onoda, upstairs in clerical, just snorted. She was the DKA office manager, had formerly been Kearny's secretary: a Japanese girl in her late twenties with classically Oriental features.

"You're a scream, Dan. I'm sending a Nate Bemel down; he wants to hire us, contingent basis, on a small lithography firm embezzlement."

Kearny snubbed out his cigarette, suddenly getting serious. "*Contingent* basis? Kathy, you know better than that."

"He's on his way down," she repeated musically. " 'Bye."

Kearny cursed and swiveled back to his desk. His office was in the basement of the converted Victorian ex-bawdy house which now was DKA, tucked away among the field agents' cubbyholes and equipped with a one-way plate-glass door. He waved O'Bannon back to his seat.

"Sit in, O'B. Man wants to hire us on a contingent basis."

"Why'd Kathy even bother to send him down? No payee, no workee."

"That's what I want to find out."

Nate Bemel proved to be a beefy man in his mid-fifties with luxurious curling black hair, a gentle face, and a huge nose.

"I'd better tell you right away, Mr. Bemel, that we normally take contingent assignments only from large financial institutions," said Kearny. "Frankly, I'm a little puzzled *why* Miss Onada sent you—"

"—down to see you?" Bemel's voice was so guttural that his English sounded almost like a foreign language. "You see, I own North Beach Litho and I got a very special sort of problem on this embezzlement."

"How much was taken?"

"Sixteen thousand, four hundred and seventy-two dollars."

O'B gave a silent whistle. "The embezzler was your bookkeeper?"

"Yes. Arnaldo Pedretti. But how do *you* know that?"

"By the size of the embezzlement," said Kearny, "he probably was coffee-canning it for months. Unless the bookkeeper was involved, he would have caught the shortages on routine audit."

Bemel nodded. "Arnaldo doesn't come to work one Monday; then I find that for six months he's been depositing only enough clients' checks to cover running expenses. The Friday before, he'd cashed all those other checks he'd been holding out and left with the money."

"When did this happen?" asked O'Bannon.

"May thirtieth. A Friday, like I said. Just nine months ago."

Kearny jerked as if a cigarette had been laid against his spine. "Nine *months* ago and you're just coming around now? The bonding comp—"

"I ain't moved against his bond." Bemel's voice saddened. "I told you—special problem. Arnaldo Pedretti is my brother-in-law."

All was suddenly clear to O'Bannon: his wife, too, was Italian. Italian wives meant Italian families. "Your mother-in-law, Mr. Bemel?"

His sadness deepened. "Seventy-four years old, gentlemen; in the Chinese New Year parade she should be the dragon, already. My Rosa says, 'Listen to Mama.' For nine months I listen." He sat up sternly. "He doesn't come back. All that money he steals, it isn't right. I want you should find him. For this, you keep half of what you recover."

Kearny lit another cigarette. Finding Pedretti would be something all right, as would half of sixteen thousand—if any of it was left. He said, "You want this undercover? Even from the family?"

Bemel bounced in his chair. "Especially from the family. Not even my wife Rosa should know. No charges against him—just my money back I want."

"We'll give it one week without retainer, Mr. Bemel. Miss Onoda will have questions and a paper for you to sign—"

"A paper I don't sign," he exclaimed. "If my wife Rosa—"

But five minutes later, assured his wife would never find out, Bemel departed for the clerical offices overhead. Kearny smeared out his cigarette. O'B, catching his eye, suddenly held up a hand palm out, like a traffic cop.

"Not *me*, Dan! I've got two flooring checks and that skip—"

"Just until next weekend, O'B," he said airily. "You're always slow the first part of the month anyway."

"That's because I'm so fast the *end* of the month," O'B said.

Monday

O'B parked on Vallejo Street in North Beach, two blocks from the apartments where the client and Rosa had the upper, Mama Pedretti—and formerly the subject—the lower. O'B reflected sourly on the two pitchers of martinis he'd downed the night before; and now *this* mickey-mouse.

Arnaldo Pedretti, 38, white, single, last known R/A, 784 Vallejo; last known B/A, North Beach Litho, 652 Vallejo. Period. No further given information. Automobile? None. Driver's license? Yes. O'B wrote *renewal date?* behind that item on the case sheet. Booze? Bemel hadn't known if, where, or with whom. O'B brightened: at least he could get a drink on expense account. Women? Only one known was Agnese Versaggi, daughter of an old friend of Mama Pedretti's, who worked at the bank where Bemel kept his account. Probably carried a rosary when she went out on a date.

There was a snapshot of Pedretti, too. Five feet seven, sallow, with his belly over his belt. Black, curly, badly receding hair, heavy horn-rim glasses. A magnificently unhappy-looking man.

O'B locked his car, walked down to Emery Lane, and cut through to the back entrance of Bank of America, Columbus Branch. He sauntered about until he found Agnese Versaggi's Paying and Receiving window. Unlike Pedretti, she had Anglicized her given name to Agnes. A big girl about 30, nearly voluptuous under a no-nonsense wool suit. Heavy-boned face, wide mouth that smiled easily, big teeth, black hair pulled back carelessly on either side of her face, dark expressive eyes.

O'B returned through the alley to Vallejo Street and selected a small mid-block tavern. A few old Italian gents were drinking red wine at the bar. O'Bannon ordered a beer.

"At least *this* neighborhood hasn't changed much," he remarked.

"You seen the joint down the block? Poetry readings every Tuesday, crazy designs all over the windows, every color you can think of?"

O'Bannon shrugged. "That's just the beats."

"They call themselves hippies now. How long you been away?"

"Since sixty-one—engineering job overseas." He paused. "Say, you know a guy named Arnie Pedretti used to live around here?"

"Pedretti? Sure. But he ain't been around for—oh, hell, must be almost a year now. Took a job out of state, his sister said."

"He used to do his drinking here?"

"You kidding? Some joint down on Bay where old Mama Pedretti wouldn't have no spies—Devlin's Dublin Pub. Member of Roma Athletic Club on Stockton, too, but that's just a gymnasium."

In succession O'B hit three more bars, a hotel, a garage, a wine company, and a dry cleaner. He got one vaguely interesting item at the garage: the subject had been hung up on sports cars.

Driving down to Devlin's, he stopped at the Roma Athletic Club to learn only that the subject had played handball, very badly, and had pitched softball, quite well, for a team sponsored by a local Italian mortician. Devlin's, however, while producing only that the subject and a black-haired gal half a foot taller than he had dropped in occasionally, proved so interesting that O'B remained until five o'clock.

At 5:12, quite tipsy, he was waiting when Agnes Versaggi emerged from the bank and crossed with the light in long strides. Like many big women, she had very shapely legs.

"Miss Versaggi? I'd like to talk to you about Arnaldo Pedretti."

She flashed an unexpected smile and said, "I know a good place on Union that won't be crowded yet. If you're buying."

Making an instant decision, O'B said, "I'm on expense account."

"I thought you were."

She downed her first martini with such ease that O'B abandoned all thought that she carried a rosary on dates.

"I've been expecting someone from the bonding company," she said, "ever since Arnie cashed those checks." Which explained who she thought O'B was. "Mama Pedretti always hoped we'd get married, but me, I knew that what I got, Arnie doesn't need. If you've lived here long—"

"Born in the Mission district."

"So you know about Italian mamas, eh? Mama Pedretti ran Arnie's life. They lived in the same apartment, went to Peter and Paul's together on Sunday—even, she insisted, 'Arnaldo' instead of Arnold. Thirty-eight years old and afraid to drink in a neighborhood bar."

"Devlin's Dublin Pub?" prompted O'Bannon.

"I used to go there with him sometimes; he went for big women, like me. Then that Friday, at the bank, he goes to another window. Always he comes to my window; so after he leaves I check up on him. Sixteen thousand dollars' worth of checks he cashed—and didn't deposit. I know what he's doing, but—what's to say? He's got power of attorney, eh? And it is maybe his last chance to get away from Mama."

Then she added darkly, "Maybe he *never* gets away from the family, eh? Even now, seven thirty at night each first Friday of the month when Mama's away at Stations of the Cross in the cathedral—he calls his sister."

"He calls Mrs. Bemel?" O'B asked sharply.

"Sure. Rosie." She gave a sudden martini giggle. "But you don't tell her

I said so, eh? She doesn't know that I know."

"Our little secret," agreed O'B gravely.

It came out so much like "Sheecret" that he decided he'd better get something to eat. But he got this excellent idea much too late. He woke up at six thirty the next morning parked in front of the DKA office, with a mouth like a mill-hand's undershirt and no recollection of how he had got there. Probably ate some gnocchi at that Italian place that disagreed with him, he decided sagely: then he spent two hours in a Turkish bath and returned at a virtuous nine o'clock.

Tuesday

Giselle Marc was a long, lean, morally upright but wicked-looking blonde in her early twenties. She had started with DKA as a part-time file girl while in college, and had gone in mortal terror of O'Bannon's winks, leers, and blatant propositions until she had realized that his weakness was liquor. Now they were close friends, and she knew that he was the firm's best investigator apart from Kearny himself.

As O'B dialed Searching Registration Service in Sacramento, Giselle said lumpily into her own phone, "My name is Mrs. Angelo Pedretti and I want the service representative for phone number 363-9810."

"Yes, Mrs. Pedretti, may we help you?"

Giselle explained in the limping accent she'd chosen for Mama Pedretti that her income tax consultant needed all available information on her long-distance calls since the previous June. The voice went icy in contemplation of the possible work involved, but finally said, "If you would hold the line, please, I'll try and get that information for you."

O'B hung up, and Giselle covered her mouthpiece. "She's buying it. Anything from S.R.S. on his license or a possible car purchase?"

"They'll check Department of Motor Vehicles files and call us."

Giselle removed her hand quickly. "Yes? I see." She began writing. "Just the one each month and . . . yes. Thank you. That should be all the accountant needs." She said to O'B, "Collect calls came from an Arnold Payne—bound to be Arnaldo Pedretti—in June, July, August, September, and October, each from a different city—"

"And from October on, all calls from Santa Rosa." O'B was reading over her shoulder. "Each from a different phone." He hid a yawn with a freckled fist. "Confirm that they'll all be pay phones, will you, doll? Also check Santa Rosa for a phone listing in either name—though I doubt he's that dumb—and find out if the calls came on the first Friday of each month. I've got a couple of hot field leads—"

"Sure you do. Have a good sleep, you fink," said Giselle.

Wednesday

O'Bannon screwed up his leathery face and began reading Giselle's memo. If he hadn't got loaded Monday night and had to spend yesterday recuperating—but to hell with it. O'B was not introspective; few detectives are. Soul searchers are not good at raking over the rubbish heaps in other human lives.

As O'B had expected, all the calls had come from pay phones, and all the calls had been made on the first Friday of the month.

June 5: Eureka, up in the north coast redwood country.

July 3: Marysville, moving south.

August 7: Napa, in the wine country.

September 4: Vallejo, 40 miles northeast of the city across the Carquinez Straights.

October 2: the jump to Santa Rosa, due north of San Francisco in Sonoma County.

Where was the pattern? If Payne *were* Pedretti, wouldn't he find better places to live it up on his stolen sixteen thou than a series of small towns?

He buzzed Giselle. "Anything from S.R.S. in Sacramento yet?"

"Negative on a driver's license renewal. They'll call back on the auto registration file check as soon as they complete it."

He then called the client at North Beach Litho. When Nate Bemel's thick accent was in his ear he said, "This is O'Bannon at DKA. I've got a couple of questions. How late do you work on Fridays?"

"Fridays? Home for supper, back here until eight o'clock."

That checked. He said, "I know the phone in your apartment is in Mama Pedretti's name, but who actually pays the bill?"

"You investigating me or—you know who? *I* pay the bill."

"But who *physically* pays it? Writes the check, say?"

"Well, Rosa pays all the household bills. I think she takes the phone bill down to Bank of America and then pays it in cash."

O'B thanked him and hung up. The collect calls made sense now. Only Rosa saw the items on the phone bill. When the call came, she could refuse it if someone else was in the apartment with her. Being sociable, she would go to Agnes Versaggi's window at the bank; Agnes would not have been fooled by Arnold Payne/Arnaldo Pedretti for a minute. But O'B was still no closer to the subject, since it was obvious that Rosa didn't know how to reach him.

Giselle buzzed on the intercom. "S.R.S. just called, O'B. Last September an Arnold Payne bought an SKE-120 Jaguar from a Vellejo dealer. The title slip was mailed in October to—" Her voice fell. "Mailed to Post Office Box 281 in Redwood City. Which is on the Peninsula thirty miles *south* of here, while the phone calls put our—"

"—our Arnold Payne in Santa Rosa, forty miles *north*. Right. How about this, Giselle: he's got a traveling sales job and the box number is his home office address?"

"Selling from a *Jaguar*, O'B? And what about Social Security, Federal withholding taxes, bonding, employment references—"

"Yeah." O'B arched an eyebrow; an idea had come to him. He said, "I'll try to pop that P.O. box, doll. There's *one* possibility—"

The telephone is the skip-tracer's most potent tool. O'Bannon in person, without elaborate disguises, was a red-headed Irishman with a hard-bitten face. But O'B on the phone could be anyone from a teenager to an octogenarian. For this call he was a truck driver.

"Ah, yeah, say, I'm out here off the Bayshore Freeway on Marsh Road. Got twelve thousand board feet of redwood one-by-six addressed to an Arnold Payne at P.O. Box 281." He paused for dramatic effect. *"Where do you want 'em?"* he asked the post office employee.

"Listen," the clerk squeaked, "that isn't mail! You can't bring—"

"Look, mister," said O'Bannon's truck-driver voice. "I picked up this load from the Sequoia Mills in Eureka last night; you're silly as hell if you think I'm just gonna dead-haul it back up there again."

"Just a minute." The postal clerk went away. This was the crucial moment, since by law the addresses of box holders are not to be given out. The man returned. "Yeah. Haney's Combined Shows, 3951 Edison Way, Redwood City."

O'B had guessed right—a traveling road show. Few carny laborers paid Social Security or even filed W-2 forms. And the little carnivals worked a swing of small-town fairs, livestock shows, and rodeos.

Giselle had an objection. "That's great, but it looks like he left it back in October to stay in Santa Rosa, doesn't it?"

"There's only one way to find out."

Forty minutes later O'B parked his car alongside a small brick building on Edison Way in Redwood City. It was a hot clear day on the Peninsula, very different from the city's March bluster, He locked his topcoat in the car and entered a door marked *C. V. Baggett, General Agent.* Behind a counter was a well-corseted woman with ruthlessly peroxided hair and a face from which time had wrung the milk of human kindness.

O'B gestured at the empty inner office. "Mr. Baggett?"

"Lunch!" The word exploded like a bullet. "I'm Madame George."

"Mr. Baggett *does* represent Haney's Combined Shows?"

"Also Phantasy Phun Phairs." She indicated a garish poster. "I was with Phantasy for twenty years before Haney took over, and twenty after that. Finally told C. V. that I wanted to sleep in a house without wheels on it, so he had me take over running the office here."

"I saw one of your carnivals in Vallejo last year, and—"

"August. Phantasy One. I was managing it then. The Phantasys are truck shows, and Haney's Combined is a railroad show."

"As president of the Erin Auld Sods of San Francisco, I—"

"—want to hire Phantasy One? We put Haney's Combined into the city usually; all the shows are *quite* similar, and they all close the third week in October for the wet months. Haney's reopens in mid-June, and Phantasy Two opened the middle of last month. Phantasy One stays in winter quarters until the fifteenth of this month. End of next week."

"Haney's is fine for us. Ah, where *are* winter quarters?"

"Santa Rosa," said Madame George.

Friday, March 7, 6:50 a.m.

Under dawn sunlight the Santa Rosa street looked dusty and disheveled, like a man who had drunk too much the night before. A lone mongrel trotted across the narrow blacktop without a thought for cars. O'B, also looking like a man who had drunk too much the night before—which he had—skittered an empty whiskey bottle across the sidewalk. His hands were deep in his faded dungaree pockets.

"It's cold," he complained, hunching his shoulders.

The dog didn't answer. It merely kept on moving, with a reproachful look as if O'B had thrown a beer can at it. O'B crossed the street toward a lot crowded with strange shapes—metal braces, odd-shaped canvas frames, long round iron poles bright with new paint.

The door of an aluminum house trailer on one side of the lot creaked open and a short, almost dapper man stepped out. His thick curly hair was grizzled at the temples, his mustache was neatly trimmed; even in T-shirt and underpants he bore the stamp of authority. A tousled blonde head appeared above his shoulder, and he turned to curse in a surprisingly deep voice. The girl disappeared abruptly with a flash of pale nude flesh like the turn of a fish deep in muddy water.

"Jug Butt!" the man roared. "Get 'em up! Gotta hump it today!"

A fat but powerful young man, barefoot, came out of the corrugated iron shed that backed the lot and stood blinking in the sunlight, scratching a remarkable expanse of gut with a grimy paw. He hawked and spat into the oil-soaked dirt, swore, and returned to the shed. From within came loud voices, curses, a thud, heavy laughter.

O'B walked up to the trailer. "You hiring here, mister?"

The stocky straw boss took in his worn clothes, lean drinker's face, red-rimmed eyes. "Yeah. Ten a day, sleep in the shed if you ain't got nowhere else. You ever been a carnival roughie before?"

"No. But I'm not green."

"God knows you ain't. I'm Carlos Ryan."

"Patrick Michael O'Bannon."

Ryan returned his grin. "Okay, Red, once the boys start in you can help Jug Butt load those Tilt-a-Whirl baskets onto a truck."

From the shed came an abnormally skinny man in his mid-twenties with a motorcycle cap pushed sideways on the back of his head. The teenager with him, called Billy the Kid, addressed the skinny man as Curly. Next was a lanky, powerful, rawboned man with mean eyes, whose accent identified him as Tex; a quizzical-faced man with a loud voice and a weak chin, named Garrison; and a toothless old duffer called, for obvious reasons, Hairless Hans. Last was Jug Butt.

No Arnaldo Pedretti. It probably had been a nutty hunch anyway, that a man with sixteen thousand would work for sixty a week, sleep-where-you-can. Still, O'B decided he'd give it a day; Payne/Pedretti, he felt sure, had spent some time with this carnival the previous season.

They worked under a sun so hot that O'B wondered if he'd collapse before he even asked a question. He lugged Tilt-a-Whirl baskets with Jug Butt; since gloves were considered cowardly, his hands soon were leaving red smears on the sharp-edged aluminum buckets. Damn Kearny!

At ten o'clock Carlos Ryan emerged, paint-spattered, from the shed. "Hell," he said, "ain't no use dyin' for a sawbuck a day."

They crossed the street to Carter's Joynt, a long narrow neighborhood bar with worn hardwood floors, boiled eggs in glass bowls, and three pinball machines. Tex bought two bucks' worth of dimes; all had beer except Carlos Ryan, who had a shot of bourbon.

Carter, the owner, looked them over, took a deep breath, and said to Billy the Kid, "Say, listen, how old are you, anyway?"

"He's a carny," growled Tex. "He don't have to be of age."

"Yeah? Try telling that to the Alcoholic Beverage Control." Looking at Tex, he subsided suddenly, drew another beer. "Aw, hell."

From ten thirty to noon they worked. Lifting, hauling, sweating, swearing, grunting, O'B learned only that Hairless Hans and Ryan had been with Phantasy One the previous season. Ryan wouldn't talk, but Hans might. O'B would try after lunch, he decided, which was sandwiches at Carter's Joynt. Ryan had another shot. O'B understood the he-mannish gesture; with a tough crew like this, the big uninhibited blonde would be honey to the bees unless Ryan were more than mere nominal boss.

At two o'clock Tex, Jug Butt, and Billy the Kid left in one of the ancient trucks to pick up some jenny horses across town. Ryan and Curly were in the paint shed doping fabric wings for the airplane ride, and Garrison was buried in the innards of the antique truck which bore the words *POPCORN, PEANUTS, SUGAR CANDY.* But as O'B sidled toward Hairless Hans, a new car pulled up and a young man with long hair got out. The pretty girl with him, who wore a Mia Farrow cut, stayed in the car.

"Hey, is there a fellow around here named Billy Weston? About my age, maybe seventeen? They call him Billy the Kid sometimes."

"Billy theh Kid?" Hans scratched where his hair should have been. "Don't recall any sech feller 'round here."

Curly brought the water jug. "Why'd you say that, Hans?"

The old man drank noisily, Adam's apple popping, water drooling from his nearly toothless mouth. He winked slyly at O'B.

"Now, Curly, say theh Kid had planted his seed in thet there orchard. An' say thet there was thet girl's brother. See? You ain't traveled wit' theh carny yit. Carny takes care of ets own. Carny don't ask questions. Why you figger ain't no tax taken outen y'r pay?" He cackled toothlessly. "Think my mother wouldda know'd me by Hans?"

So much for trying to pump *you*, O'B thought to himself.

Tex's semi grunted around the corner, struck the curb, and blew a tire with a sound like a mortar being fired, then to stop smashed into a tree. Tex jumped from the doorless cab and strode to the shed.

"Hey, you, Carlos Ryan!" When the dapper boss emerged, Tex bellowed, "I thought you said that there truck was fixed up!"

"I did. Garrison's a mechanic and he did it yesterday. He—"

"Who the hell told him?"

"Told him what?"

"That he was a mechanic. Brakes went out on the way over and the clutch on the way back, hadda drive it by ear. He may a' been a mechanic somewhere else, but he ain't but a bigmouth around here."

At 6:00 p.m. they lined up outside the trailer for their pay. A week before, O'B had been drinking bourbon with Dan Kearny; now he was hot, flushed, sunburned, and tired. He stank. His hands were cut, and where they weren't cut they were blistered. And he was no closer to Arnaldo Pedretti than he'd been that morning. Or was he?

Some nagging thing made him go over to Carter's Joynt to drink beer, listen to the ping of Tex's pinball machine, and talk with Carlos Ryan.

"You must have seen 'em come and go, Carlos," he opened.

"Yeah, Red, been with it long enough to know better," Ryan grinned. "Y'see, I'm half Irish, half Spanish, and half carny."

"That makes three halves," objected O'Bannon.

"You better believe it," said Ryan.

A large laborer with his yellow safety helmet on the stick beside him, the bar's only other customer, gave a snort. "Did you say *carny*?"

Tex said suddenly, "One hundred free games! An' I'm buyin'!"

"Mark 'em off." Carter disgustedly jabbed *NO SALE* on the register.

"I ain't drinking with no carnies," said the laborer.

"Your privilege," said Ryan quickly, but Tex already had set down his glass of beer and was staring at the construction worker.

"You ain't drinking with us, buddy-buddy? Down in Texas a man don't refuse to drink with another man unless he's meanin' to—"

"Texas?" The laborer leaned back against the bar with his elbows on it. "Feller tole me once that the way to find Texas was to go east far enough to smell it, and south far enough to step in it, and I'd—"

The heel of Tex's hand, swung by a strap-steel right arm, exploded on the other's jaw, upsetting man and stool. The laborer's head rebounded from the hardwood floor with a great ka-thunk as Tex surged forward, giving his battle cry: "*YAHOO! SAN ANTON'!*"

Ryan flicked O'B's half-full beer off the bar in an underhand arc. The spinning bottle caught Tex just above the right temple; he went over sideways against a dark-varnished plywood booth. He lay still for a time, then sat up rubbing his temple with a horny callused palm.

"Aw, hell, Carlos," he said plaintively, "what'd you have to go an' do that for?"

"We don't want law trouble. C'mon; I gotta make a phone call anyway." He dropped a twenty on the bar and jerked a thumb at the fallen warrior. "You never saw us before, right, Carter?"

Carter grinned. "Total strangers to me, Carlos."

Outside, O'B check his watch: 7:30. Night had fallen and it was chilly again. He hobbled around the block twice on work-stiffened legs, cursing but glad to be using his head instead of his back once more.

The missing Jaguar bothered him, but there would be an explanation. In the dark he crossed to the aluminum house trailer where, he hoped, Carlos Ryan would supply the answers he needed.

The blonde peered at him with incurious eyes. She was dressed in a sweater and such impossibly tight jeans that she reminded him of Little Annie Fanny in the *Playboy* cartoon satires; nobody could be that dumb but somebody was. Ryan was working at the small fold-down kitchen table; through the doorway was a narrow living room with a television set, and beyond that the bedroom with an unmade bed. O'B jerked his head.

"Could she go change the sheets or something, Carlos?"

"I'll watch TV," pouted the blonde, pausing at the miniature refrigerator to get a can of beer and wiggle a petulant behind.

"That's a good girl." As *Hogan's Heroes* blasted from the set, O'B flopped his identification open on the table in front of Ryan.

"About your embezzlement last May thirtieth from North Beach Litho—"

Ryan leaped erect, crashing his chair back against the stove. His powerful fingers were clawed for throat gripping, but O'B managed to retain his carefully careless pose.

"Sit down, Pedretti. You're not a killer, just a cheap carny straw boss. God, I never knew roughies worked so hard. Sit down, man."

Carlos Ryan, tough little dude, gave the sort of sob that Arnaldo Pedretti, mama's boy, thief, and sometime bookkeeper might have given, and all the starch went out of him. O'B had seen it a thousand times: you hit the subject with the inevitability of your presence and he reacted blindly, with panic. That was the dangerous time. Then his mind began to function, he made a mental adjustment to the new situation, and you could begin to deal with him on a rational basis again.

"I—how did you find—"

"It's our business to find people. Your sister didn't mention us when you called her an hour ago because she didn't know about us. What happened to the Jaguar, by the way?"

Pedretti's color was returning. "Gladys totaled it three months ago." He considered for a moment. "She's too dumb to live."

"Agreed." O'B laid down the snapshot. "I almost missed you because I was after an overweight, mousy guy with soft hands, horn-rims, and not much hair. But five months as a roughie toughened you up and slimmed you down. Add a mustache and a good hairpiece and contact lenses—and *presto*, Carlos Ryan."

Pedretti was looking at his picture. "God, that *is* me?"

O'B, busy pouring two bourbons, nodded. "Little things gave you away. I'm enough of a boozer to know you were playing a role with those straight shots. Then the phone call tonight, seven thirty—on the first Friday of the month. You threw that bottle at Tex underhand—like a softball pitcher. Finally, your woman is six inches taller than you—like Agnes Versaggi. She said you liked 'em big."

"I've found I also prefer 'em like Gladys," he said drily. "With their brains in their backsides. I should have just left, you know? But without taking the money I never would have made the break. I *had* to take it, so I couldn't ever go back."

"How'd you get your job here?"

"Just chance. I've always been sort of a romantic, so when I ran across Phantasy One up by the Oregon border, I got a job as a roughie. An old gal named Madame George was running it then." His grin was a fleeting Carlos Ryan grin. "Used to be in a skin show, when she got fat she worked a mentalist act. She got the whole story out of me and decided to help me. She set it up for me to run the section this season." He swallowed suddenly. "What happens now, Red?"

Funny: while Pedretti had thought of himself as Carlos Ryan, he had *been* Carlos Ryan—tough, jaunty, uncomplicated. Now he was mush. O'B had preferred Ryan to Pedretti.

"How much money is left?" O'B asked briskly.

"Something over ten thousand. The rest went for the Jag, the contact lenses, the wig. Now—"

"Now we have a drink." O'B fitted actions to words. "And a talk."

Forty minutes later he was on the horn with Dan Kearny.

"Ten thousand is in a Santa Rosa safe-deposit box. He'll turn that over to me on Monday, along with a promissory note for the rest, bank terms at two hundred a month."

"Any chance he's planning a skip, or some rough stuff?"

"He's just damned grateful to get out from under. Besides, there's this other guy, a real old carny type—"

"Dammit, O'Bannon," Kearny bellowed in sudden comprehension, "if you think you're going to run up a big expense account on booze—"

"I'm telling you, Dan," said O'B virtuously, "this other guy will make us a *great* carny contact. His name is Carlos Ryan and he says he's half Irish, half Spanish, and half carny—"

"Wait a minute," objected Dan Kearny, "that makes three halves."

"You better believe it," said O'Bannon.

FILE #4: LINCOLN SEDAN DEADLINE

Preface

When I made the repo fictionalized in "Lincoln Sedan Deadline" very early in my career as a private eye, DKA did not yet exist. Dave Kikkert was still San Francisco manager of the L.A. Walker Company and I was working for him. The case was my introduction to the culture of the American Gypsies.

It was a deadline deal for Crocker Bank: three payments delinquent, the fourth coming due at midnight the following day. If we didn't return the car to the dealer who had sold it before that midnight deadline, he would be off the hook and the bank would have to "eat" it—take the car back no matter what shape it was in. Banks frown deeply on that sort of thing.

So Dave gave me a crash-course in telephone skip-tracing. By seven the next morning, he had located the subject in Palm Springs. He immediately stuck me on a plane going south, with orders to grab the car and get it back to the dealer's lot in San Francisco before the midnight deadline had passed.

When I located the subject, a striking Gypsy fortune-teller, and told her I was taking her car, she first tried to seduce me. When that didn't work, she brought down a Gypsy curse on me. From that point on, fiction takes over, and the story unfolds in a way reality never did.

"Lincoln Sedan Deadline" was not the first use I made of that Palm Springs adventure, nor the last. Long before the File Series was conceived, my second published story, "Killer Man," sends a hit man down to Palm Springs to dispatch a woman with knowledge dangerous to a mob boss. It appeared in 1958 in Manhunt, *last of the pulps, under the title "Pro." And in 1999, I cannibalized "Killer Man" again, as I had for this story, to make up one segment of a suspense novel,* Cases, *set in 1953.*

I worked many more Gypsy cases after that first one, and returned to this fascinating subculture fictionally in 32 Cadillacs *and the forthcoming* Cons, Scams & Grifts.

One final, funny note. Most repo agencies in the '50s and '60s used a private investigation firm called the GYPSY LOCATE SERVICE for help in Gypsy cases. It was only years later that Dave and I learned this outfit was itself a Gypsy front, a con to get repo agencies to harass Gypsy clans that were feuding with those running the locate service. Or, if P.I.s were looking for Gypsies from their clans, to feed them false or outdated info.

FILE #4: LINCOLN SEDAN DEADLINE

Dan Kearny laughed and said, " 'Bye!" in a bright and jocular voice. Then he tossed the receiver toward the phone and cursed aloud in his basement cubbyhole at DKA. That made it just a perfect morning.

Item: the new receptionist had blithely let in a process server, and Kearny had been slapped with a damage-suit summons.

Item: Marty Rossman had lost a repossessed auto from the tow-bar coming down Cathedral Hill, and had wiped out three parked cars.

Item: Kathy Onoda, office manager ever since Kearny had quit Walter's Auto Detectives nearly eight years before to form Daniel Kearny Associates, was off sick again. Hell, she was run-down from a full-time job, two kids, and supporting a deadbeat husband, but it still put them in a bind. Now this!

Kearny jabbed Giselle Marc's intercom button viciously; as it buzzed upstairs in clerical, he shook a cigarette from his pack and lit it. He was a hard, pugnacious man with a square face and icy gray eyes; his slightly bent nose and massive jaw gave him the look of an aging middleweight club fighter.

"Yes, Dan," said Giselle musically. She was a tall stimulating blonde, 24 years old, whose looks kept most men from realizing that her wits matched her other attractions. Kearny was one of the few who wasn't fooled.

"Who's the field agent on this Jennifer Poteet skip?"

"Larry Ballard."

"Where the hell is—" He broke off; through the one-way glass of his cubbyhole he had seen Ballard entering the garage. "Skip it."

"Dan, don't jump on Larry! This is a Gypsy case, and you know what Gypsy cases are."

"Somebody oughta tell Lou Cassavette at Crescent Lincoln-Mercury what Gypsy cases are, so he doesn't get on the horn to blow smoke at me about making California Citizens Bank eat this one because it won't be back before the deadline. So I—" He caught himself, but not in time.

"Dan, did you bet Lou Cassavette that we'd have that car back?"

"Bet?" he asked innocently. "Why, I—yeah. Fifty iron men. Hell, I won at the track Saturday." Over her expostulations he hung up, buzzed Ballard. "Get in here—with your case file," he growled.

Larry Ballard, tall and energetic and in his mid-twenties, had a surfer's build and sun-bleached hair. He reminded Kearny of himself twenty years before at the same age: smart, ready to work around the clock, slowly gaining the successful investigator's necessary detachment. In his nine months with DKA, Ballard had become a damned good field agent, but he still didn't know how to really dig on skip cases. He'd learn on this one.

Kearny offered a cigarette, began silkily, "Ballard, what are *you* DOING ON *JENNIFER POTEET?*" His voice thumped the words like a ring opponent's jaw.

"I—well, er—that's a tough one, Da—Mr. Kearny."

"It's a deadline deal, Ballard." Kearny's voice was deceptively soft. He suddenly roared: *"AT ONE MINUTE PAST TWELVE TOMORROW NIGHT CAL-CIT BANK IS GOING TO HAVE TO EAT THAT CAR!"* His voice dropped. "The dealer recourse expires then, three months since initial delinquency, and Lou Cassavette isn't about to take back a seven-thousand-dollar car once it's gone over the wire. Not from a Gypsy."

Ballard hadn't really *forgotten* the Poteet Lincoln sedan, just had—well, let it slip by. A bounced down payment, three months delinquent. Now a deadline deal, with the deadline just 38 hours away.

"Dan, I can't get a live lead on this one."

"Ballard, I don't care if you boot one," said Kearny coldly. "Everyone does. But none of *my* men tell me they 'can't'."

Reviewing the Jennifer Poteet file under Kearny's critical eye, Ballard mentally cringed. The reports were pathetic. *Followed to given address, cruised the area. Vehicle not in sight. Returned several times during late evening and early morning hours without success.* A dozen such reports in the file, all written by himself. All he'd really discovered was that the 28-year-old subject was gone from her residence address in the Mission district, and that she had walked off her job at a North Beach topless joint.

Dropping a dime for Information would have told them that much.

"We also know she's a John clan Gypsy," Kearny pointed out.

"How can we be sure of that?"

"The residence address is a storefront joint where only John clan Gyps live. If I'd seen this file sooner—" He looked up. "Why didn't I?" It was just a question, not badgering.

"This is the first Gypsy file I've worked."

"It isn't the first one Giselle's worked."

Private investigators, law-enforcement officers, auto dealers, and retail credit men all know there is a flourishing Gypsy subculture in this country, with its own royalty, its own unique clan structure, and a moral code relating only to other Gypsies. Punishments for those who break the code can range up to ritual murder. Piercing this spider web is not impossible, for money talks as loudly to Gypsies as to anyone else; but it takes time. And time was just what Kearny didn't have.

"Let's get at it," he growled. "Deadline's tomorrow night."

To Larry Ballard the hours until midnight, with sandwiches sent in, were a crash course in skip-tracing as opposed to field work. They also explained why the DKA phone bill ran twenty grand a year.

Kearny began with long-distance calls to the motor vehicle departments of Georgia and Mississippi, where cars sometimes are licensed without actual proof of ownership. No record. Then he called Louisiana, where such fraudulently registered vehicles sometimes get a clear title which bypasses original lien holders such as Cal-Cit Bank. No record.

"So it probably still has California plates," said Kearny.

Ballard learned that the seven main western Gypsy clans—John, Miller, Ristick, Costello, Ephrem, Ellis, and Steve—use some fifty regular aliases and, on fraudulent credit applications, such supposed occupations as boilermakers, brass workers, coppersmiths, church vestment salesmen, silversmiths, photographers, and many others.

"Did you ask around that go-go joint in North Beach where the subject was supposed to be the house photographer?"

"She worked at the club, Dan," said Ballard, "but as a topless waitress. She was so kooky that they were glad to see her leave."

Kearny gave him a list of sheriffs, state police agencies, repossessors, skip-tracers, and local cops to phone around the country. He discovered that the Jones and Stanley clans were attending the funeral of a Gypsy prince in Toledo, Ohio; that the Blake clan had been operating a florist shop in Buffalo, New York, to establish credit for a big color TV set haul; that the Nicholas and Mitchell clans were in Clearwater, Florida, waiting for the carnival season to open; and that more than 50 wanted Gypsy vehicles had been discovered on a farm near Clear Lake, Indiana. Of Jennifer Poteet, however, he discovered nothing.

At 3:30 p.m. he got his first break: an Arizona policeman once had arrested the subject for operating a fraudulent mitt camp at a County Fair midway. With this information, Kearny learned from another fortuneteller near Santa Rosa that the subject had a brother named Rudolph Marino. Then the lead seemed to die.

At 8:00 p.m. Marino's wife, reached by phone at Portland, explained that Marino had been in the Oregon state pen for nearly a year on a charge of assault with a deadly weapon while in commission of a felony.

At midnight Kearny leaned back and knuckled his reddened eyes. The desk was littered with papers, the ashtrays were overflowing, the soundproofed office was close and stale.

Ballard rubbed the back of his neck. "What do we do now? Punt?"

"We keep digging. Cassavette has the idea we can't produce; he wants to be sitting in his used car lot tomorrow at midnight when we *don't* bring in that Lincoln sedan. Which wouldn't help us at the bank one damned bit." He grinned wolfishly. "Be here at six in the morning."

✕ ✕ ✕

It was 6:01 a.m. Although DKA wouldn't open for another hour and a half, Giselle Marc stuck her gleaming blonde head into Kearny's cubbyhole. "Any luck, guys?"

"What are you doing here?" In the same tone Kearny said to Ballard, "Larry, this is the girl I was telling you about."

"No kidding? And she looks like such a sweet kid, too."

"All right, you cats—" began Giselle.

"We haven't turned up a thing," Kearny said. "Did you see Kathy last night?"

She nodded. "I'm worried about her, Dan. She looks terrible but she won't see a doctor. Says she's just tired."

When she left, Kearny pushed aside his very real concern for Kathy Onoda. He began, "Poteet must not be using any common Gypsy alias." His eyes suddenly gleamed. "Larry, what was that number for Marino's wife in Portland?"

Ballard told him, objecting, "But Marino's in the pen, Dan."

"His wife isn't." Kearny used the area code so that it would seem like a local call. "Hello? Mrs. Marino? This is Morning Wake-Up from station KXWR in Portland. Have you been listening? My phone call woke you up? Well, Mrs. Marino, you—can I call you something besides Mrs.? —Neya? A lovely name. And for being such a good sport, Neya, we are giving you an electric carving knife *ab*solutely free—you just have to pick it up here in Studio C at KXWR. Oh, could we have your maiden name for identification purposes? That's right, Neya. And could you spell that? Z-L-A-T-C-H-I. Fine. Thanks and 'bye, Neya."

Ballard shut his mouth, which had been hanging open wide enough to catch flies. "What if she'd asked for the studio address?"

"I'd have made one up," said Kearny airily. "Like I made up the studio." He leaned forward to pluck a cigarette from the pack on the desk. "The subject was busted once for running a fortune-telling skam, right? She's not traveling with other Gyps or our informants would have turned her up, right? So what's she doing for eating money? We start checking for a palm reader named Madame Neya or Madame Zlatchi."

"Seems like an awfully long shot, Dan."

"We don't have any short ones left," grunted Kearny.

His third phone call broke the case. A San Pedro Gypsy informant, grumbling about being got out of bed, said a Madame Neya was reading tea leaves at a joint a few miles from Palm Springs.

"We've got a field agent in Riverside—" Ballard began.

"—who's too brittle to find the Lincoln and get it back up here in seventeen and a half hours. No." Kearny jerked his wallet from his inside jacket pocket. "Here's fifty bucks, Larry. I'll drive you to the airport, you get the jet shuttle to L.A.—it only takes forty minutes. You can catch the eight-twenty Palm Springs flight from there." He stood up, gesturing impatiently. "C'mon. Let's move."

They moved. Larry Ballard was in Palm Springs by 9:14 a.m.

✕ ✕ ✕

From the airport he called San Francisco. Kearny came on.

"I've contacted The Green Cactus, Larry. They only know that the subject has a shack in a date grove near Rancho Mirage, and that she shows up for work at six o'clock every night. You'll have to find that shack if you're to get the Lincoln back here in time."

On the blacktop beyond the airport Ballard pushed his rented Mustang up to 70; but an open Cadillac deVille rocketed past him like an errant moon probe, its pilots a pair of bleached blondes goggled with wrap-around sunglasses. They waved airily; marvelous what sunshine and an assured income did for your outlook, Ballard thought.

At a stationery store in the rich, still somnolent town he got a blow-up map of the area, and at a gas station he got directions to the nearest firehouse. The red trucks gleamed in a driveway still puddled from their morning bath. A lean browned man in heavy rubber boots like a buccaneer's was wiping the chrome grille of a truck.

"Dirt roads through the date groves near Rancho Mirage that might have shack on 'em?" He dropped his chamois into his bucket and dried his hands. "Let's go inside and take a look at the wall map."

Twenty minutes later Ballard was on his way, his head full of local lore and his map full of wavy pencil squiggles, on one of which he hoped to find Madame Neya.

It took him just under two hours.

✕ ✕ ✕

He had turned off a dirt road between the Thunderbird Club and the Shadow Mountain Club on a pair of hardened ruts meandering off into the date groves. Clouds of tan dust swirled around the car when he drove across a dry wash and then stopped abruptly. Just ahead, some 30 yards, the tail of a black Lincoln sedan protruded from behind a date palm.

He drove on, slowly. Yes. The Lincoln had the correct license number, and the shack was there, too, like something out of the Oklahoma migrations of the '30s. 12:01 p.m.: 11 hours, 59 minutes left.

Ballard returned to the highway, locked the Mustang, and laid the keys on top of the left-rear wheel. Then he walked back, trying to steel himself. Mustn't blow it by being soft. One girl he'd been soft with, Jocelyn Mayfield, had ended up killing herself.

Palm fronds tickled the roof drily; his shoes were soundless in the soft dust. As he quietly opened the door of the Lincoln the screen door on the porch slammed. The woman was as tall as Ballard, nearly six feet, with a striking face—straight nose, high cheekbones, thin lips.

She pointed a carmine-tipped finger. "You are accursed!" Her deep, rich, angry voice raised the hairs on the back of Ballard's neck.

"Miss Jennifer Poteet?"

"I am Madame Neya," she intoned.

Thin loops of beaten gold gleamed in her pierced earlobes, and set inside the edges of the ears, which also were pierced, were small beads of gold. Her legs were superb, and her plunging neckline suggested that she wore no brassiere. Her very femaleness lessened her impact.

"Madame Neya, huh?" said Ballard. "Jennifer Poteet to the bank."

"Ah." She expelled a breath, again drawing his eyes to her neckline. "You have come to take poor Madame Neya's car."

"That's it—come all the way from San Francisco."

She led him through a living room, furnished only with a beaten-down couch, a new color TV, and a dozen garish hippie posters, through a small dark bedroom, and into the kitchen. It was very dirty, with dishes piled high in the sink. She leaned back against the stove, arms crossed; her eyes were such a deep blue they were nearly violet.

"Now, Mr. Car Thief man, what can I do to keep my Lincoln?"

"You should have done it four months ago. All you can do now is to remove any personal property and give me the keys. I have to get it back to San Francisco by midnight."

She smiled warmly; her eyelashes were very long, and very dark. Outside a desert bird called brokenly in the noonday heat. "Don't you want to go to bed with me?" she purred.

Ballard was not really successful in putting boredom into his voice; she was a lot of woman. "Where are the keys, Jennifer?"

She realized then that he actually meant to take the car, and her face got momentarily ugly; her eyes flashed and her fingers worked, like a cat sheathing and unsheathing its claws. Then she suddenly laughed.

"So. You take Madame Neya's beautiful car. I gave them the good run for it, eh?" She turned to the stove, her face calculating but her eyes dancing with some arcane Gypsy delight. "Anyway, a cup of coffee before you go, eh? To show there is no hard feeling?"

"Okay." She obviously was playing for time—for the arrival of a friend, perhaps; but the coffee already was hot. She added half-and-half and a lump of sugar for Ballard, drank hers black like a woman conscious of her figure. Ballard knew he certainly was conscious of it.

"Still not too late to change your mind, Mr. Car Thief man."

Maybe she really *was* a mind reader; but Ballard said, "Sorry, Jennifer, just the coffee. But I can give you a ride to work."

She shrugged, finally giving up. "My boyfriend picks me up every day. I thought maybe today he would come early."

He'd been right about her stalling for time. He guzzled his coffee, which was vile, just remembering that he'd left the coil wire in the Lincoln instead of removing it as he should have.

"You giving me those keys, Jennifer?"

Her face was sullen again. "They're on the counter."

He got to the living room before she called out behind him. The odd resonance of her voice turned him almost against his will. She was standing in the center of the dim bedroom like a nighttime animal in its den; her violet eyes gleamed ferally, her magnificent breast heaved.

"You hope to get that car to San Francisco by midnight? You will not get it there . . . *at all*." Her eyes rolled up and her voice rose, to pierce his eardrums like an eagle's cry. "Oh, ye who sow discord, where are you? Ye who infuse hatreds and propagate enmities, I conjure you: fulfill your work—so that *never again shall this man go in peace*."

Ballard tried to speak, but his throat was dry; he tried to laugh, but her voice still echoed in his brain. She was rigid, one arm extended, a blood-tipped finger pointing him out for her private Evils.

Then the spell was broken and Ballard was through the door and off the sagging, unpainted porch. His shadow seemed to hunch at his feet uneasily as he scuffed through the dust toward the Lincoln; he drove away with his eyes unconsciously fixed on the rearview mirror.

Jennifer Poteet. Some woman. He checked the time: over eleven hours to drive 500 miles. At a gas station he filled up, made out the vehicle condition report, and called the sheriff about the repo, the rental agency about the Mustang. He felt better once he was on the open highway. How about that chick? *Cursing* him! And in broad daylight!

✕ ✕ ✕

It started about an hour later—a little after 2:00 p.m. At first he thought it was just the broiling sun, so he switched on the air conditioner. It didn't help. His palms were sweaty and when he took a hand from the wheel it was tremoring. He kept his mind carefully away from the curse; after all, how silly could you get?

But the sun *was* intense. Why? What did it have against him? He was squinting. This time of year the sun set about 4:30; he'd be glad when it was gone. The Lincoln whispered down the freeway at 80. The damned thing was *drinking* gas. What reason did it have?

Ballard began to laugh softly. A curse, huh? He said aloud, "What are you laughing at?" To reassure himself he added, "Don't worry, I'm not laughing at you."

The last five minutes by the dashboard clock had been longer than the preceding five minutes. This struck him as funny, so he laughed once more. Why worry about getting the car to San Francisco before midnight when the minutes were getting steadily longer?

On a sudden whim he pushed down the automatic door lock. No use taking chances. At this speed it was doubtful if anything dangerous could get into the car with him, but it paid to be sure. He felt a slight chill at the thought, and thrust his hands into his pockets to warm them, and the perverse Lincoln swerved wildly. He grabbed the wheel. What the hell was going on? He shook his head to clear it of the light dancing from the chrome-work of approaching cars. Marvelous colors in that supposedly silver gleam of reflected sunlight —and how loud the sound of his tires was on the pavement! By stretching his ears he could even hear the tires of approaching autos.

Los Angeles. Intensely vivid streets. And then, waiting at a light, he saw Madame Neya. She was tiny, viewed through a telescope turned wrong-end to, but even at this distance he could see her great violet eyes. Eyes? Or empty sockets?

The head whipped toward him at sickening speed. It was huge. Then the lights changed, and the cars behind began to blare their hostility; but how could he drive right through that giant balloon face bobbing right in front of his windshield? Had to. Gritting his teeth, he jammed down the accelerator. The tires shrieked.

No, not the tires. Madame Neya, rolling over and over in his rearview mirror, her mouth distended, her teeth gleaming, her larynx working to form the screams. The words, rather.

ye who infuse hatreds—fulfill your work—never go in peace

Jocelyn Mayfield, screaming for peace, had slashed both her wrists because Ballard had taken her car and her man had beaten her

a Lincoln—he looked about the car—*this* Lincoln?

in San Francisco

Strength flowed through him. He had to get to San Francisco, help Jocelyn. Tell her not to do it. San Francisco by midnight

Somehow he got through Los Angeles

Serenity brushed him with gentle wings as he climbed into the darkening Tehachepi mountains on The Grapevine. How had he let a curse frighten him so? Jennifer, after all, was behind him, run down in Los Angeles, bleeding in a gutter—only Jocelyn was ahead—Jocelyn dead—but death, birth, decay—all were natural processes

Staring at the great clustered rock formations flanking the highway he realized that even stone decayed. It was a monotheistic universe: God was good, God was everywhere. But how to reach Him? How to say "sorry" to Him?

Ballard glanced at the gas gauge, and terror shattered serenity. Nearly EMPTY. Only a theistic, vengeful God would do that to Larry Ballard—Larry Ballard—guilty—guilty

don't panic— He regarded the gauge cunningly. Had to stop for gas, had to act natural. Station ahead. Breathe deeply—*don't panic*

He pulled in on the cement apron and waited while the attendant came around to the driver's side. Through the closed window he mouthed the words, "Fill 'er up." He watched the attendant set the hose, wash the windshield. The wrist of the hand wiping the paper towels back and forth was delicate, like a woman's. Like Jocelyn Mayfield's wrist. My God! The wrist was bleeding—green blood was washing down the glass

"Okay under the hood, sir?"

"What?" The blood was gone. "Oh. Yes. Okay. Fine."

"Eight-fifty, sir."

He was just a kid; how did they corrupt them so young? Ballard touched the button to lower the window an inch. It took twenty minutes, but the attendant did not hold out his hand. Hiding that slashed wrist—then as he reached for Ballard's ten-dollar bill his left eye popped out on his cheek—Ballard could see into the socket—into the brain—could see the thoughts forming sluggishly in the convoluted lobes

accursed—the word glowed redly

The grease-rimed fingers took an hour to close over the bill and all that time the eyeball swayed gracefully on its cable of optic muscle—the fingers moved away with the bill—the eye swayed

Ballard slyly had left the ignition key on to check that the tank actually was filled. Now he saw his chance. He twisted the key, slammed the accelerator to the floor while he snapped the transmission into DRIVE. Fishtailing wildly, the Lincoln screamed back out onto the highway. Safe.

Time, which was eternity, stretched ahead to midnight and the deadline. Darkness had come. Lights. From the cavern of his headlights, thrown down the blackness ahead, came life—from Cambrian seas to Devonian slime to Carboniferous forests.

He drove on—one hundred and fifty million years passed in a single hour by his watch—then with a sudden sob Ballard admitted it all—he was guilty—accursed.

when the night of action has arrived, the operator shall gather up his goatskin, the stone called Ematille, two vervain crowns, two candles of virgin wax, and four nails from the coffin of a dead child

Time passing. Half-remembered greenglow freeway signs. Bakersfield. Fresno. Modesto. Must have stopped for gas again—gauge all right. He couldn't make it—had to atone—had to save Jocelyn—but the razor blade was laid full-edge against the pulsing blue veins on the wrist of the girl seated beside him on the front seat

No, Jocelyn! Not because of an *automobile!* I won't

A sudden convulsive movement—blood bubbling up and running down the slim white arm—glowing eyes solemn beneath dark brows gazing sadly into his as her blood ran free

Staring in terror, Ballard suddenly became aware that the top of the car had begun lowering, like the canopy of that terribly strange bed in that story he'd read in high school. It was pressing on his head now—intolerable pressure

He began sobbing—the flesh was melting from his hands—what had begun as a soft suety look around the edges of his fingernails had become drops of hot tallow running down his wrists—like the blood down Jocelyn's wrists to the cold tiles of the bathroom floor

He wrenched the wheel over. Had to stop before the flesh was gone, before the marrow dried and the bones fell apart. Had to atone for Jocelyn for Jennifer for a hundred others. He was accursed damned. Had to stop get out walk in front of the next passing car

he waited

Better now—areas of the headlights which had been detached and revolving like mobiles, giving him glimpses of the eyeless sockets from which they had come, had begun to steady. Soon now he would atone. He watched the headlights through closed, opaque lids. Soon now—Soon

✕ ✕ ✕

The door, jerked open, nearly spilled Ballard onto the ground. The overhead light dazzled him, but the headlights now were normal. So was the gruff voice, demanding, "Hey, buddy, you okay?"

"What? Huh?" His head ached slightly. "Oh." He could see the gleaming leather belt and starchly crisp uniform of the highway patrol.

"I said, you okay, buddy?" The patrolman's nose was quivering, trying to smell booze. As Ballard watched, the nose began to lengthen and hair began to sprout on the man's cheeks—he was turning into a fox—

Ballard rubbed his eyes. The face was normal again.

"Sure. Thanks, officer. I got—sleepy." He yawned involuntarily. "Thought I'd better pull off the road. What time is it?"

"Ten forty-five."

Ten forty-five? Urgency shook him. "How far to San Francisco?"

"Just under seventy miles; you're right out of Manteca."

Ballard watched the lights of the parked police car in his rearview mirror as he pulled away. If that cop hadn't stopped—What the hell had happened? Jennifer's curse? He shuddered. As he roared on through the night, holding the big Lincoln sedan at 85, occasional demons still lurched beyond his arc of headlights, but they dissolved when he turned his face to meet them.

Would he make the deadline? He used Highway 50, taking the MacArthur freeway rather than the Nimitz. After the tricky interchanges at Oakland he swept down to the Bay Bridge's gold-lit toll plaza. On the bridge he shattered the 50 m.p.h. speed limit; using the Ninth Street off-ramp gave him a straight shot across Market and over to Van Ness Avenue.

At 11:56 p.m. he turned sedately into the Crescent Motors used car lot on Van Ness and Eddy, cut the motor and lights, and got the condition report from the glove compartment. The small shed at the rear of the lot spilled out light; he needed only carry the condition report up those three wooden steps, get it signed, and he'd make the deadline.

But he couldn't move. His hands shook on the wheel with delayed reaction; his body refused to function. Sweat stood out on his face.

Then from the darkness came a Negro. He was grinning. The breadth of his shoulders and the thickness of his chest gave an impression of bulk, but his hips were narrow and he moved with the grace of an athlete. Ballard released a long sigh. Bart Heslip, ex-boxer, for three years a DKA field agent. He'd trained Ballard, and was Ballard's best friend. Heslip opened the door.

"Hey, dad, what the hell you doin'? Waiting for the deadline to pass?" Ballard didn't speak. "What's the matter, man, you stoned?"

Then he saw the sweat on Ballard's face. He grunted, reached in to grab the condition report, and strode away without looking back.

Inside the shed a broad, heavy man in his thirties was reading a girlie magazine, one leg cocked on the dusty surface of his desk. A dead cigar jutted from a corner of his mouth. Heslip opened the door.

"Yeah?" The cigar switched corners without apparent volition.

"Cassavette?"

"Me." The big man stood up and yanked the cigar from his mouth and was balanced easily on the balls of his feet in one smooth movement.

"DKA's man. The Jennifer Poteet repo is outside. Keys are in it."

"I'll be a bird." From the doorway he looked out at the black gleaming auto. "I'll be a *dirty* bird. I tried to turn up this chick myself; would have sworn *nobody* could find her before the deadline—"

"How about kind of checking it in now?"

"Yeah, yeah," he muttered absently, scrawling his name and the magic numerals 11:59 p.m. across the bottom of the condition report. "Hey, look, where the hell did you find her?"

"It'll all be in the field report," said Heslip smoothly.

Ballard had finally got out and was leaning against the fender, wiping his face on his jacket sleeve. Heslip punched him lightly on the arm in passing, and they walked away, leaving Cassavette shaking his head over the DEALER copy of the condition report.

Heslip silently drove the company car out through the darkened Western Addition on Fell Street. He'd planned to drive over to his apartment on Steiner, where Corinne Jones was waiting for them, but it seemed better now to get Larry out to his own place on Lincoln Way near the Park. Corinne could wait. When you worked this job, your woman did a lot of waiting.

Finally he turned to Ballard. "Okay, baby. Give."

Ballard gave, his voice quickening over the recital, becoming compulsive, almost hysterical; he talked as fast as he could form the words. The curse. The strange derangements of the drive up.

"Cursed, huh? And you feel good now? Just a little headache?"

"Yeah. Bart, this Madame Neya said—"

"It started with sweaty palms, irritation at light, anxiety, physical disorientation, feelings of guilt and oppression—"

"That's it," Ballard exclaimed excitedly. "Do you suppose—"

"Don't suppose. *Know.* That wasn't any curse, baby. You've been on a bad trip."

"Bad trip?" Ballard's face had gone slack with surprise.

"LSD. Acid. Lysergic acid diethylamide tartrate. She gave it to you in the sugar cube, and an hour later—*VOOM!* Tripsville."

"But *why,* Bart? I could have smashed up the car, been killed—"

"Just what she wanted; hell, *she'd* lost it anyway. She *wanted* you to think you'd been cursed. Mumbo-Jumbo, god of the Congo, all that jazz." He shook his head admiringly. "Chick plays *rough,* man."

When the light at Stanyan stopped them, Ballard suddenly realized where they were going. "Hey!" he exclaimed, "isn't Corinne waiting for you over at your place? I don't want you to—"

"Cool it, dad, I'll get you home, pour some coffee into you—"

"Coffee!" exclaimed Larry Ballard. His face suddenly was sick.

Heslip looked over at him. After a moment Heslip began to shake. Then he couldn't hold it in and let out a roar of laughter. Yeah, man! The Lincoln sedan car was in the barn by the deadline, all right, and Larry Ballard had put it there. But Larry Ballard, boy acid-head, was going to be hearing about curses, and sugar in his coffee, for a long, long time around DKA. Bart Heslip would see to that.

FILE #5: BE NICE TO ME

Preface

In "Be Nice to Me," Larry Ballard gets emotionally—though not sexually
—involved with the subject, Maria Navarro, the woman whose car he is
supposed to repossess. Maria turns up in later DKA tales and Larry keeps
trying to get her into bed, which I use as a sort of running gag: he is always
unsuccessful, and is always swearing that he will never go out with a Catholic
girl again. He comes home just too damned frustrated. In the novel Gone, No
Forwarding, Larry loses his Maria Navarro obsession for good.

While "Be Nice to Me" was based on a real case, I wrote it mostly because
I thought it was time to show Ballard operating in a thoroughly unprofessional
manner, as every repoman I've ever known occasionally does. Note that I
didn't say unethical; merely unprofessional by repo agency standards. Which
are based on getting the job done. I also wanted to show how such a lapse
would be handled at an agency such as ours. Neither morality nor legality
enter into it; the field agents had a saying, "A felony a week whether we need
it or not."

That Trin Morales is even more unprofessional doesn't excuse Ballard's
failure. Morales appears only in this story, but popped up again in 32
Cadillacs and subsequently became an integral if unliked member of the DKA
team.

Giselle Marc's skip-tracing is based on Ronile Lahti's skip-tracing to find
the real-life Maria Novarro for me. Unlike Morales, when I spotted her car at
a branch library, I took it. And, unlike Ballard, I never offered to pay Maria's
overdue car notes for her. The real-life Maria prosaically redeemed the
vehicle and never let it get delinquent again.

A few years after this story appeared, I put poor little Maria's place to
hellacious purpose. To furnish my 1974 novel Interface with a jazzy opening
chapter, I moved Maria's apartment to the 1700 block of Bryant Street from
Linda Alley, stripped it of most of its furniture, and very carefully removed the
phone alcove with its little shrine. Then I set up a drug deal in the front room,
and made it go sour so a man died of a broken neck. Sic transit probita Mundi.

Also, waste not, want not.

FILE #5: BE NICE TO ME

Trinidad Morales had a brown moon-face, clever brown hands, and precise feet in brown oxfords. He was 29 years old, considerably overweight, and had been a field agent with Daniel Kearny Associates of San Francisco for two years. By the coming February, he figured, he would have enough experience to pass the California private investigator's examination and get his own license. Then no more skip-tracing, no more embezzlement investigations or repossessions. Divorces, then. Insurance frauds and electronic snooping. The meaty stuff that paid the real dough.

Morales sighed and rolled another snap-out form into the typewriter. After his reports there was a repossessed Mercury to go down to the Florida Street storage lot, and then cases to work.

At 9:00 p.m. a key grated in the street door of the basement below DKA's old Victorian building on Golden Gate Avenue. Morales stuck his head out of his cubicle just in time to see a tall, well-built, blond man closing the heavy door behind him. Morales' small brown eyes lit up. It was Larry Ballard, who had been with DKA just over a year and was getting quite a rep as an investigator. Ballard's blue eyes were oddly hard for his 24 years—and yet he was an easy mark when you needed somebody to help with your work.

"Hi, Trin. I didn't know you were here."

"Doing reports." Morales had a heavy, breathy voice as if he were recovering from an asthma attack. He added, with elaborate nonchalance, "Got a minute to run a repo down to Florida Street with me?"

"Sure. And then maybe you could help me with something."

"Jeez, Ballard, I'm really jammed up—"

"It's right near the Florida Street lot. A re-open for Cal-Cit Bank. The subject's skipped and the old Mexican lady in the lower apartment doesn't speak English."

Morales, deciding that Ballard was uptight about something, let his lips curve in a grin that showed a glint of gold from one of his broad white teeth. His eyes became almost sly. "As long as we're working *your* cases, Ballard, we might as well take a look at a couple of mine."

× × ×

The 300 block of Shotwell in San Francisco's Mission district was a row of gingerbready old houses, narrow, flat-roofed, crammed shoulder to shoulder. In the darkness their flaked pastel colors were a uniform mud-gray.

Morales parked in front of a hulking warehouse across the narrow street from 356; glass from the stone-pocked windows crunched under the wheels of his company Ford.

"The subjects are José and Maria Navarro," said Ballard over the hum of the two-way radio. "It's a '67 Pontiac Bonneville convertible, license L-S-G-1-5-1. When I worked it before, Navarro had skipped out and Maria had the car. She's got twin daughters about three years old and is trying like hell to raise them up right."

Crossing the litter-strewn street, Morales wondered idly how Ballard would know what kind of mother the subject's wife was. The front steps of 356 had collapsed and had been replaced with bare wood risers. Unpainted two-by-fours had been used as hand railings. Ballard gestured toward the right-hand door, which opened on an inner flight of stairs and was flanked by a brassy new mailbox with no name on it.

"Maria lived up there before."

Morales laid a stubby finger against the left-hand bell. After a few seconds the vestibule light went on and a shuffling Spanish woman appeared. She wore a black shawl and her seamed face was sullen. Morales spouted Spanish at her which contained the name of Maria Navarro. The old woman shrugged.

"Antes, si; pero se largo hace un par de meses."

"She cut out two months ago," Morales explained to Ballard. He turned back to the old woman with another question. Her answer was a gesture which seemed to suggest the vast reaches into which such patently unsavory women might disappear.

"Ask if Maria had any friends around here," Ballard suggested.

Morales did. The old woman spat a final reply, then slammed the door. The overweight, slightly bow-legged investigator rocked on thoughtful heels; he had heavy shoulders and a solid meaty torso. "She says this Maria broad was a cheap tramp who hung around the neighborhood bars. Sure your little chick ain't been nighthawking?"

"A prostitute? *Maria?*" Ballard shot a murderous look toward the closed door. "Why, that lying old—" He drew a breath, then said in a very different voice, "Hell, Trin, Maria had a job as a domestic over in Pacific Heights."

What gave with Ballard, anyway? Jumpy as a canary at a cat show. Morales started to say that he would snoop around, then remembered that it would mean a lot of work to satisfy a little curiosity; so he merely grunted, "Yeah, well, she's long gone from here. C'mon, Ballard, I got addresses to check on a couple of cases."

× × ×

On Monday, June 1st, Giselle Marc reviewed the Navarro file as part of her normal office routine, and then began skip-tracing on the case. The subjects showed a previous residence on Griffith Street, and Maria had been a domestic for a Mrs. Hosford on Scott Street in the exclusive Pacific Heights area. The husband José, who had worked in a warehouse on Market Street, had parents living on Harper Street in Berkeley. Giselle assigned the Berkeley lead to the DKA East Bay office and put a memo carbon of the other information into Larry Ballard's IN box.

She got in touch with the dealer who had originally sold the car and with the credit bureau; then she made a traffic-citation check with the San Francisco police, and ran the subject, his wife, and the car through the California Department of Motor Vehicle files in Sacramento for possible new addresses. No leads developed from this preliminary skip-tracing.

By Friday, June 5th, Ballard had turned in only a single report announcing that José had been gone from his employment for several months and had been dropped from Warehousemen's Local #860 for nonpayment of dues. Giselle read it, frowned, then scrawled *See me* across the spare report carbon and turned it back to Ballard.

At 5:30, when the clerical staff had gone home, Larry sauntered in to hook one hip on the edge of Giselle's desk.

"What's the gripe on the Navarro file?"

"*One* report in a week? What about the Shotwell Street address? What about Maria? Last time you worked it she had the car, not José."

Ballard said defensively, "Trin Morales and I talked to the old lady who lives downstairs on Shotwell. She didn't know anything."

Giselle leaned back in her chair and tapped her pen on the desk. She was a very bright and very handsome blonde, tall, slender, reserved, about Ballard's age; but three years at DKA had developed the hunter's instinct that all good investigators must possess.

"Morales said the old lady thought Maria was a prostitute."

"She's no prostie!" yelped Ballard. "She—"

Giselle nodded, tapping the file with her pen. "C'mon, Larry give to Mama. Are you playing around with the girl?"

"I'm not and I never was," snapped Ballard. "I don't even know where she is right now. I only wish I did."

"This is a re-open, Larry. When you worked the case two months ago, the girl all of a sudden brought the contract up to date. Did you make her payments?"

Ballard stood up abruptly and went to the yard-square map of San Francisco which hung on the wall behind Giselle's desk. He kept his back to her, seemingly immersed in the detailed streets.

"What if I did?" he asked without turning around.

"So you'll be looking for a new job if the Great White Father finds out.

You know how Dan is, Larry. *No personal involvement. Ever.* Did you think that by not working it you'd make it disappear?"

Ballard sighed, finally returning to the desk. "No. I know she's going to have to pay or lose the car. I just don't want to be the one who takes it away from her. You'd have to meet the girl to understand, Giselle."

"Try me."

"Well, okay. Her husband was a real deadbeat, just walked out on the three of them. The twins are absolute dolls. I took the two of them to the park one afternoon while Maria tried to raise the cash for the payments among her friends. She couldn't, so I lent it to her."

"And never asked for it back. So then she lets it get two down and skips again—for whatever reason." Giselle shook her head in wonderment. "Larry Ballard, the knight on a big white horse."

Just then Dan Kearny walked in. He was a square-faced, heavy-jawed man in his forties who drove himself and his crew too hard because he didn't know any other way to operate. Now he shot his hard, level gaze from one to the other, sensing the tension in the room like a hunting cat sensing its quarry.

"What's up?" he demanded bluntly.

"Larry and I were just talking about Kathy," said Giselle quickly. Kathy Onoda, the Japanese office manager who had been with DKA ever since the firm had started, had been missing work lately because of illness. "About how run-down she looks."

"She does that," agreed Kearny, put off the scent. He turned to Ballard. "Johnny Dell in Bakersfield needs a few days off, Larry, so I want you to go down there tonight and cover for him. He'll be back a week from Monday—the fifteenth. How's your work load right now?"

"Only one bad one," said Ballard unwillingly. "Maria Navarro."

Kearny's slate-gray eyes narrowed as his mental computer flashed. "That's a re-open for Cal-Cit. Okay, give it to Morales—he worked it with you one night anyway."

It was 6:00 p.m. when Ballard went down the steep narrow stairs from the second-floor clerical layout to the street. Morales was pulling up in a blue Buick Skylark, and Ballard paused to grin at him. He realized how pleased he was at being sent out of town; it resolved his division of loyalties. Morales would find Maria, repo the car, and Ballard could forget all about it. And about Maria.

"I'm going to Bakersfield for a week, Trin, so you're getting that Navarro skip to work."

"Don't do me no favors." Morales pursed lips and scratched the side of his nose as he watched Ballard walk off. "Now, why ain't *you* turned her yet, hotshot?" he muttered under his breath.

× × ×

Over the weekend Morales had some private business with a certain dancer from a Bush Street topless joint, so it wasn't until Monday that he got around to reworking the Navarro case. At Scott Street he ignored the breathtaking Bay view to learn from Mrs. Hosford that Maria had been a domestic with them for a year, but had been discharged following some anonymous phone warnings about her morals. The Griffith Street address was in the Hunter's Point projects —one of the institutionalized slums the city called low-cost housing—and here Morales spoke with a bountiful black woman who had never heard of the Navarros. Morales checked with the Housing Authority: no forwarding address.

It was still daylight when he parked across from 356 Shotwell again. Now the street was crowded with noisy brown and black children. Morales poked his nose up against the garage window: the Navarro chick might have stashed the Pontiac there before she skipped. Inside there was a car, all right, but it was a 1956 Ford station wagon with two flat tires and only one headlight.

As Morales stretched a finger toward the old woman's bell he realized that her curtains were gone from the bay windows; through the bare dirty panes he could see that the place was empty. *Que pasa?* Had the old lady skipped, too?

Then he saw that the door to the top stairs was ajar. He slipped inside and cat-footed up the interior stairs to the apartment.

"Hey!" he yelled. "Anybody home?"

"Front room," called an answering voice.

Morales entered a room which reeked of new paint. Two Caucasians about his own age were there, wearing Nehru jackets, peace beads, slacks so tight he could almost count their pocket change, and highly glossed ankle-length boots. Their dark hair was too neat, their eyes were too bright, and the skin over their cheekbones had an odd polished look.

"I'm looking for Maria Navarro," grated Morales, darting his eyes about melodramatically. Fruiters. Soft as mush, easy to push around.

"Do you think we're hiding her under the *molding?*" asked one with an affected simper. "After all, we don't know who *you* are—"

"Private investigator."

"Do you have anything to prove it?"

Morales geared down abruptly. The second man was tougher, older than he looked, probably wore a toupee, and did yoga exercises to keep his girlish figure. He had dark watchful eyes that gave nothing away. Morales knew the look; he had it himself Yeah, this would be the landlord.

"We're looking for the Pontiac—she's two down with the third due this month. She burn you for the rent?"

The landlord shook his head, his lean face clearing. Morales realized that he was wearing a carefully applied cosmetic base. "She was good pay with us until she lost her job. Try the corner grocery store."

"What happened to the old lady downstairs?"

"She died." He suddenly laughed. "Are you looking for her, too?"

"Yeah. She ain't paid for her coffin yet."

Morales walked slowly over to the grocery store. He'd grown up here in the Mission District, in one of the Mexican ghettos where the rents were high and the water pipes leaked and nearly every family was shielding a wetback uncle from Immigration. The store was rich with the smells of chile powder, onion, garlic, bay leaf, and drying strings of red peppers. The food shelves featured *tamales, enchiladas* and *tortillas*, and Morales automatically spoke Spanish to the shopkeeper.

"Old man, do you remember a girl named Maria Navarro?"

"Truly." He had silky white hair and an old-fashioned gunfighter's mustache. The gnarled hands gripping the counter were still strong; many years of field work had gone into them. "Who is it wishes to know?"

"I am her brother. Our mother desires that she come home now."

The old man nodded. "Truly," he said again. "Her man was of a badness—" He spread his hands in a vain attempt to encompass the badness of José Navarro. "It is he who caused the end of her employment, with his telephone calls. So she had to turn to the Welfare to live."

Welfare. Dammit. Not even a cop armed with a felony warrant could get into Welfare's files. The old man had gone on, his voice brightening as he talked of Maria Navarro.

"Welfare has found her a job. A very proud girl, that one." Morales, who had turned toward the door, stopped abruptly when the old man added, almost dreamily, "The checks she cashes, they are not in the name of Navarro."

"Then in what name, old one?"

Hidden malice lifted in the voice. "Her unmarried name. Which you know, of course, brother of Maria."

Que caray, thought Morales indignantly as he returned to the Shotwell Street address. That old man had caught on that Morales was not Maria's brother. Her *maiden* name, for chrissake! How was he supposed to find that out? The landlord, maybe?

But the landlord was gone. And then Morales saw some junk mail sticking out of the mailbox that had been Maria's. And folded over in the bottom of the box was a letter from Nogales, Arizona, addressed in a pencil scrawl to a name that might have been Maria Escajodo. Worth a try. At least it would give

Giselle Marc something to work on.

× × ×

Like all DKA field agents, Morales carried a heavy case load; so it was not until Thursday, June 11th, that he was able to review the Navarro file with Giselle and ask her to pop Welfare for Maria's work address.

"Okay, I'll make a couple of phone calls."

Giselle dialed the General Assistance office of Social Services and asked for Mr. Smith, thus learning there was a Charles Smith who was a field case worker in Aid to Families with Dependent Children. She then became Miss Simmons of the *Chronicle* to speak with Mr. Charles Smith, asking him about the Social Services "job placement program." There wasn't any, he said, but Social Services had been placing selected Welfare "clients" in a public library training program on an experimental basis.

Then it was a phone call, as Constance St. John of Social Services, disturbed over a misplaced file, to learn from the public library personnel office that no Maria Escajodo had been placed with the library. A Maria Escajeda—that was E-s-c-a-j-e-d-a—had been placed, however, and assigned to the Catalogue Section. Giselle called Morales.

The Catalogue Section was at 45 Hyde Street behind the main library building—a cavernous room crowded with females of every age and description except that of the subject. Morales stopped a fresh-faced girl who was passing by with an outsized armload of folders. He knew he had a better chance with her than with the hard-eyed woman who ran the place.

"*Señorita*, I look for Maria," he announced in guttural English.

"Do you mean Maria Escajeda?"

"*Sí.*"

"She's working at one of the branches now. Out on Potrero Hill."

× × ×

On Monday, June 15th, Trinidad Morales parked in front of the 20th Street Medical Building, across from the modernistic-pink branch library sandwiched between two much older private residences. On the previous Thursday, Morales had learned that Maria was off until today because her daughters were ill with the flu. It was against library policy to give out home addresses or phone numbers.

He drummed the steering wheel impatiently; the library would open in a few minutes, at noon. A beer truck pulled up, and its driver began to stack cased cans on a handcart as a red three-wheeler whipped into the curb behind the truck. The rider was a fortyish woman in a blue jacket, sunglasses, a hairnet, black Frisko jeans, hack boots; she jerked a pack of X-ray negs from the cycle box and clumped into the medical building with them.

A 1967 Pontiac, white with a black convertible top, passed and turned right into Connecticut. License: LSG 151. Driven by a petite Mexican girl. Two minutes later she reappeared, walking briskly toward the library. Her cheap, plain red dress showed the full exciting figure of so many Spanish girls; her eyes were huge and dark.

Seeing her, Morales thought, explained a lot about Ballard's handling of the case. Ballard probably had got next to her last time around; which meant that Morales ought to be able to do the same.

He walked around the corner to the Pontiac, got into it with the use of a window pick, and ran his bulky chain of 64 GM master keys on the ignition. Key 19 fit. Then, grinning, Morales re-locked the car and went away.

When Maria left work that evening and drove the Pontiac to Linda Alley in the Mission district, where the close-packed houses had an oddly Old World flavor, Morales was close behind. By the time she had found a parking place and walked back to number 74, he was standing in a shadowy vestibule across the alley. Even when Maria's head appeared in the second-floor bay window as she lowered the shades, he still waited. Finally a teenage Mexican girl emerged. The babysitter. Then Morales moved.

The house was white stucco, two apartments. Dead tendrils of ivy clung to the front; the decorative roof over the tiny porch showed missing shingles. The owner had probably kicked off, not leaving much insurance, and his widow had converted the upper floor into a rental unit to make ends meet.

He rang the old ornate brass doorbell for the upper apartment. In a few moments the stairwell light went on and Maria descended.

"Who is it?" she called through the front door.

"From the bank," said Morales pushing inside. "About the car."

He heard her sharp intake of breath. He was only five eight, but her richly waved raven hair barely reached his chin. She began to talk in rapid-fire Spanish, but Morales snapped, *"Hable ingles."* Being forced to speak English would keep her off balance. He jerked his head. "We'd better go upstairs, huh? You wouldn't want the landlady to know."

Maria's front room was crowded by its couch, overstuffed chair, portable TV, and a single floor lamp. In the old-fashioned phone alcove there was a plaster cast of the Virgin, with a votive candle flickering in front of it. The furniture was the sort usually found in furnished apartments. Through an archway he saw a spotless but makeshift kitchen; the other doors would lead to the bedroom and the bathroom.

Maria sat down on the couch, but Morales remained standing over her. "Any personal junk you wanna take outta the car?"

"Can I not keep it?" Her eyes were very large and liquid and troubled. "I have a job now again, soon I can pay—"

"I got my orders."

Her eyes flashed defiantly. "Orders! Then here are the keys. I will ride the bus to work from now on."

Morales should have remembered the old shopkeeper's remark about her pride. Well, there were other ways. Moon-face bland, he sat down.

"You know, Maria, all us investigators, we got our little arrangements. Take Welfare, now. They tell me where you're living, I tell them if José is sneaking in here on the sly."

Sudden anger darkened her eyes. "I spit upon José!" she exclaimed. "It is he who lose me my job with his phone calls."

Morales nodded. "*You* know you spit on him, and *I* know you spit on him, but what will Welfare do when I say he's still living here?"

"But it is false!" she gasped.

"Remember, you swore out a criminal warrant against José." Such failure-to-support warrants were a legal prerequisite for all dependent support payments, but she wouldn't know that. It would help convince her that Morales really was working with Social Services. And then he remembered Ballard. Perfect. He leaned forward to nail it down. "And *then*, when I tell 'em about you and Larry Ballard, they'll take your kids away from you."

"No!" Her voice was almost a shriek. Face contorted, she began sobbing out broken Spanish phrases. *". . . por favor. . . no me denuncies . . ."*

Yeah, she'd come around. She'd do anything to keep those kids. Very deliberately Morales put one clever brown hand on her knee. She stiffened at his touch, but made no other movement; the hand seemed to mean no more to her than a glob of mud thrown by a passing auto.

"Be nice to me, Maria," he said breathily, "and maybe you'll get to keep your kids."

"My children are asleep in the bedroom. We cannot . . ." She used the flat voice of the defeated down all the ages; but there was a defiant gleam in her eyes that Morales was too elated to notice. "Tomorrow night I will get Beatriz to stay with the children."

Morales quit grinning abruptly; by the shaded light of the floor lamp his face became sullen. Finally he nodded.

"Okay, tomorrow night. But I'm still taking the car tonight."

After he had gone, Maria crossed to the phone quickly. Her face was set, but her hands shook slightly as she dialed.

× × ×

Larry Ballard felt really beat. He had worked flat out in Bakersfield for ten days, and then had driven home. It was after 11:00 p.m. when he parked on

Lincoln Way and trudged across the street to his two-room apartment which peered from bay windows toward the green reaches of Golden Gate Park. Yawning, he dropped his suitcase just inside the door, crinkled his nose at the musty smell of the apartment, and went to the refrigerator for a beer.

Beat. He kicked off his shoes. Anyway, he'd left Johnny Dell's Bakersfield area in a hell of a lot better shape than he'd found it. It would be nice to relax and read a newspaper again, and even get back to his own cases. He grunted. Such as Maria Navarro. He hoped Morales had found her and got the car. He'd really dug that chick, though he'd never laid a hand on her.

The phone rang.

"To hell with you," muttered Ballard. But he got up and crossed the threadbare carpet of the front room on stockinged feet. "Ballard," he snarled into the phone. Then he started listening.

Two minutes later he was running across the street to his Fairlane. That pig, he thought to himself as he drove toward the Mission district, that dirty pig.

It was nearly an hour later, well after midnight, when he tried the basement entrance of DKA and found it unlocked. At the far end the one-way glass door of Kearny's private office was open enough so that he could see Kearny and the back of O'Bannon's flaming red head. Working late, those two. As he had expected, the white Bonneville with the black convertible top was blocking the middle of the garage.

Ballard went down the narrow aisle the convertible left in front of the field agents' cubicles, stuck his head into the one that Morales habitually used, and gestured at the car.

"How did you turn her, Trin?" he asked. His voice was deceptively tranquil, considering that the hand which gripped the doorframe was white-knuckled with tension. The chunky investigator glanced up from the report he was filling in and leered with self-satisfaction.

"I know how to dig, hot-shot." He tossed the case assignment to Ballard. "Here, read how you're supposed to do it."

Ballard leaned his long frame against the fender of the Pontiac to scan the report carbons stapled face-out to the back of the assignment sheet. Neither of them saw Kearny and O'Bannon emerge from the private office. O'B, a red-headed Irishman about Kearny's age, had been with him ever since the old days at Walter's Auto Detectives and was DKA's best field agent.

"So you caught up with her at work, huh, Trin?" asked Ballard.

"Yeah." Morales' eyes twinkled. "I ran the keys on it there today, see, so I could push it off tonight without no trouble."

"Why didn't you just take it then, Trin?"

"I had other ideas, man." He stood up to get confidential. "I tailed her home tonight, see, and then I told her that Welfare had asked me to check if her old man was still living with her. Get it? Then I said *maybe* I'd report negative—if she was nice to me."

"That was awfully clever, Trin," said Ballard silkily.

Morales uttered a heavy complacent laugh. "Yeah. This works out even better, waiting until tomorrow. I've already got the car, and she's too dumb to know I'm just stringing her along. So she'll think I'm doing her a big favor by not reporting her to Welfare, when really—"

Ballard's fist caught him under the left eye and knocked him backward into a chair, which upset to dump him under the desk. The heavy agent burst out in a scrabbling crouch, roaring, to butt Ballard in the midsection. Ballard went to his knees against the Pontiac, his face distorted, and Morales aimed a vicious kick at the head.

O'Bannon's freckled hand flicked up and dumped Morales back on the desk top. O'B went in fast, got a forearm clamped across the throat, his wrist gripped by his other hand for added leverage. "Cool it, baby," he said.

Morales thrashed helplessly until Kearny appeared in the doorway; then O'Bannon released his grip and stepped back.

"You'd better go on home, Trin," said Kearny mildly. "You can finish those reports in the morning."

Morales began sullenly gathering up his case sheets. Ballard was leaning against the Pontiac, very pale and with sweat standing on his forehead, but with his jaw set stubbornly. As Morales started out with the folders bulging untidily under his arm Ballard stopped him.

"Don't try going over there again, Morales. She called me right after you left. Know why? Because she planned to pack up and run, so you'd just find an empty apartment when you got there; but she was worried that I might get into trouble about making her payments for her the last time. I told her to stay right where she was—but to call the cops if you ever showed your face around there again."

Morales clumped out without a response, but Kearny looked Ballard over with a grimace. "Playing games with a subject, huh?"

Larry shrugged uneasily; his color was gradually returning. No use trying to explain that he'd made the payments because he'd felt sorry for Maria—just that, and no strings attached. Not to Kearny. Kearny never worried about motives; just results.

As if on cue Kearny jerked his thumb at a board which was fastened to the partition between two of the cubicles. It was lined and divided to show each field agent's name, radio call number, and monthly work breakdown.

"You see that tally board, Ballard? You see the number of repos Morales has made this month? The skips he's turned? The hours and mileage he's reported? The total of cases he's closed?"

"I—yes, sir."

Kearny rapped his knuckles on the Navarro car. "Morales put this Pontiac here—you didn't. All you did was a damned sloppy job on this case while you had it. If you pull something like this again, you're out, get me? O-U-T. You're looking for a new job."

"Yes, sir," said Ballard.

"I'm on your back, Ballard, and don't you forget it."

They stared after the retreating field agent until the door closed, then O'B cleared his throat. His leathery drinker's face was mapped with the topography of a lifetime. "Say, Dan, weren't you a little hard on the kid? Think what our liability exposure would have been, say, if Morales had gotten away with it tomorrow night and that girl later yelled to the Welfare people."

Kearny's rugged features broke into a grin. "Well, O'B, think what sort of laugh would go around the circuit if our client ever found out that one of our own agents made a subject's car payments for her!" He shook his head. "I guess I'm getting soft. I sort of wanted to bust Morales one myself."

"You sure hid it well," said O'Bannon drily.

They went out, setting the alarms and locking the solid-core hardwood door behind them. The fog was swirling in, around the parked cars, muffling the headlights and the mournful rumble of the traffic which shook the cement skyway above their heads. Kearny paused.

"I lit into Ballard because he's going to be a damned good man, O'B, and I don't want to see him get really hurt one of these days because he gets personally involved with a subject. As for Morales—" He slapped the redhead abruptly on the shoulder. "I'm giving him the sack in the morning. He's out. O-U-T. C'mon, I'll buy you a drink."

O'Bannon stared at Kearny for a long moment; then his irrepressible smile lit up his features.

"You know I never take *a* drink, Dan," he said happily.

The two men drew their topcoats about them and sauntered off into the fog like a pair of scarred and wise old alley cats out on the prowl.

FILE #6: BEYOND THE SHADOW

Preface

Many of Ellery Queen's novels contain a "challenge to the reader," so I thought it would be fun to try a mild challenge to the readers of a DKA File story. If it all worked as planned, the final twist would come in the final three words of the story.

Fred Dannay got a big kick out of the attempt. I hope you do, too. My AFTERWORD following the story is taken from my cover letter to Fred when I first submitted "Beyond the Shadow," and should make clear whatever you haven't figured out by then.

FILE #6: BEYOND THE SHADOW

Christmas Eve in San Francisco: bright decorations under alternating rain and mist. Despite the weather, the fancy shops lining Union Square had been jammed with last-minute buyers, and the Santa Claus at Geary and Stockton had long since found a sheltered doorway from which to contemplate his imminent unemployment. Out on Golden Gate Avenue the high-shouldered charcoal Victorian which housed Daniel Kearny Associates was unusually dark and silent. Kearny had sent the office staff home at 2:30; soon after, Kathy Onoda, the Japanese office manager, had departed.

Sometime after 9:00, Giselle Marc stuck her shining blonde head through the open sliding door of Kearny's cubbyhole in the DKA basement.

"You need me for anything more, Dan?"

Kearny looked up in surprise. "I thought I sent you girls home."

"Year-end stuff I wanted a head start on," she said lightly. Giselle was 26, tall and lithe, with a master's degree in history and all the brains that aren't supposed to go with her sort of looks. That year she had no one special to go home to. "What about you?"

"I've been looking for a handle in that Bannock file for Golden Gate Trust. There's a police A.P.B. out on Myra, the older girl, and since she's probably driving the Lincoln that we're supposed to repossess—"

"An A.P.B.! Why?"

"The younger sister, Ruth, was found today over in Contra Costa County. Shot. Dead. She'd been there for several days."

"And the police think Myra did it?" asked Giselle.

Kearny shrugged. Just then he looked his 44 hard-driving years. Too many all-night searches for deadbeats, embezzlers, or missing relatives; too many repossessions after non-stop investigations; too many bourbons straight from too many hotel-room bottles with other men as hard as himself.

"The police want to talk to her, anyway. Some of the places we've had to look for those girls, I wouldn't be surprised at *anything* that either one of them did. The Haight, upper Grant, the commune out on Sutter Street—how can people live like that, Giselle?"

"Different strokes for different folks, Dan'l." She added thoughtfully, "That's the second death in this case in a week."

"I don't follow."

"Irma Carroll. The client's wife."

"She was a suicide," objected Kearny. "Of course, for all we know, so was Ruth Bannock. Anyway, we've got to get that car before the police impound it.

That would mean the ninety-day dealer recourse would expire, and the bank would have to eat the car."

He flipped the Bannock file a foot in the air so that it fell on the desk and slewed out papers like a fanned deck of cards. "The bank's deadline is Monday. That gives us only three days to come up with the car."

He shook a cigarette from his pack as he listened to Giselle's retreating heels, lit up, and then waved a hand to dispel the smoke from his tired eyes. A rough week. Rough year, actually, with the state snuffling around on license renewal because of this and that, and the constant unsuccessful search for a bigger office. There was that old brick laundry down on 11th Street for sale, but their asking price . . .

Ought to get home to Mama and the kids. Instead he leaned back in the swivel chair with his hands locked behind his head to stare at the ceiling in silence. The smoke of his cigarette drifted almost hypnotically upward.

Silence. Unusual at DKA. Usually field men were coming in and going out. Phones were ringing, intercom was buzzing. Giselle or Kathy or Jane Goldson, the Limey wench whose accent lent a bit of class to the switchboard, calling down from upstairs with a hot one. O'Bannon in to bang the desk about the latest cuts in his expense account . . .

The Bannock Lincoln. Damned odd case. Stewart Carroll, the auto zone man at Golden Gate Trust, had waited three months before even assigning the car to DKA. That had been last Monday, the 21st. The same night Carroll's wife committed suicide. And now one of the free-wheeling Bannock girls was dead, murdered maybe, in a state park on a mountain in the East Bay. One in the temple, the latest news broadcast had said.

Doubtful that the sister, Myra, had pulled the trigger; if he was looking for a head-roller in the case he'd pick that slick friend of theirs, that real-estate man down on Montgomery Street. Raymond Edwards. Now there was a guy capable of doing anything to . . .

The sound of the front door closing jerked Kearny's eyes from the sound-proofed ceiling. He could see a man's shadow cast thick and heavy down the garage. It might have belonged to Trinidad Morales, but he'd fired Morales last summer.

The man who appeared in the office doorway *was* built like Morales, short and broad and overweight, with a sleepy, pleasantly tough face. Maybe a couple of years younger than Kearny. Durable-looking. Giselle must have forgotten to set the outside lock.

"You're looking hard for that Bannock Lincoln."

"Any of your business?" asked Kearny almost pleasantly. Not a process server: he would have been advancing with a toothy grin as he reached for the papers to slap on the desk.

"Could be." He sat down unbidden on the other side of the desk. "I'm a cop. Private tin, like you. We were hired by old man Bannock to find the daughters, same day you were hired by Golden Gate Trust to find the car."

Kearny lit another cigarette. Neither Heslip nor Ballard had cut this one's sign, which meant he had to be damned smooth.

"The police found one of the girls," Kearny said.

"Yeah. Ruth. I was over in Contra Costa County when she turned up. Just got back. Clearing in the woods up on Mount Diablo, besides the ashes of a little fire." He paused. "Pretty odd, Stewart Carroll letting that car get right up to the deadline before assigning it out."

"He probably figured old man Bannock would make the payments even though he wasn't on the contract." Then Kearny added, his square hard face watchful, "You have anything that says who you are?"

The stocky man grunted and dug out a business card. Kearny had never heard of the agency. There were a lot of them he'd never heard of, mostly one-man shops with impressive-sounding names like this one.

"Well, that's interesting, Mr. Wright," he said. He stood up. "But it *is* Christmas Eve and—"

"Or maybe Carroll had other things on his mind," Wright cut in almost dreamily. "His wife, Irma, for instance. Big fancy house out in Presidio Terrace —even had a fireplace in the bedroom where she killed herself. Ashes in the grate, maybe like she'd burned some papers, pictures, something like that."

Kearny sat down. "A fire like the one where Ruth died?"

The stocky detective gave a short appreciative laugh. "The girls got a pretty hefty allowance—so why were they three months' delinquent on their car payment? And why, the day before they disappeared—last Thursday, a week ago today—did they try to hit the old man up for some very substantial extra loot? Since they didn't get it—"

"You checked the pawnshops." It was the obvious move.

"Yeah. Little joint down on Third and Mission, the guy says that Myra, the older sister, came in and hocked a bunch of jewelry on Friday morning. Same day she and her sister disappeared. She had a cute little blonde with her at the pawnshop."

Kearny stubbed out his cigarette and lit another. The smoke filled the cramped office. Cute little blonde didn't fit the dead Ruth at all.

"Irma Carroll," he said. "You think her husband delayed assigning the Lincoln for repossession because she asked him to. Why?"

"So old man Bannock wouldn't know his daughters had financial woes," beamed the other detective. "We got a positive ident on Irma Carroll from the pawnbroker. Plus she was away from home Friday—the day the sisters disappeared."

"And on Monday she killed herself. When did Ruth die?"

"Friday night, Saturday morning, close as the coroner can tell."

"Mmmm." Kearny smoked silently for a moment. James (Jimmy) Wright —according to the name on his card—had a good breadth of shoulder, good thickness of chest and arm. Physically competent, despite his owl-like appearance. With a damned subtle mind besides. "I wonder how many *other* local women in the past year—"

Wright held up three fingers. "I started out with a list like a small-town phonebook—every female suicide and disappearance in San Francisco since January first. Three of them knew the Bannock girls *and* the Carroll woman, and all three needed money *and* burned something before they killed themselves. No telling how many more just burned whatever it was they were buying and then sat tight."

Kearny squinted through his cigarette smoke. He had long since forgotten about spending Christmas Eve with Jeanie and the kids.

"I figure you've got more than just that. Another connection maybe between your three suicides and the Bannock girls and Irma Carroll—" He paused to taste his idea, and liked it. "Raymond Edwards?"

The stocky man beamed again.

"Edwards. Yeah. I'd like to get a look at the bird's tax returns. Real-estate office on Montgomery Street—but no clients. Fancy apartment out in the Sunset and spends plenty of money—but doesn't seem to make any. What put you on to him?"

"Two of the hippies at that Sutter Street commune gave us a make on a cat in a Ferrari who was a steady customer for psilocybin—the 'sacred mushrooms' of the Mex Indians. On their description I ran Edwards through DMV in Sacramento and found he holds the pink on a Ferrari. A lot of car for a man with no visible income not to owe any money on. And—no other car."

"I don't see any significance in that," objected Wright.

"You don't sell real estate out of a Ferrari."

The other detective nodded. "Got you. And Edwards made it down to his office exactly twice this week—to pick up his mail. But every night he made it to a house up on Telegraph Hill—each time with a different well-to-do dame."

"But none of them the Bannock girls," said Kearny.

The phone interrupted. That would be Jeanie, he thought as he picked up. But after a moment he extended the receiver to Wright.

"Yeah . . . I see." He nodded and his eyes glistened. "Are you sure it was Myra? In this fog . . . that close, huh?" He listened some more. "Through the cellar window? Good. Yes. No. Kearny and I'll go in—what?" Another pause. "I don't give a damn about that, we need someone outside to tail her if she comes out before we do."

He hung up, turned to Kearny.

"Myra just went into the Telegraph Hill place through a cellar window. She's still in there. You heavy?"

"Not for years." You wore a gun, you sometimes used it. "And what makes you so sure I'll go along with you?"

The stocky detective grinned. "Find Myra, we find the Lincoln, right? Before the cops. You get your car, I get somebody who ain't shy to back my play. I'd have a hell of a time scraping up another of my own men on Christmas Eve."

Kearny unlocked the filing cabinet and from its middle drawer took out a Luger and a full clip. A German officer had fired it at him outside Aumetz in 1944, when the 106th Panzer SS had broken through to 90th Division HQ.

He dropped it into his right-hand topcoat pocket, stuck Wright's card in his left. He had another question but it could wait.

The fog was thick and wet outside, glistening on the streets and haloing the lights. They walked past Kearny's Ford station wagon, their shoes rapping hollow against the concrete. He felt twenty years old again. From a Van Ness bus they transferred to the California cable, transferred again on Nob Hill where the thick fog made pale blobs of the bright Christmas decorations on the Mark and the Fairmont. A band of caroling youngsters drifted past them, voices fog-muted. Alcatraz bellowed desolately from the black bay like an injured sea beast.

They were the only ones left on the car at the turn-around in the 500 block of Greenwich. Fog shrouded the crowded houses slanting steeply down the hill. Christmas trees brightened many windows, their candles flickering warmly through the steamy glass. The detectives paused in the light from the tavern on Grant and Greenwich.

"Which way?" asked Kearny.

"Up the hill. Then we work around to the Filbert Street steps. My man'll meet us somewhere below Montgomery."

They toiled up the steep brushy side of Telegraph beyond the Greenwich dead end, their shoes slipping in the heavy yellowish loam. Kearny went to one knee and cursed. When they paused at the head of the wooden Filbert Street steps, both men were panting and sweat sheened their faces. The sea-wet wind off the bay swirled fog around them, danced the widely-scattered streetlights below.

Just as they started down, the fog eddied to reveal, beyond the shadow of clearly etched foliage, the misty panorama of the bay. Off to the left was grimly lit Alcatraz, and ahead, to the right of dark Yerba Buena Island, the 11 o'clock ferry to Oakland, yellow pinpoints moving against the darkness. The foliage closed in wetly on either side. The Luger was a heavy comfortable weight in Kearny's pocket. He could see only about two yards ahead in the bone-chilling fog. When they crossed Montgomery the air carried the musty tang of fermenting grapes. The old Italians must make plenty of wine up here. There was another, more acrid scent; somewhere an animal bleated.

"They ought to pen up their goats once in a while," chuckled Kearny's companion. "They stink."

More wooden steps in the fog. They paused where a narrow path led off into the grayness.

"Catfish Row," muttered the stocky detective in Kearny's ear. "My man ought to be around some—" He broke off as a short dark shape materialized at their elbow. "Dick?"

"Right."

"She's still inside?"

"Right."

The newcomer pulled out a handkerchief to wipe the fog from his sharp-featured irritable face. Kearny got a vagrant whiff of scent.

"We're going in," breathed the stocky detective. "If the Bannock girl comes out, stick with her."

"Right," said Dick.

They started along an uneven brick path slippery with moss, then began climbing another set of narrow wooden steps which paralleled those on Filbert.

"Your man is talkative," said Kearny drily.

"Canadian," said the other. "A good detective."

"But you don't trust him in this." Kearny then asked the question he hadn't asked back in the office. "Why?"

Wright shrugged irritably. "I've got enough to do without having to watch him." He didn't elaborate.

They stopped and peered through the gloom at a three-storied narrow wooden house that looked egg-yolk yellow in the fog. Dripping bushes flanked it both uphill and down. There was a half basement; the uphill side had not been excavated from the rock. Myra Bannock must have entered by one of the blacked-out windows which flanked the gray basement door.

The two detectives climbed past it to the first-floor level. Here a small porch cantilevered out over the recessed basement. The front door and windows were decorated to echo the high-peaked roof of the house itself.

A big black man answered the bell. The hallway behind him was so dark that his face showed only highlights: brows, cheekbones, nose, lips, a gleam of eyeballs. He was wearing red. Red fez, red silk Nehru jacket over red striped shirt, red harem pants with baggy legs, red shoes with upturned toes.

"As-salaam aleikum," he said.

"Mr. Maxwell, please," said Wright briskly.

The door began to close. The dumpy detective stuck his foot in it and immediately a gong boomed in the back of the house. Kearny's companion sank a fist into the middle of the red shirt as Kearny's shoulder slammed into the door.

The guard was on his hands and knees in the dim hallway, gasping. His eyes rolled up at Kearny's as the detectives stormed by him.

A door slammed up above. They climbed broad circular stairs in the gloom, guns out. Their shoulders in unison splintered a locked door at the head of the stairs. The room was blue-lit, seemingly empty except for incense, thick carpets, and strewn clothing of both sexes. Then they saw three women and a man crowded into a corner, a grotesque frightened jumble, all of them nude.

"Topless *and* bottomless," grunted Kearny.

"But no Myra," said Wright in a disgust that was practical, not moral. "Let's dust."

As they came out of the room, feet pounded down the stairs. They'd been faked out—drawn into the room by the slamming door so that someone who was trapped upstairs by their entrance could get by them. Peering down, Kearny saw Raymond Edwards' head just sliding from view around the stairs' old-fashioned newel post. Edwards. The real-estate promoter who didn't promote real estate.

Kearny went over the banister, landed with a jar that clipped his jaw against his knee, stumbled to his feet, and charged down the hall. He went through an open doorway to meet a black fist traveling very rapidly in the other direction. The doorkeeper.

"Ungh!" Kearny went down, gagging, but managed to wave Wright through the door where Edwards and the black man had just disappeared.

There was a crash within, and furious curses. A gun went off. Once more, Kearny tottered through the doorway, an old man again, to see another door across the room just closing and the stocky detective and the guard locked in a curious dance. The black man had the detective's arms pinned at his side, and the detective was trying to shoot his captor in the foot.

Kearny's Luger, swung in a wide backhand arc, made a thwucking sound against the black man's skull. The black man shook his head, turned, grabbed Kearny, who dropped the Luger as he was bounced off the far wall. A hand came up under his jaw and shoved. He started to yell at the ceiling. His neck was going to break.

The black man shuddered like a ship hitting a reef. Again. Again. Yet again. His hands went away. Wright was standing over the downed man, looking at his gun in a puzzled way.

"I hit him with it four times before he went down. Four times."

"Edwards?" Kearny managed to gasp.

"That way." He shook his head. "Four times."

The door was locked. They broke through after several tries and went downstairs to the empty cellar. But there was another door; the durable detective kicked off the lock. A red glow and a chemical smell emerged.

"Darkroom," said Kearny.

A girl came out stiffly, her eyes wide with shock. It was Myra Bannock. A solid meaty girl in a fawn pants suit with a white ruffled Restoration blouse. Square-toed high heels made her two inches taller than either of them.

"Did you kill him, sister?"

"Y-yes."

Over her shoulder Kearny could see Edwards on the floor with one hand still stretched up into an open squat iron safe. He was dressed in 19th century splendor: black velvet even to his shirt and shoes. Once in the temple, a contact wound with powder burns. Kearny looked at his watch automatically. They'd been in the house exactly six minutes. *Six minutes?* It seemed like a weekend.

"Why'd you come here tonight?" demanded the other detective.

"Pic-pictures. I wanted—" Her jaw started to tremble.

"What kind of scam was Edwards running?" Kearny wondered.

"Cult stuff, I'm sure," said Wright. "Turning on wealthy young matrons to the Age of Aquarius or something. Getting them up here, doping them up, taking pictures of them doing things they'd pay to keep their parents or husbands from seeing." He turned sharply to the girl. "What kind of pictures?"

"Ter-terrible. Nasty things. We—he would give us 'sacred' wine to drink. It—distorted—able to see beyond . . . beyond the shadow. At the time everything seemed *right*." A long shudder ran through her flesh like the slow roll of an ocean wave.

"You and Ruth both?"

"Yes. Both. Together, even. With my own sister, with Irma—" She drew a ragged breath. "I sneaked in to get the negatives. I found the safe—but it was locked. Then Raymond ran in. I was behind the door." She suddenly giggled, a little girl sound. "He opened the safe and I saw the pictures inside, so I walked up and—and I shot him. Just shot him."

Without warning she started to cry, great racking sobs that twisted her face and aged her. The stocky detective was on his knees at the safe, dragging out a thick sheaf of Kodacolor negatives and a heavy stack of prints.

"Where'd you get the gun?" he asked over his shoulder.

"On Third Street," she got out through her sobs. "We pawned our jewelry to pay for the pictures."

"Same gun your sister was killed with?" asked Kearny.

"Does this have to go on and on?" she demanded suddenly, with an abrupt synthetic calmness. "I killed him. Just take me in and—"

"We're private," snapped Wright. "Hired by your father to find you girls. Tell us what happened up on Mount Diablo."

His tone got through and started words again.

"I—we opened the pictures we bought—Friday morning after we pawned the jewelry to pay for them. Just prints. No negatives. We knew then that he planned to ask for more money. Irma was trying to raise it, but Ruth and I decided to just—well, kill ourselves. So we drove up to the mountains to—" Her face was starting to crumple, but the detective held her with his eyes. "To do it. But then I said I wouldn't give him the satisfaction. I would burn the pictures and then come back with the gun. But when I started burning them—when I—"

"Keep going," said Kearny.

"Ruth just grabbed the gun from the glove compartment and ran across the little clearing. I ran after her but she stopped and—and—" She started to cry.

"There's no time for that now!" snarled the stocky detective to her tears. "Let's have it."

"She put the gun against her head and it made such a little noise." Her eyes were puzzled now. "Like a twig breaking. Then she fell down."

"Where have you been since then?" asked Kearny.

"I paid for a Lombard Street motel with a credit card and just stayed there. I wanted to shoot myself but I couldn't. Tonight the radio said they had found Ruth. I knew then that I had to come here and get the negatives, so she wouldn't have died for nothing."

"Just dumb luck she made it here without being spotted by the cops," said Kearny. He swung back to her. "Where did you leave the Lincoln?"

"On Montgomery. In front of Julius's Castle."

"Give me the keys." She did. He said to Wright, "The pawnbroker isn't about to identify the gun, since he sold it to her illegally in the first place. So if the cops find it here beside the body with only Edwards' fingerprints on it—"

The squat detective's eyes narrowed. He paused in his picture shuffling. "Yeah. It'll work. And they'll think Edwards burned whatever was in the safe before he did himself in. Yeah. Hand her over to Dick, tell him to take her back to her old man so his doctor can knock her out before they call in the police. I'll—"

"You'll burn the pictures," said Kearny. "While I watch."

Wright laughed, then handed a slim sheaf of them to Kearny. As Myra had said, they were indescribably nasty—acts performed by people strung out on the mind-altering psilocybin. The things people got themselves into while looking for kicks. It was lucky Edwards was dead or Kearny might have been tempted to do the job himself. He handed the pictures back.

"Burn them," he said harshly. "All of them."

The squat durable detective did. A good man, good when the trouble started. Myra drifted away into the fog with Dick's hand on her arm. The Lincoln was parked by the closed restaurant, as she had said, and the key started it. No cops spotted Kearny getting it back to the DKA garage . . .

× × ×

Kearny came to with a start, found himself slumped in his chair, his head hanging over the back at an odd angle, the edge of the typing stand digging into him. He groaned. His stomach hurt, his neck was stiff. Must have fallen asleep after getting the Lincoln—

Mists of sleep and dream cleared. He dug strong fingers into the back of his neck. Midnight and after, and he and Jeanie still faced a night of trimming the tree. The kids were at an age when Santa arrived while they slept, so Christmas morning dawned to awe and delight.

He stood up. Damned neck. Sleep and dream. Dream.

Dream.

Dammit! He'd fallen asleep over the Bannock file, with Stewart Carroll's wife's suicide on his mind, and Ruth Bannock's death, and had dreamed the whole crazy thing! Fog. Cable cars. The house on Telegraph Hill.

He rubbed his neck again. So damned vivid; but there was no Greenwich Street cable car. Had there ever been? Catfish Row was now Napier Lane. And the Christmas trees now had, not candles, but strings of electric lights. Goats and the smell of wine were both long gone, fifty years or more, from Telegraph Hill.

He flipped through the big maroon *Polk Cross-Street Directory* to 491 Greenwich. *Mike's Grocery.* In the dream an Oakland ferry: they had stopped running a dozen years before. No Bay Bridge either—it had been built in the '30s. As had Treasure Island, also missing from the dream, man-made in 1938, '39, as a home for the San Francisco World's Fair.

All so damned vivid. Usually a dream faded in a few minutes, but this one had remained, sharp and clear.

Kearny started to sit down, frowning, then stood up abruptly and felt his topcoat hanging on the rack. Damp. It should have dried off from the rain he'd ducked through this afternoon. Well, it hadn't, that's all. A better way to check: merely pull open the middle drawer of the filing cabinet to look at the Luger—

The Luger was gone.

Kearny stood quite still with the hairs tingling on the back of his sore neck. Then he slammed the drawer impatiently shut. Hell, it could have been missing for weeks.

But what if the Luger was found in a yellow house on Telegraph Hill, a house with a dead body in the basement and a safe full of ashes? So? The gun had never been registered, and it was tougher to get fingerprints off them than people realized.

Dammit, he thought, stop it. It had been a dream, just a dream. And despite the dream he still had to find the Bannock Lincoln before the deadline. He strode around the desk, slid back the glass door, stuck his head out to look down the garage.

Kearny's face felt suddenly stiff. Bright gleam of chrome and black enamel. Correct license plate. He went out, stiff-legged like a dog getting ready to fight, rapped his knuckles on the sleek streamlined hood. Real. The Bannock Lincoln. How in hell—

Larry Ballard, of course. Larry had been working the case, had spotted the car, repo'd it, dropped it off in the garage without even knowing that Kearny was asleep in his sound-proofed cubbyhole.

But what if Ballard *hadn't* repo'd the car?

Well, then, dammit, Kearny would dummy up some sort of report for the client. They had the car, that was the important thing. And—well, there would be some rational explanation if Larry *hadn't* been the one who'd brought it in.

Kearny left the office, setting the alarms and double-locking the basement door to activate them. He walked slowly down to the Ford station wagon. What did it all add up to? A crazy dream that *couldn't* be true, because it was mixed up with San Francisco of fifty years ago. Certain things seemed to have slopped over from the dream into subsequent reality, but there was a rational explanation for all of them—there must be. He would take that rational explanation, every time. Dan Kearny was not a fanciful man.

He reached for his keys in the topcoat pocket and touched a small oblong of thin cardboard. He looked at it for a long moment, then with an almost compulsive gesture he flipped it into the gutter between his car and the curb. It had probably been in his pocket for a week—people were always handing him business cards. Especially guys in his own racket, guys with little one-man outfits sporting those impressive-sounding names.

Kearny snorted as he got into the station wagon. What was the name on his business card? Oh yeah.

Continental Detective Agency.

AFTERWORD

Below is part of my cover letter to Fred Dannay at EQMM:

"Dear Fred: I am trying to write a new kind of procedural story here—what might be termed a 'procedural fantasy.' While it uses the dream 'story within a story' idea that antedates even William Langland's 14th-century Vision Concerning Piers Plowman, *it is also a DKA File Series procedural.*

"There are numerous clues that suggest it is a dream—or is it? —beginning with Kearny and Jimmy Wright walking past Kearny's car as if it doesn't exist in the time-continuum the two men now inhabit. Some clues—candles on Christmas trees—should be apparent to all. Others—the nonexistent Bay Bridge, goats penned on Telegraph Hill—will obviously have more significance to those familiar with San Francisco.

"Because the story grew out of my personal conviction that San Francisco-in-the-fog still belongs to Dashiell Hammett, I have inserted quite a few clues pointing to the identity of Jimmy Wright.

"First, the plot was frankly adapted from Hammett's masterly Continental Op story, "The Scorched Face." Even DKA's client, Golden Gate Trust, was borrowed from that story, as were the first names of certain characters.

"Next, the detective on stakeout was obviously that old Continental hand, Dick Foley. Besides retaining his first name, I described him essentially as Hammett did in Red Harvest. *(It was in* Red Harvest, *you'll remember, that Foley suspected the Op of murder and was sent away with the remark, 'I've got enough to do without having to watch you.')*

"As for Jimmy Wright himself, his physical description, reiterated throughout "Beyond the Shadow," is that of the Continental Op. His slang is the Op's slang, not that of Kearny's era: 'private tin' for private investigator; 'bird' for a man (instead of a girl); and 'let's dust' instead of today's hipper 'let's split.'

"We know the Continental Op was nameless in Hammett's tales, but I would like to point out the name itself as the clinching proof of his identity. As evidence I submit your own editorial remarks, Fred, that preceded "Who Killed Bob Teal?" in the July 1947 issue of Ellery Queen's Mystery Magazine:

" 'One night Dashiell Hammett and your editor were sitting in Luchow's Restaurant on 14th Street . . . Anyway, about this character known as the Continental Op: who was he, really? And Dash gave us the lowdown. The Continental Op is based on a real-life person—James (Jimmy) Wright, Assistant Superintendent, in the good old days of Pinkerton's Baltimore Agency, under whom Dashiell Hammett actually worked . . .' "

FILE #7: O BLACK AND UNKNOWN BARD

Preface

I wrote this story early in the 1970s, when I was no longer a full-time repoman for DKA. By then I was trying to make my living as a writer, but then, as now, it was very difficult to do so. As a result, I had an arrangement with Dave Kikkert. Any time I needed rent or living money, I would go in and work a 24-hour non-stop day, grabbing every car I saw, closing as many cases as I could, writing up my reports, then going home to crash before returning to the typewriter. Sometimes, if I had a really tough or tricky case, I might work a second straight day. Dave paid me $100 a day, which in the '70s seemed generous indeed.

I usually did this at the end of the month when my rent came due, and when the banks were faced with "item accounts"—contracts that would become two months delinquent on the first day of the following month. The efficiency rating of the bank's "zone men" who handled the auto contracts was based on how few "items" they carried over on any given month. A repoman's dream! You didn't have to talk to anyone, you just thugged cars!

It was on one of those 24-hour days that I got handed the case I turned into "O Black and Unknown Bard." For reasons obvious in the story, I couldn't close it out in one day. So I stuck with it until the resolution of the case.

Our client, as in the story, was in Louisiana, and the subject, who was black, had come from there. So I gave it to Bart Heslip because the racial angle made it a natural for him, and because I knew he could handle the opponents in the story with a great deal more aplomb and bravery than I did. I got the car pretty much as happens in the story, but there was no physical confrontation after I was lucky enough to repossess it. I wasn't that dumb.

In real life, naturally, I stole it and just kept going. Or did I? I know I was chased down by the CHP and was enraged as a result; but if anything else happened afterwards, I sure as hell didn't ever tell the Great White Father about it.

FILE #7: O BLACK AND UNKNOWN BARD

Dan Kearny raised flinty gray eyes to the stiff-faced man in front of his desk.

"Well?"

"Hoss, you ain't paying me enough for that."

J. Small laid the Elton T. Lang file on the desk. He had been a field investigator with Daniel Kearny Associates (Head Office, San Francisco, Branch Offices in All Major California Cities) for just three weeks; his name didn't go with his lanky six feet of height. He paused now at the door of Kearny's cubbyhole of an office deep in the basement of the converted Victorian bawdy house.

"Y'all mail my check to my rooming house, hear?"

Kearny, his square massive-jawed face expressionless, watched the lean Southerner's retreating back through the one-way glass. Kearny's eyes were deep-set, his nose was slightly flattened and bent to give him the appearance of an overage fighter rather than a detective who had spent a quarter of a century investigating frauds and defalcations, recovering delinquent chattels, skip-tracing deadbeats, missing relatives, and embezzlers.

He sighed, then opened the Elton T. Lang repossession file to search for whatever had scared Small off. First report, September 17th: J. Small had "upon receipt of this assignment this date" gone to "the above subject's address but at this time could not make contact." He had returned "to effect repossession" of the subject's 1968 Ford Galaxie in "the early morning hours of 9/18 but to no avail as unit was not on location." Similar reports detailing further Small sorties to 532 Grennan Street, Vallejo, "in the early morning hours to no avail" were dated 9/19, 9/21, 9/24, and 9/27.

That was all, except for a letter from the client, R. Williamson, Vice President of Dixie Fleet Leasing in Baton Rouge, Louisiana, demanding action. Kearny had ordered Small to go talk to people on the case. Apparently he had— only to be scared off somehow.

Kearny's buzzer sounded; Barton Heslip was waiting outside. Heslip was a totally black man, black as the grinning black kids that the movies used to depict with their faces buried in watermelons—but without the "yassah boss." He had been with DKA for nearly four years.

"Small turned belly-up, huh?" To Kearny's raised eyebrows he added, "His company car's parked across the street in the red; meter maid was hanging a ten-buck tag on it when I came in."

Kearny cursed almost absently as he pushed the Lang file across the desk.

"This is supposed to be the reason he wandered off."

Heslip buried his nose and hairline mustache in the folder. His features were unmarked, even though he had been a professional fighter before coming with DKA; he still trained three days a week.

"Nothing else? He didn't even give you a verbal?"

Kearny, cremating a cigarette, extended the pack to Heslip as he invariably did; Heslip refused, as he invariably did.

"You're looking at what we've got. You'd better cover Vallejo until I can shake one of the Oakland men loose, Bart. And wrap this one up, will you? The client's screaming on it."

Heslip went into his detachable accent. "Lord in hebben, Marse Dan'l, mah high-yaller gal jus' *spect*in' Ah'm gonna take her to de *talk*ies dis ebenin'. Ah don't do dat, she gwine sell me into slab'ry."

"I'll give her two acres and a mule for you," said Kearny.

Before leaving, Heslip called Corinne at the travel agency where she was secretary-receptionist, and hung up rubbing his ear. That Corinne, she just didn't understand that manhunting was Heslip's profession, the only substitute he'd found for the excitement of the ring. With DKA, it was your knowledge and your cuteness and your toughness against the adversary's. Sometimes he won, usually you won. And that's the way Heslip liked it.

× × ×

Vallejo without Mare Island Naval Shipyard would be just another sleepy town 40 miles northeast of San Francisco. Because of the shipyard Vallejo's population had exceeded 65,000 and its small, crowded, old-fashioned downtown was being jostled by sprawling subdivisions. The major streets were getting big-townish, sprouting used car lots, trailer parks, and drive-ins.

Heslip found that 532 Grennan was the standard California bungalow on the standard lot in an older, middle-income neighborhood—which meant you could lean against the wall without sticking your elbow through it. A teenage black girl answered his ring, bringing a murmur of living-room television to the door with her.

"Elton Lang here?" asked Heslip casually.

"You want Senior or The Third? Don't matter *which*, really, 'cause neither of 'em's here. Just me and my homework."

"The young one. He owes me."

Her face closed up. "Like I tole the man yesterday, don't know nothin' 'bout no owing."

But she hadn't shut the door. She had something further to say. The man yesterday, J. Small, finally knocking on the door.

"Elt, he's my cousin," she said, then added almost maliciously, "He got him a girl he been living with. Ain't got her address, but the phone is, um . . . 635-7825."

From a pay phone Heslip called Ma Bell's Vallejo business office to learn that 635-7825 was registered to a Marylee Beatty, 223 Contra Costa Street. This proved to be a new, cheaply constructed apartment building with twelve units and underneath carport parking. No Ford Galaxie. The mailboxes told him Marylee had 2-A. No one home. In 2-B there were two black men drinking beer.

"Elton Lang? Naw, don't know the cat. Know Marylee." He rolled wide eyes bloodshot from too much daytime TV. "Wow, man, that Marylee! Sure, she drove a '68 Ford Galaxie for a week or so. Don't no more. Secretary somewheres, that's all I know."

Back at 5:45. Marylee was home, wow indeed, her hair natural, her skirt very mini over lovely, honey-brown legs. Even features and severe glasses gave her a schoolteacher look.

"That cousin of Elt's, she hates my—okay, sure, he was staying here for a while. He was broke, in big trouble." She stopped abruptly, face almost scornful. "Hey, how do I know you ain't from the Man?"

Searching for a role Heslip snarled, "Get yo' head together, girl! I *look* like I'm from the Man?"

Apparently he didn't. She said, "*You* people ought to know where he is better than me." Her eyes suddenly troubled, she added, almost to herself, "Made his choice, made it plain to me." She raised her still-scornful face to Heslip. "You still here? Maybe his sister knows. Over in the projects, 1122 Monterey Street."

"Right on." Heslip added casually, "That honkey cat was around yesterday, you send him over to the sister's, too?"

"I sent *him* down to Headquarters."

Headquarters. Of what? What did she assume Heslip was part of, for which she despised him? What had Small run into, apparently at Headquarters, heavy enough to scare him off so completely?

Maybe the sister knew.

He got no response at 1122 Monterey, so he knocked at 1120 as the streetlights went on behind him. A black woman in her fifties opened the door. She was tall and lean and stooped, with a grayness of recent illness laid like dead ash over her brown skin. Her hair was white and kinky.

"They all out next door, it's my boy's place, he's married to Elt's sister, Helene. But Elt ain't living here anyways; staying with a friend name of Wilson, some such, out to Flora Terrace." A fairly new subdivision north of town by the municipal golf course, Heslip knew. The woman was slanting a look at him from the corner of her eye. " 'Course you ain't just *said* what you want with Elt . . ."

Her voice slid off. The stew bubbling richly on the gas stove behind her was a tangible presence in the apartment.

"I'm here to repossess the Galaxie. He owes on it."

"Mmmmph." Nothing showed in her face. Some time went by. She said, "How come you put down a man of your own color this way?"

"Color doesn't mean you don't pay your bills, Mama."

"Bills don't mean you go arrestin' a boy like Elt, neither."

The story, told over bowls of incredible beef-hock stew, was taken up halfway through by the subject's sister, Helene, after arriving with groceries.

Elton T. (for Truscott) Lang had been attending Louisiana State University in Baton Rouge, majoring in English and working nights and weekends as a mechanic for Dixie Leasing. When he'd wanted a car following his graduation, he'd financed one of Dixie's used lease cars through them. Then he'd decided to come to California and live with his grandparents on Grennan Street while writing the Great American Black Novel.

"Nothin' for that boy," said Helene, "except pickin' away at that typewriter. Moved in with us 'cause Granny couldn't take it, all hours of the day an' night. Me it didn't bother any."

"Did he tell Dixie Leasing he was taking the car from Louisiana?"

"No." Eyes that rivaled Lena Horne's dominated Helene's pinched face. "But he tole them a month after he got here. Called 'em long distance from my phone, nineteen dollars' worth. He wanted to register the car in California—"

"And Williamson demanded a payoff," Heslip supplied. It was standard procedure: by forcing a local refinance arrangement, the original lien holder was assured of getting his money.

"Thirteen hundred dollars he wanted—gave Elt twelve hours to raise it. Never did hold with Elt's college, jus' wanted him to stay there as a mechanic. Elt, he offered to make *double* payments, would of paid off the note in nine months. But Mr. Williamson, he said he was gonna get him a warrant."

"And he *did*?" Heslip was astounded. In four years he had never heard of a dealer really going for Grand Theft. Helene was nodding.

"Two days later here comes the FBI busting right into my living room where Elt was sleeping on the sofa, and they clapped the handcuffs on him right in my house, and took him off to Municipal Court. Illegal Flight to Avoid Persecution, they said—something like that. Our Granny, she put up her house as surety for the bailbond man."

"How long ago did this happen?"

" 'Bout a month. Elt, he changed after that. First he quit bangin' that typewriter, then he moved over to that Marylee's place, then out to that Wilson's place in Flora Terrace. We just got the phone number out there, not the address." Distress twisted her face, but Heslip was untouched. You got involved, you didn't do your job right. "They gonna make Elt go back to Louisiana even if you take his car away?"

"Of course not," said Heslip with an assurance he didn't feel. "All Dixie Leasing wants is the car."

Helene took him next door for the probably worthless phone number. Flora Terrace had garages, so he couldn't just cruise to spot the car.

"Could he have written the address down anywhere?"

Helene chewed her lip for a moment, then led him down the hall. "If he did, it'd be in here. I ain't moved anything since he left."

Project housing doesn't run to elegance. The room was small, furnished with a broken-down cot, neatly made, a table and chair. On the table was a dusty typewriter and a pile of manuscript. Taped to the wall was a verse.

O black and unknown bards of long ago
How came your lips to touch the sacred fire?
How, in your darkness, did you come to know
The power and beauty of the minstrel's lyre?

Unexpectedly, the lines touched Heslip. He reread them, then shrugged them off almost irritably and returned to his search. No memo pad on the table or in its single drawer, no address book. Heslip pawed briefly through the manuscripts; the top one was different from the rest.

As-Salaam-Alaikum, Beloved Brothers and Sisters of the Simba Black People's Party:

It is time that you became aware of the unjust treatment given a fellow Black in the struggle against this devilish pig society. On August 27, Black Brother Elton T. Lang was illegally arrested by the Federal pigs. The People's Revolution cannot

Heslip read it through, ebony face expressionless, then folded it and stuck it in his pocket. Lang's sister might not have seen it. He also drove downtown before returning to San Francisco for the night. The Simba Black People's Party Headquarters was on a littered side street near the Greyhound Station, a storefront building with boarded-up windows and no lights showing. No 1968 Galaxie in sight, either.

✕ ✕ ✕

The next morning Heslip called Williamson in Baton Rouge. "It would make my job a lot easier if that warrant was vacated," Heslip explained. "The way it is now—"

"I don't understand your concern over this Nigra's well-being," said Williamson coldly. He had a heavy Southern drawl that Heslip didn't like.

"Some of my best friends are whites."

"What? You mean that *you're* a—" Williamson paused. "Very well. I'll— ah—ask our lawyer to withdraw the complaint."

"I don't think one would want to marry his daughter," said Heslip after reporting the conversation to Kearny. "At least not this one."

"Our concern is the car," said Kearny sharply. "*Just* the car."

By 10:30 a.m. Heslip was in Vallejo and had learned from Ma Bell that Wilson's phone in Flora Terrace was unlisted. What he had expected. That left Simba Headquarters, the staging area for the black power radicals who talked incessantly about black pride, who wore quasi-military uniforms and snappy berets, and who ran around with carbines and rifles.

Not for Heslip. In the ring, that stud was there to whup your butt, just as you were there to whup his. Didn't matter what color that butt happened to be. Heslip was proud of *him*. Being black was an integral part of being Bart Heslip, but it wasn't the *source* of that pride. *He* was. He himself. Too bad it wasn't that way for Lang.

He got out of the company car and crossed the street. The Simba Black People's Party Headquarters didn't look any better by daylight than it had by night. A narrow storefront building, with a defunct record shop on one side and a boarded-up warehouse with double doors on the other. Passing the warehouse, Heslip checked suddenly, then went on, grinning to himself. Cool, man. Should have guessed.

Headquarters were so under-furnished as to be nearly barren. Straight ahead was a curtained partition to divide the single long room into a public front section and a private rear one. From behind the partition came male voices and the smell of coffee. In front of it was a bookshelf of unplaned pine boards bearing piles of revolutionary newspapers, including the *Simba Community News*.

To the left was a battered wooden desk with a plump black teenage girl behind it, a pencil in her Afro-cut hair. Her round, vacant face was intent as she hunt-and-pecked envelopes slower than she could have hand-lettered them.

"What you want, Brother?"

Heslip jerked his head at the curtain. "Elton Lang, Sister."

"You ain't a Simba?" When Heslip just shook his head, so did she. "Then you cain't talk to him, man."

Before Heslip could argue, the curtain parted and a man sauntered out. To merely call him a man was to call a battleship a boat. He stood an easy six foot six, and wore GI fatigue pants under a violent purple shirt stretched skin-tight by tremendous blocky weight-lifter shoulders. He outweighed Heslip's 158 by 100 pounds.

"You heard the Sister," he said. His face was a block of black granite scarred on one side by an ancient knife fight and decorated with a nose that had nothing left to fear from club or bottle. "Simbas only here, jes' like I tole the honkey cat I run off yesterday."

No wonder Small had split after running into this stud. But Heslip didn't move. The giant's head sank down between yard-wide shoulders; his breath abruptly began to hiss between his teeth. The girl was staring at him so raptly that her mouth was hanging open.

At the last possible moment Heslip said, "I'll be across the street. On city property."

Which left purple-shirt nothing to attack but a back already retreating. Across the street Heslip leaned against his fender, arms folded, and waited. He had a hunch it wouldn't be long. It wasn't. Ten minutes later a slim young black man in slacks and sports shirt came out of Headquarters alone. He had a handsome angry face, even-featured, with high cheekbones and his sister's huge melting eyes. Right now they snapped with scorn.

"Helene *said* some Tom want to take my car away from me."

Heslip just laughed. "You living like this because you got busted? Man, *I'm* blacker than you—but I pay my bills."

"Sure, you're a good Tom," said the boy bitterly. "You—"

" 'O black and unknown bard,' " quoted Heslip softly, " 'How came your lips to touch the sacred fire?' "

The boy went into a furious crouch like an angry Doberman and cursed him, bitterly, foully, but Heslip didn't even unfold his arms. He merely craned forward, as if examining a rare exotic animal.

"What you, boy, some kind of writer or something? Or you just a talker?"

Lang drew a deep ragged breath and straightened up. Good stuff in him, Heslip had to admit. Only the shakiness of his voice betrayed him.

"You through?" Then he blew it. He yelled, "We Simbas are *men! Black* men, ready to fight and die for freedom *now!* You're a corrupted traitorous counter-revolutionary who's sold out to the racist pigs!"

"Because I work for a living?"

The boy threw two more words at him, then stalked off stiffly across the street. Heslip got into the company car. His hands were shaking. Then his face lost its sullen ferocity and he chuckled. Hell, baby, you make them play your game in this business. He'd shook the boy up good, and if the Simbas run true to form—

Yeah, man. Four of them, all there were in the building, he hoped. Lang. Purple-shirt—probably Wilson—and two others wearing fatigue jackets and berets. No guns. They all got into an old Chevy panel truck at the curb, very carefully not seeing Heslip.

The truck pulled away; when it was nearly to the corner, Heslip U-turned to fall in well behind. It swung north, through town. Toward the Flora Terrace subdivision where Lang and Wilson lived—where the Galaxie might reasonably be.

But the instant the truck made the turn out of sight, Heslip pulled over quickly, was out of his car with his repossession order in one pocket and pop keys, window picks, and jump wires in another. It was a matter of minutes now, possibly just seconds.

Item: they'd wanted him to follow, wanted to lead him away.

Item: four was the ideal number for stomping somebody who unsuspectingly followed a panel truck to a garage where there wasn't any Galaxie after all.

Item: the warehouse double doors were barred on the inside, and were wide enough to admit a full-size sedan. A Galaxie, say.

Item: Heslip had seen treadmarks across the curb and sidewalk in front of the doors when he had first walked by.

Now if the Simbas would just take several minutes to realize that he wasn't behind them and if the vacant-faced girl now (hopefully) alone in Simba Headquarters was as dumb as she looked—

He was halfway to the partition before the pudgy receptionist had found enough of her wits to start up behind her desk, yelling.

"Hey, you, Simbas only! What—"

A groove, man. A girl yelling couldn't be phoning for help. He was through the partition—no one there! —past the triple hotplate and wisping coffee pot. Yes! The door in the right-hand wall *did* open into the warehouse. Unlocked. If—

The Galaxie was there. Yellow in color. Louisiana plates. Doors— *unlocked!* Keys—*in it!* Heslip ran to the big double doors, flipped aside the two-by-four barring them, violently shoved, and they swung open, wide.

"Damn you, *stop!* You can't—"

No brains, that girl, but nothing wrong with her lungs.

Heslip was into the Galaxie as the girl came around the front of it, his eyes already confirming the last four digits of the motor number on the doorpost, solid man, a groove, right on, he was pumping the foot feed, twisting the key.

It started instantly, he floored it, out it went, back end slewing, horn yelping under his hand, right out through the doors and across the sidewalk as the girl leaped aside like an out-of-condition matador. Heslip slammed the wheel hard over, left, taking the car in the opposite direction from the panel truck. One eye on the mirror, the other on the street on which he was traveling too fast. No time to call the repo in to the cops, not now; get to the freeway and out of town.

Hot damn! He pounded the steering wheel in elation. Try that on your Simba rhetoric, baby.

But sixty-fiving south on Interstate 80, Heslip felt his triumph evaporate. He had got the car in the only way possible, short of sheriff's replevin; Williamson would be delighted and Kearny might even act pleased. And yet—Elton T. Lang was going to be pushed further into the revolutionaries' control. Further from his family and Marylee, further from his dream of being a black Hemingway.

To hell with it, Heslip thought as he started across the bridge spanning the Carquinez Straits. Not his problem. He checked the mirror and saw a highway patrol car far behind him. Had to report the repossession to the police by phone from Richmond or somewhere.

The black-and-white was coming up fast, red lights flashing, so Heslip pulled into the middle lane. Man, they were in some kind of a hurry. Must have got a hot one on the radio.

The patrol car hit the middle lane, too. Okay, cats, the slow lane to let you by.

The patrol car switched.

After *him*, for God's sake? Damn! Should have phoned from Vallejo. But who would have thought the Simbas would have reported it as stolen? A grim irony there.

As he got out of the Galaxie to walk back to the cruiser, the driver, out first, threw down on him. Heslip froze; the muzzle of the .38 looked as big as the rain barrel under the eaves of the old farmhouse where he had been born back in Missouri.

"Okay, hands on the car, feet back and spread, lean forward. *Move!*"

Heslip moved, rage boiling up as rough hands frisked him. He began to speak, but the cop cut him off.

"Just get that right hand on top of the head, Lang." Cuffs bit coldly at his wrist. "Now the left hand on—"

"Dammit, *NOT* Lang!" Heslip shouted, finally breaking through their ritual. "Barton Heslip, with Daniel Kearny Associates of San Francisco. I repossessed this vehicle in Vallejo twenty minutes ago."

That stopped it. He showed them his driver's license, private investigator's registration card, and the repossession order on the Galaxie. The older patrolman, who had a hard tanned face with a white bank around his forehead marking where his cap covered, abruptly removed the cuffs.

"We're—er—sorry, Mr. Heslip. Spotted the car on the hot sheet, saw a black man driving, assumed—"

"We all look alike to you?" snapped Heslip, rubbing his wrist. "Okay, not your fault. That damned FBI Flight to Avoid warrant was supposed to have been killed this morning. It—"

The older patrolman had returned to the cruiser; the younger one was frowning. "We got it as Grand Theft against Lang. A Louisiana warrant, teletyped out just today."

Williamson had sent out the warrant *after* talking to Heslip! He apparently didn't like blacks, not even when they were doing his work for him. Damn him. If that cat wanted to push, Heslip would push back.

The other patrolman returned from running Heslip through CLETS—the new California Law Enforcement Telecommunications System. His face said the detective was clean.

"Since you represent the vehicle's legal owner we have no further cause to detain you. Or the vehicle. I hope you will accept our apologies for any inconvenience—"

"Part of the game," said Heslip. Then he added casually, "But you *will* get the Galaxie off the hot sheet, won't you? I don't want to get stopped by every patrol unit between here and San Francisco."

They assured him the car would be cleared through the CLETS network, the three men shook hands, and returned to their respective cars. Heslip used the Rodeo turnoff to get back on Interstate 80 north—back toward Vallejo. Kearny was going to flip if he ever heard about this little maneuver, because Heslip stood a good chance of losing the car again. Or of getting beat up. Or both. It went against all his own carefully ingrained professional habits, too: but there was a chance. Lang had wavered there for a moment.

The four Simbas were gathered on the sidewalk in front of the still-gaping double doors when Heslip stopped the yellow Galaxie across the street. As he got out they saw him and came at him fast, Lang and purple-shirt in the lead.

"Oh, baby," crooned the giant, "did you mess it up!"

"Did I?" Heslip's voice was nonchalant, as was his pose against the car's fender, but his guts were churning. Well, use your fear, use the adrenaline it pumped into your bloodstream; use your heightened perceptions and quickened pulse and sharpened reflexes.

"Why did you come back?" yelped Lang in a frightened voice.

Yeah, man! Scared of what the others would do to Heslip.

"Why, to get a driver to take my car back to the city, of course," he said as if surprised at the question. "Want the job? I'm getting all the charges against you dropped, so—"

"Man, you really too stupid to know what's gonna happen to you?" demanded purple-shirt.

They were poised, set on a knife-edge. They could go either way. And then purple-shirt made his move.

"*Hai!*" he yelled, flicking the karate chop known as the backhand lash at Heslip's neck.

A few hours of hand-to-hand combat instruction, however, don't make any amateur the equal of a professional fighter, and Heslip had won 39 out of 40 career fights.

As the plank-like rigid hand exploded toward him, he just wasn't there anymore. He came off the car to his own left, pivoting so the hand would whoosh harmlessly past his shoulder, countering while purple-shirted Wilson was still at full stretch, off balance, moving into it.

Heslip, spurred by fear, had never hit anyone harder. His fist, thumb down and knuckles parallel to the ground, caught Wilson right in the throat. No knuckles would be broken that way.

The huge man went backward and sideways right across the hood of the Galaxie as if struck by a .45 slug. He landed on one shoulder in the grease-rimmed street with a sickening crack of breaking bone, rolled over once, tried to get up once, sprawled on his face. A sound like escaping steam came from him, the closest thing to a scream his larynx was capable of producing.

"Any other takers?" asked Heslip in a terrible soft voice that robbed the question of theatricality.

No takers. The other two Simbas were nothing, ciphers, they didn't exist. Him against me, his knowledge and his cuteness and his toughness against mine. Purple-shirt hadn't had enough of any of them.

"You coming, kid?"

Lang turned a stunned, blinded face toward him.

"Here's the keys." To Lang's own car. If it was going to work, it would work all the way. "Meet me at Golden Gate and Gough in the city. Got that?"

"Gol-Golden Gate—"

"Good man. Driver's fee is ten buck plus a bus ticket back."

He walked to his company car without a backward glance.

× × ×

"You *what?*" roared Dan Kearny.

Heslip had told his story. He shrugged almost sullenly. "The car's in the barn, isn't it? It worked. And I'll tell you something else, Dan. I'm gonna call that guy in Baton Rouge and tell him I've got his car and I'm gonna hold it until those warrants are voided, and he isn't gonna get a payoff or any bids until—"

Kearny had stood up; he inclined abruptly across the desk so that his heavy blunt features were a scant six inches away from Heslip's face.

"*I* will call the client, Mr. Heslip, and I will tell him what I feel is in the best interests of DKA, and nothing more. Got that?"

"I—"

"Got that, Mr. Heslip?"

"I—yes, sir."

But in his cubicle, after he had ratcheted a report form into his typewriter, Heslip found himself unable to type. Dammit, Kearny was *wrong*. Lang thought the warrants had been cleared, and—

Kearny's phone extension had lighted up. Probably calling Williamson. Business as usual, Heslip thought bitterly. As if by its own volition his hand snaked out to jab the lighted button, then lightly and guardedly lifted the receiver. Kearny was in mid-speech.

"…surprised at your attorney's action, Mr. Williamson. I know that *you* would never have any part in hounding that poor black boy, but even so, Dixie Leasing has been laid open for a civil rights suit. I *think* our man Heslip has gotten Lang to drop the Criminal Persecution charges he was going to file, but—"

Almost reverently, Heslip slipped the receiver back into place. Beautiful, man. Walk all over Heslip for getting out of line, then call up Williamson and make him swallow what Heslip had wanted. Take him right down to the nitty-gritty without ever quite pushing his embarrassment to anger. Yeah, man! Bart Heslip still had a lot to learn.

Meanwhile Dan Kearny was one sweet cat to work for. The black field agent began typing reports, whistling softly through his teeth.

In his cubbyhole Kearny had finished his conversation. Years back, he remembered, he'd called a client himself because he was sore about something. Just as Heslip had wanted to do. They'd lost the account, and Old Man Walters had racked him up but good.

His mouth quirked at the corners. Bart had listened in, of course; Kearny had heard the receiver being raised. Good. The kid was learning the detective's basic maxim: never trust anyone entirely, not even yourself, because just being human made you full of surprises.

Kearny shook a cigarette from his pack and dragged over a stack of files due for review. The top one was labeled Elton T. Lang. He tossed it into the CLOSED bin. When the final field report and the auto condition report came in, he could bill that one out.

FILE #8: THE O'BANNON BLARNEY FILE

Preface

I had been stuck with running the DKA Oakland office for several weeks because our office manager had crashed and burned, and there was nobody else to do it. I hated it: I had always been a field man, and was uncomfortable behind a desk doing "business" rather than being out in the field thugging cars.

So I jumped at the chance to break in a new man by taking him on a swing up Sacramento Way. We had to clean up cases left unworked since our local man had been so inept as to let an enraged subject slam a car hood on his back. This kid riding with me was just 20 years old, and he was fantastic. I'd never worked with anyone who had such an instinctive aptitude for the game. As a result, it was one of the funniest, best days of my repoman life.

Of course it was too good to be true. When we got back to the office the next morning (the story explains why it took us all night), his father was waiting. He insisted his son quit after only one day: it was too dangerous, don't you know, it was grungy, and besides, Junior had to get back to college.

This goofy day on the road seemed a natural for the DKA File Series. I gave the story to O'B and Larry Ballard on St. Paddy's Day—O'B in my role, Larry in the kid's role. I thought it was deliriously funny. More than any other story in the series, this one gives you an inkling of why I loved being a repoman, and why I found it so hard to quit the game even to fulfill my lifelong ambition of becoming a writer full-time.

So I was feeling really good when I sent it in. But what did I know? Fred Dannay rejected it out of hand—my first turn-down from EQMM! Why? I demanded. Fred said each File Story had to deal with only one case; something about dramatic unity.

I was peeved; I needed the money.

At the same time, an old friend named Dean Dickinsheet was putting together an anthology of original stories to be called Men and Malice. *I was mad at Fred, so I gave Dean "The O'Bannon Blarney File" for his anthology. It is the only File story that did not first appear in EQMM. But alas, once I was over my mad, I felt secretly ashamed to have shattered the DKA/EQMM tradition.*

FILE #8: THE O'BANNON BLARNEY FILE

"March seventeenth!" Dan Kearny fell back weakly in his chair, cold gray eyes fixed in disbelief on his desk calendar. "My God, Giselle, it's—"

"—St. Paddy's Day," she said hollowly. Giselle Marc was a tall, slender, wickedly curved blonde who was much too intelligent to be so attractive. "To O'B, it's Christmas and New Year's and the Fourth of July and Happy Hanukkah and his Saint's Day all rolled into one."

"And *you* send him off to Sacramento! Out of town, on St. Paddy's Day, with one of the new men . . ."

"Larry Ballard isn't exactly *new*, Dan. He's been a field investigator with DKA going on two years."

They were in Kearny's soundproofed cubbyhole in the basement of the old narrow Victorian ex-bawdy house which served as head offices for Daniel Kearny Associates. Kearny scowled, hunched ex-prizefighter shoulders, stuck out his ice-breaker jaw. He was a stocky, thick-chested, compact man with thinning curly hair.

"Too new to ride with O'B on St. Paddy's Day. Remember last year? O'Bannon came off the freeway, loaded, at seventy miles an hour and broadsided a new Polara with a cop standing on the corner—"

"An *Irish* cop. And by some miracle the other guy was driving on a suspended license." He shook his heavy graying head bitterly. "How could you *do* this to me, Giselle?"

× × ×

It must be admitted: O'Bannon Had Been Drinking. But, as he pointed out to Larry Ballard, Kearny was to blame. Expecting O'B to work on St. Paddy's Day! And worse, in *Sacramento* instead of San Francisco! As well Dismal Seepage, Arkansas.

"It isn't *Dan's* fault that our Sacramento man let that guy slam a car hood on his back," Ballard pointed out.

"I'm not so sure," said O'B darkly, leading the younger man into yet another bar's cool shadowing interior. It seemed to Ballard that they had spent the day playing liar's dice for drinks in a succession of undistinguished bistros; yet they had somehow closed out a disconcerting number of open cases.

"Sacrilege!" exclaimed O'Bannon.

Ballard, who admitted to no ethnic affiliations, stared about in bewilderment. "What do you mean?"

The Rathskeller, as its name implied, was a German-style *Bierhaus* of darkly varnished woodwork, a back bar lined with heavy steins, and imported beer on tap. Now, however, the place was wildly decorated with giant shamrocks, cardboard Leprecauns, and twisted streamers of green crepe paper. Behind the stick was an apparently Teutonic gentleman with thick hairy forearms and the pale butch-cut hair of a Hitler Youth. He was just raising a mug to his lips; festive green food coloring had been added to the beer therein.

"Sacrilege," repeated O'Bannon brokenly.

The bartender lowered his tankard, did a slow take around his establishment, then took in the Irishman's shamrock green tie, flaming red hair, and lean freckled drinker's face. Finally he nodded.

"I'll lay you a double shot of Bushmill's that I'm more Irish than you are, Red."

An unholy light came into O'Bannon's eyes; he began shamelessly gargling his r's. "Holy Mither presairve us." He rubbed his hands briskly together, then laid his driver's license on the bar beside the three doubles the bartender was pouring. "Faith, and 'tis Patrick Michael O'Bannon I be, begorra—as confirmed by the Department of Motor Vehicles of this gr-r-reat state."

"Man, you're a Mick, all right. But . . ."

The bartender almost regretfully produced his own license and laid it next to O'Bannon's. Their heads drew close over it. After a long moment, O'B heaved a bitter shuddering sigh, and very slowly laid a ten-dollar bill on the stick next to the three double Bushmill's.

The publican's name was Seamus Sean Irish.

× × ×

"We should have phoned in *hours* ago," Ballard said weakly.

O'B, in the outdoor phone booth next to The Rathskeller, was having a little trouble finding the slot with his dime. He paused to pontificate. "The trouble with you, Ballard me lad, is that you're too cautious. *Strike . . .*" His gesture would have carried him outside the booth if the metal-flex from the receiver hadn't stopped him. His dime popped from between his fingers and catapulted into the slot. ". . . while the iron is hot. Observe people, Ballard me lad. Study them. Every man has his weakness . . ."

"What's my weaknesh . . . ah, weakness, O'B?"

"Sad-eyed women who either kill themselves or put something in your coffee." He paused to give the long-distance operator the collect call. "Mine is never taking *a* drink. Dan Kearny's is a deplorable lack of faith in my ability to . . . what? Hello?"

Ballard could hear Giselle, clearly speaking with her mouth pressed close to the phone. "The Great White Father is on the warpath, O'B! He wants—"

"O'BANNON, WHY IN HELL HAVEN'T YOU PHONED IN? WHERE ARE YOU?"

O'B held the blaring phone from his ear, wincing, then answered in a tour-guide's singsong. "Sacramento, the historic capital of California, is center of the 'forty-nine gold rush—"

"DON'T GET CUTE WITH ME, O'BANNON! I sent you up there to work cases, not get Ballard drunk in some cheap gin mill. What about that Drake Plymouth? We've been chasing that guy for three months—"

"Plymouth's in the barn, Dan. It was laying on the residence address with two flat tires and cobwebs on the steering wheel." He tipped a wink at Ballard; they actually had spent two hours digging the guy out of the woodwork by convincing a relief mail carrier that they were telephone repairmen.

"Oh." Kearny sounded almost crestfallen. "The client thinks the MacDonald woman who embezzled those negotiable bonds skipped—"

"Her new address is 6316 North Rosebury, St. Louis, Missouri."

"I . . . see." Then Kearny's voice became triumphant. "What about the Wellman Toronado, huh? The client's really *screaming*—"

"Toronado's on the two-bar, Dan. I'm looking at it right now."

Ten minutes later, slouched in the rider's side of O'Bannon's Chev Caprice with a headache, Larry Ballard wondered why O'B was the only person he'd ever met who could leave Dan Kearny speechless. Hell, here was Ballard, twenty-five years old, half an inch under six feet and weighing 184 pounds; but when Kearny cut loose, he just hung on grimly, like a barnacle on a rock. There was O'B, forty-two years old, just touching five-eight, 155 pounds, whose only admitted sports were bar whiskey at night and steam baths in the morning. But *he* calmly ignored Kearny's outbursts as an umpire ignores heckling from the stands.

Was it because O'B had heard all of the world's sad tales at least twice, and had never believed any of them? While Ballard believed almost all of them?

"I thought you were going to tell me what files we have to work on the way home," said O'Bannon from behind the wheel.

Ballard studied the cases as the linked Caprice and Toronado sped southwest through the Sacramento River flatlands. There were two of them. First was a 1972 Cougar registered to a Dorothy Soderberg, last known address of 458 West D street, Dixon. Client was Fairfield First National Bank.

"Where the hell is Dixon, O'B?"

"Little burg twenty miles down the road."

Orders were REPOSSESS ON SIGHT, which meant they didn't have to talk to anyone, just grab. If, of course, they could spot the car. Fairfield, home of their client bank on the Cougar, was a somewhat larger town another twenty miles beyond Dixon. Fairfield was also where the second case was located.

But first, *la* Soderberg and her 1972 Cougar; one case at a time was all his aching head could encompass. Then he realized that O'B, who had taken the Dixon overpass, was pulling off on the shoulder.

"What's the matter?"

"Let's drop the Toronado off the two-bar here by the overpass. We can pick it up again on our way back out after we work the Cougar."

Dixon reminded Ballard of his own home town. The same grid of north-south streets intersecting similar east-west streets; the same drive-in where the teenagers would congregate; the movie house, volunteer fire department, drugstore, bars, churches, supermarket; trees arching over frame-housed residential streets.

The address on West D was the O-Kay Kleaners. Closed.

"Let's try the volunteer firemen," said Ballard.

On duty was a teenage boy watching television. "That'd be the Soderbergs," he said. "Two blocks past the stop sign, right-hand side on the street. They just seeded the front lawn . . ."

They drove past the Soderberg house, circled the block, went down the alley. No Cougar. Dusk had fallen, lights were winking on; through the front window they could see a middle-aged man watching TV. He wore old-fashioned arm garters. A fresh-faced girl of high school age opened the door. "Dorothy Soderberg?" Ballard asked.

The girl's dark eyes slid away. "I . . . she isn't . . ." She turned toward the front-room TV-watcher. "Pops . . ."

The man asked them in as a gray-haired stocky woman came from the kitchen to appraise them with shrewd faded eyes.

"Dorothy owe you, too?" she demanded harshly.

Ballard hesitated, but O'Bannon said immediately, "That she does, ma'am, that she does. For the Cougar."

"She's our daughter-in-law," said Soderberg. "She's a *good* girl, but our son was killed in Vietnam, and Dot . . . well, she . . ."

Sorrow and scorn had been battling in the woman's face; sorrow lost. "Six weeks, and already she's dating other boys!"

"Now, Mother, these men aren't interested in—"

"Well, I don't care. She got the government insurance money, and she just went crazy spending. Big fancy car, running up to Tahoe weekends to ski . . ." Her shrewd eyes pried at the investigators. "If we tell where she is, do you intend to take that car away from her?"

Again Ballard hesitated; again O'Bannon spoke immediately. "Yes ma'am, that's what we're here for."

She looked defiantly at her sad-eyed husband.

"She's moved back in with her pa out west of town—three miles beyond the freeway overpass. Tudor, his name is. Can't probably read the mailboxes in the dark, but being it's a chicken ranch . . ."

It was dark out. As they drove back out past their parked Toronado, Ballard opened his window. Through it came clean fresh country air, the scent of new grass, the rich smell of damp earth, the . . .

"Whew!" exclaimed O'B. "That's *got* to be our chicken ranch."

From the road they could see lights; O'B played his spotlight across the barnyard, the coops, the open-ended machinery shed. No Cougar. They stumbled across a rutted yard; faint light through the screen door showed that a long and skinny man wearing bib overalls was sitting on the top step in the dark.

"Mr. Tudor?" asked O'Bannon.

"Yep." He uncoiled his length until he was an easy six-and-a-half feet tall, slat-thin. He thrust a thumb through his overalls bib. "Pointa fac', *Royal* Tudor. *De*scended of the Tudors of England. Lookin' fer Dot, ain'tcher? Men come, nights, it's gen'ally fer her. T'other one's too little yit—least, hope she is. Dot's in town . . ."

The screen door creaked open, then slammed three diminishing times. A girl about fourteen paused where the light from inside would clearly outline her shape through her thin cotton dress.

"Bet she's drivin' 'round after a *boy*." She turned to silhouette her precocious bustline. "Taldy *Ben*son. *He* works at the garage, an' *he's* got a new Corvette Stingray auto*mo*bile."

They returned to the scattered lights of Dixon, where O'B parked across from the drive-in and changed places with Ballard. "I've just got a feeling this is going to call for a finesse from the Old Maestro." He chuckled. "How did you like the little sister? Tobacco Rhoda. Makes you feel that old lady Soderberg probably had a point about Dot. She must wear those widow's weeds pretty lightly."

Ballard stiffened. "There she is."

A new Corvette had passed, tail-gated by a screaming red Cougar with a laughing blonde behind the wheel. She had good facial bones and wide-set reckless eyes. Beside her was a round-faced brunette.

"Next time around, join the parade."

Within a few minutes, Taldy Benson had pulled into the drive-in. As O'B had expected, Dorothy kept going.

"The Old Maestro is about to strike. Pull alongside."

Ballard gunned up even with the red car. The girl looked over, then slammed on her brakes and called through her open window.

"Why are you following us? We'll tell the police!"

"*Do*rothy *ba*by!" yipped O'Bannon.

"Who . . . are you?" But her wide, go-to-hell mouth was already quirking at O'B's lean, freckled, equally go-to-hell features.

"This is *Red!* Don't you remember? Tahoe . . ."

"Were . . . you the man who helped us with the tire chains . . ."

"That's right!" cried O'B. He muttered, "Follow us," to Ballard, and slid from the Chev. He opened Dorothy's door, in a moment was behind the wheel with the girls emitting shrill squeals of laughter beside him. Ballard heard, "Your Old Man said . . . in town . . . my car conked out . . . the overpass . . ."

But it wasn't until the taillights of the red Cougar, a quarter-mile ahead, brightened just behind the parked black Toronado that Ballard understood. He cut his lights, drifted closer in the dark. They were clearly visible by the glare of the Cougar's headlights. It was pulled up close behind the parked Toronado, and the brunette was out on the shoulder to check the match of the bumpers. That left Dot . . .

Ballard went slowly by, tires crunching gravel. O'B was gesturing. "Dot . . . check on this side, will you?"

Ballard pounded his steering wheel gleefully. The Old Maestro indeed! She had slid obediently out, was standing in the road to watch the bumpers come gently together.

"Don't scratch . . . car . . ."

She was out of earshot by then, but Ballard could see in the rearview mirror that the cars were nose-to-tail. Then the red Cougar moved. It shot *backwards*, away from the car that the open-mouthed girls had thought O'B was going to push. He paused momentarily before whipping a U-ie to speed safely away.

"Lady," he declared solemnly, "you've just been repossessed!"

× × ×

"Gailani Funeral Home." Ballard was reading aloud from the file. He stifled a satisfied belch; his headache was gone. "Client is California Citizens Bank, San Mateo Branch. Hmmm . . . Short $76.85 on the January payment, down $193.75 each for February and March..."

"And we're after a 1969 Oldsmobile hearse," mused O'B.

They had rendezvoused at a pizza joint in Fairfield. Ballard had driven the Caprice, with the recovered Toronado dragging behind on the tow-bar. In the unencumbered Soderberg Cougar, O'B had been half a pizza and a whole pitcher of beer ahead when Ballard finally had arrived.

"What are the instructions?"

"*Contact subject, collect all delinquent funds or store unit. No exceptions.* O'B, why in hell wouldn't a funeral home pay for its hearse?"

O'Bannon shrugged. "Maybe the guy's got expensive tastes. Let's hit the residence address first; he's probably home this time of night."

It was just after midnight when they pulled up across from the rambling ranch-style house. Ballard parked his linked vehicles behind the Cougar, joined O'B on the walk. A dog thundered inside. O'B punched the bell, to be rewarded with a female voice asking who it was.

"Sorry to bother you so late, Mrs. Gailani, but it's important that we speak with your husband."

The dog growled softly. The woman said, through the closed door, "He's down at the shop, finishing up some work"

"The *shop*?" muttered O'B as they returned to the cars.

Gailani's Funeral Home was a fine new box of aluminum, glass, and Permastone, set off Massachusetts Street between a hospital and a branch bank. It looked like a liquor store with pretensions. Ballard made a loop through the hospital drive to end up behind the red Cougar. He grinned as he noted the name of the bank next door. Fairfield First National. Talk about coincidences! In the mortuary's blacktop lot gleamed a row of three hearses. O'B jerked a thumb at them.

"I'll check if it's one of those—you go talk to the man like the instructions say. Remember, cash only."

"Hell, O'B, he won't have cash tonight."

O'B winked. "I've always wanted to repo a hearse."

The night bell brought forth a fortyish man in white shirt, no tie, and black trousers. His shoes and his eyes gleamed blackly; his hair was too black to be convincing. Ballard was assailed by the rolling chords of an organ and warm air cloyed with too many flowers.

"Mr. Gailani?"

"Yes." His voice was a well-oiled baritone.

"I represent the San Mateo Branch of California Citizens Bank." The subject maintained his oily beam, so Ballard said in a harder tone, "About the Oldsmobile hearse."

A frown marred Gailani's hitherto tranquil brow. "Ah. Of course. Come in."

A coffin was laid out in the same chapel as the organ; flowers and ornate candlesticks bearing dull orange tapers flanked it. The upper half was open to display a stern waxy profile, but it was the organ which made Ballard's hackles rise.

No one was playing it.

"Runs off a tape," beamed Gailani. "I've just been . . . ah . . . clearing up a few odds and ends . . ."

Which one was the corpse, Ballard wondered. An odd or an end?

"Ah . . . there was something?"

"There was—is—$464.35 in cash, Mr. Gailani, plus my charges. Or I'll be forced to store the vehicle."

"The Olds hearse? Oh dear. You didn't receive word I'd paid?"

"Do you have proof of payment, Mr. Gailani?"

"I spoke with Mr. Verdugo on the phone at four-thirty today." Ballard surreptitiously checked the case sheet; Verdugo was indeed the bank zone man who had assigned it. "I asked if my check for the payment had arrived, and he said it had." Gailani frowned. "He said investigators from a . . . Kenny Associates? Kearny? That was it, Daniel Kearny Associates, were on the case, but that he would call them and tell them to close their file."

Ballard sighed inwardly. O'Bannon had called in *before* 4:30, so they had not gotten the cancellation. No hearse-repossession for O'B that night. Gailani was shoving an open checkbook under his nose.

"See? There's the check stub, dated yesterday, made out—"

"I believe you, I believe you," said Ballard.

"I'm *most* relieved. You've no idea how I feel about my hearses." His mouth pursed erotically. "That Olds is a . . . mighty . . . fine . . . *piece* . . . OF . . . *IRON!* And business has been so *brisk* that I need it! Tomorrow the departed in the next room makes his final journey; there's a delivery to San Francisco early in the morning . . ."

Ballard paused outside to breathe air not cloyed with death's cosmetics. After 1 a.m., fifty miles to the city towing that damned Toronado. He pulled open the door of the red Cougar.

"O'B, the guy already paid—"

He stopped. O'Bannon was not within. Ballard swiveled to look at the three hearses in the parking lot, feeling distinctly unwell as he did.

Only two hearses were left. The Old Maestro had struck again.

× × ×

O'B would wait for him—but where? Fairfield was too small; the subject might see his repossessed hearse parked outside a bar and just take it back again. A bar it would be, of course. But . . . Yeah. A bar in the next big town south toward San Francisco. Near the freeway.

Ballard drove at the even 50 m.p.h. the law allowed vehicles with a tow, took Vallejo's Magazine Street off-ramp, pulled into a slanting blacktop lot beside a bar, from which he could swing the linked autos easily back onto the freeway. His hunch had been right. Behind the building, out of sight, was the hearse.

Inside, on a stool, was O'Bannon. "You have the makings of a detective after all, Ballard me boy." He clapped a dice box on the bar. "I'll fight you for last call."

Ballard sat down, shook his dice box idly until the bartender had departed for their beers. He said, "O'B, the guy paid."

O'Bannon's freckled face paled. Repossessing a vehicle on which the payments were current could lead to lawsuits; lawsuits led banks to quit using the investigation firm which got them sued.

"What proof did he have? Certified check carbon? Stamped payment book? Canceled check?"

"Just a check stub. But . . ." Ballard outlined the facts, concluding, ". . . and he obviously *had* talked with Dick Verdugo at San Mateo. Do we try to sneaky-pete the hearse back to his lot—"

"No way. I reported the repo to the Fairfield police; they'll have an official record of it." He brightened. "After all, Larry, check stubs aren't *proof* of payment. If we take it back to DKA, in the morning get to Verdugo before the subject does—"

"That isn't all, O'B." Ballard stared glumly into the mirror. "I moved the Soderberg Cougar to the mortuary lot, but—"

"So? Hell, one of us can pick it up tomorrow..."

"The bank? Next door? That's our client on that car."

Watching O'B take the news was like watching one of the Roadrunner TV ads, where the coyote ran into a wall and then cracked apart and fell into several separate pieces. Finally O'Bannon sighed deeply.

"So if our client happens to look out the window tomorrow and recognizes that red Cougar—which isn't exactly inconspicuous—he'll wonder why it isn't safely in the DKA storage garage in San Francisco where it's supposed to be, and . . ."

Ballard nodded. "Scratch one client."

"So I've blown both of them. And on St. Paddy's Day, yet." Then O'B shrugged and stood up. "Well, let's get the hearse down to the city. We can make out the condition report right here—there's plenty of light in the lot."

They circled the hearse, noting dents, scratches, general mechanical condition, the amount of usable tread left on the tires. They checked mileage; extras such as power steering, brakes, seats, windows; the condition of the interior upholstery. That left the itemization of all personal property found in the vehicle.

"I'll check the back end," grunted O'B.

But when he drew aside the curtains behind the seat, there was one of the long pauses of the sort Victorian novels delighted in characterizing as pregnant.

A casket reposed in the curtained hearse.

Ballard began, in a hushed voice, "You don't suppose . . ."

O'Bannon lifted the display half of the coffin's top. He shone his flashlight within. They craned forward, then pivoted to look at each other. O'B lowered the lid reverently.

"Now *that's* what I call personal property," he breathed. Then he snapped his fingers, began rummaging through the glove box. "Just a second, I thought . . . yeah." He read aloud, *"George: consign to Eternal Rest."* He looked up at Ballard. "Gailani said they had one to deliver to San Francisco, didn't he? There's an SF directory in the Caprice . . ."

Larry Ballard returned riffling the Yellow Pages. "Here it is! Eternal Rest Funeral Home, Geary Boulevard at Twelfth Avenue. But we can't just—"

"We sure as hell can't store it in the personal property lockers at the office." O'Bannon rummaged again, came up with a chauffeur's cap. He touched the visor with a diffident finger. "Call me George."

× × ×

Eternal Rest was to be found in a narrow rose-colored building flanked by a florist's shop and a bank parking lot. An alley slanted up between the florist and the mortuary to a small concrete loading platform with double doors. Ballard was beside O'Bannon in the hearse; the Chev and Toronado were parked a black away. At 3:30 a.m. the boulevard was deserted and dark.

"Now, as the Great White Father says, we shall play it by ear."

O'Bannon backed the hearse's long shining shape up the alley. Cap in place, he mounted to the double doors and tapped on the glass with his ring. Finally the single caged light bulb over the platform went on, a bolt snicked, handles clanked, and the doors opened outward. A short dumpy man appeared, egg-bald and wearing a rumpled morning face armored with bad breath.

"You guys are early enough." He shivered, clicked porcelain teeth together. "Which one's this?"

"From Fairfield," said O'Bannon with a picturesque yawn.

"That'd be Anna Osborne—died all over the cake at her daughter's wedding reception. Chapel B. Lemme get my shoes on, this cement's cold."

When he returned, Ballard and O'B had the rear doors open and the casket slid out on its oiled telescope runners. The three men wrestled it onto a wheeled dolly. Then the two detectives stole quickly away.

"Like falling off a log," chortled O'B as they drove away. He sobered. "After we dump this and the Toronado at the storage lot let's find an all-night Turkish bath. We have to be on Verdugo's phone when he comes into the office at eight-thirty."

Four hours later, at 8:20, they arrived at the DKA basement rumpled but refreshed. Along the left wall were the field agent cubicles; along the right, banks of screened personal property lockers into which Anna Osborne would not possibly have fit. As they entered, the sliding glass door of Kearny's office at the far end of the basement opened to let his massive jaw emerge. It was followed by Kearny. Kearny was beaming, like a spitting cobra about to spit.

"You lads are up bright and early," he said toothily.

"You know us, Dan. Company Time is Company Money."

"I'll bet you fellows repossessed a Cougar from a little girl named Dorothy Soderberg up in Dixon last night, didn't you?"

O'B and Ballard exchanged glances. O'B cleared his throat. Dan Kearny beamed invincibly.

"And you know what? Fairfield First National Bank has been on the horn. Our clients. Miss Soderberg came into their Auto Contracts at eight o'clock— beat on the doors until they opened them up. And she *paid off that car!* In cash. And *now*—she wants her car. *Right now* she wants it. AND I SUPPOSE YOU HAVE THE CAR DOWN HERE—"

It was O'Bannon at his finest. He cut in airily, "Tell them to look out the window."

"DOWN HERE AND . . . . What?"

"Tell our client to look out of his side window and he'll see the Cougar parked in the lot that's . . . ah . . .next to the bank."

"But . . . how did you . . . .."

O'B spread deprecatory hands. "I *knew* she'd pay it off this morning, so I left it there. We had a long chat with her before the repo—right, Larry?"

Ballard had trouble with some obstruction in his throat, but finally nodded.

"Right," he got out.

Kearny looked from one to the other, rapidly, like a tennis spectator. Dammit, O'Bannon had done *some* unorthodox thing that . . .

The intercom buzzed. He snatched up the closest phone, listened to Giselle from the clerical offices above. He nodded, eying O'B and Ballard malevolently. When he spoke, there was honey in his voice.

"Tell Mr. Verdugo that we have the field agents on that Gailani repossession right here. Yes. Assure him that any charge-backs will come right from their salaries . . ." He said crisply to O'Bannon, "Take extension three."

O'B picked up the phone as if it were booby-trapped, but his voice bubbled with carefree *bonhomie*. "Dicky Verdugo! How's tricks, reverend?"

He listened, nodded, then finally spoke with virtuous horror. "A *corpse?* In the hearse *we* repossessed? Dicky, I can *personally* assure you that there's no corpse in that vehicle. And . . .."

Kearny jerked his own phone back to his ear. Dammit, O'Bannon *couldn't* be getting away with it after all! If . . . He heard Verdugo speaking.

". . . real *relief*, O'B. A stray stiff would make some real *waves*." Admiration filled his voice. "What I can't figure out is how the hell you *knew* that guy's check was rubber, and repossessed the hearse anyway. I mean, he conned me *plenty* on the phone yesterday. It was only when our Vallejo branch called this morning that I found out he's been sailing kites all over Solano County . . ."

Kearny had no stomach for further listening. He tossed the receiver in the general direction of the phone and stalked majestically back into his cubbyhole, slamming the door behind him hard enough to rattle it on its padded runners. Once safely alone, he plucked a cigarette from his pack with outraged fingers, then flopped in the chair behind his big blondewood desk.

By God, how in *hell* did O'Bannon do it? Pull all sorts of cute crap, ignore proper procedure, give a younger man like Ballard every sort of bad example— and come out rosewater. St. Paddy's Day, that had to be it. What had Giselle called it? O'Bannon's Saint's Day?

He puffed furiously at his cigarette, stubbed it out, lit another. And there would be more to come, he knew. The redheaded Irishman would try to ram an eye-popping expense account from the Sacramento foray down his throat. And expect him, Dan Kearny, to swallow it.

Yes, and even *that* wasn't the worst of it. Hell no.

The *worst* of it was that Dan Kearny would.

FILE #9: FULL MOON MADNESS

Preface

In the preface to the previous story, I mention how bad I felt about getting sore at Fred Dannay for rejecting that story on the grounds that it dealt with two cases at once. In the fullness of time, I was getting all sentimental and warm and gooey with delicious guilt feelings.

Well, that didn't last long. Because I did it again. In checking through my case files for repo adventures that would translate into good File Stories, I came across two repos that were each a lot of fun, but neither of which I felt could stand alone as a 5000-word story. So I combined them in a longer story I titled "Double-Header." In "The O'Bannon Blarney File" I'd had O'B and Larry Ballard working the cases together; in "Double-Header" I had each man independently working his own repo, but I intercut the cases into a single short story.

I did it again—and Fred did it again. Again he rejected the story out of hand, on the same grounds that he'd used before: he wasn't going to have two separate repos in one story.

This time I didn't shop the story off to another market. I just stuck it back in the folder and forgot about it. I had sold a script to the popular TV crime drama Kojak, *and it had won the MWA Edgar for Best Episode of the year. This got me more television assignments, and then film assignments. Francis Ford Coppola bought film rights to my novel* Hammett, *and hired me to write the screenplay. I was enamored of this new kind of writing. In wanting to learn how to do it as well as I could, I virtually quit novel- and short-story writing for several years.*

In 1976, when I did get around to doing another File Story for EQMM's *new Managing Editor, Eleanor Sullivan, it was an entirely new story: "File #10: The Maimed and the Halt." I had finally admitted to myself that Fred had been right and I had been wrong: "Double-Header" hadn't worked as a single story.*

As it developed, I didn't rewrite it as two separate stories until 1983, when I sent Eleanor the cleanly separated halves of the original story. She published the Ballard half as "File #9: Full Moon Madness," in February 1984, and published the O'B half as File #11 that July.

Meanwhile, "Full Moon Madness" has another distinction: it is the first appearance of Beverly Daniels, who goes on to become Larry's friend and lover in subsequent DKA stories and novels.

FILE #9: FULL MOON MADNESS

Beverly Daniels opened one big blue eye and for the first time in months wished she were in love. Then she moved a shapely sun-browned dancer's leg under the covers and felt Caliban's solid inert weight against her knee. She flexed the leg. Caliban complained.

"You're a clown," she told him unfeelingly.

Caliban's square whiskered face came into view above the tumbled covers. He yawned prodigiously, stretched fore and aft, and padded up to sit on her chest and purr.

"Get your tail out of my eye," Bev said.

Caliban sprang over the edge of the bed and was gone on silent cat feet to the living room, where he already had discovered a strategic windowsill giving him total command of the street below. Bev swung her legs out of bed, padded barefoot through the new flat with its new paint smell, to the kitchen to make coffee.

Why was she thinking rather wistfully of sleeping with someone besides Caliban? Her last boyfriend had been a disaster. Maybe it was being twenty-five years old and doing sensible things like moving two blocks from work, and investing in her own business. Or maybe it was the full moon or something. She put coffee into the inverted paper cone and started heating water. The full moon unleashed all sorts of craziness in people.

Or maybe it was just that the tavern was taking every cent she could raise, she was two payments behind on her car with a third coming up and the bank was going to do something about it very shortly, and she had no shoulder to cry on.

Maybe she'd go open up the bar early. Maybe some really cute guy would come in.

× × ×

Larry Ballard would once have been characterized as a really cute guy. Twenty-five years old, just under six feet tall, conditioned like an athlete, with a thatch of sun-whitened hair shading even features. Watchful blue eyes. Then the language had changed, and he would have been called a real hunk. It had changed again, and he now probably would have been noted as a very fine unit. He opened his frayed lace curtains to look across Lincoln Way to the fog-shrouded morning reaches of Golden Gate Park, and wished that he had time to find someone to fall in love with.

Maybe next week. He settled down in his broken-down old easy chair, a steaming cup of exquisite coffee balanced on the arm—he gave his coffee the same care Chippendale had given his sideboards—and considered twenty-three open files screaming for action and reports. Daniel Kearny Associates investigated almost anything involving people, money, or chattels, in any combination, and DKA (Head Office, San Francisco, Branch Offices in All Major California Cities) expected twenty-four-hour first reports, with written updates every three days.

Ballard had spent the last five days investigating some abalone up the coast. His files were a mess.

He put the assignments into sequence by address—only in detective stories does an investigator work one case all day long—and found he was looking at a REPO ON SIGHT on a yellow 280-Z. Since the chick was supposed to live over in North Beach but was gone from there, and was supposed to work in a bar on Lincoln Way just a mile from his apartment (but the car never showed up there), she was first up.

In his run through his cases, he missed a file on something called Full Moon Madness, which had a key stapled to the assignment sheet and somehow had gotten sandwiched between two other files in his Hold folder by mistake.

× × ×

Dan Kearny was a compact, late-forties, hard-bodied man, with a tough square face, an iron jaw, hair, and mind, and a nose that once had met, with considerable force, something harder than itself. He slammed down the phone receiver in his basement cubbyhole at DKA. Cal-Cit Bank was threatening to give all future fieldwork to the competitors unless something happened on Full Moon Madness *right now.* He jabbed the intercom button so hard he broke a fingernail.

"Full Moon Madness," he said into it.

"I beg your pardon?" said Giselle Marc, upstairs in her office in the narrow old Victorian on Golden Gate Avenue which once had been a specialty cat-house but which now headquartered DKA. She was a wickedly lean and leggy blonde with soft lovely features and a hard lovely mind.

"A rock group that has a Maserati Bora Coupe from Cal-Cit Bank, thirty-four thousand owing on it, three payments back, they ran off the bank's man . . ."

"Oh, *that* Full Moon Madness."

"It was assigned to Larry Ballard *five days ago* and there isn't even a report in on it yet." Sudden decision entered his voice. "Have the girls hold my calls, Giselle. I'm going out on this one myself."

× × ×

Last time Ballard had been in the place it had been a run-down dump with three or four rummies draped over the stick like laundry left out in the rain. Now there were green hanging ferns, brightly polished back-bar mirrors, Tiffany-style lamps, and old photos opening faded black-and-white windows on a San Francisco long dead.

The petite girl behind the bar was the same shade over five feet that Ballard was under six, with cornsilk hair as pale as Ballard's, sharp-featured, and exquisitely made under a sweatshirt and slacks. She moved like a dancer and gave him a smile he felt all the way to his toes.

"What can I get you?"

"A yellow Datsun 280-Z," said Ballard with an inward sigh at the cruelty of a fate which would let them meet this way.

The good cheer left her face. "And it was such a nice day." A little hope returned. "Look, we just opened the place last month, it's taking every cent I can scrape up. But . . ."

Ballard said sadly, really feeling sad for a change, "You know I'm going to have to store the car, don't you."

"You don't know where it is."

"You do."

She thought that one over for a while. "I'll get the keys."

Waiting, Ballard wondered wistfully whether she might be able to fall in love with him even though he had repossessed her car. Fall in *like*, maybe?

× × ×

Full Moon Madness was to be found at 24 Urbano Drive, a perfectly oval street just off Ocean Avenue which, before it had entered the city as an exclusive residential area, had been a racetrack. The area had then gone black, but Urbano had remained WASP black: six-figure mortgages, five-figure IRS estimate payments, Montessori School for the kids. A sprinkler system hazed silver across a kelly-green lawn as Kearny got out of his car. He checked the garage. The Maserati was locked inside. He felt no trepidation, even though the bank's man had been run off by the members of Full Moon Madness. In his experience, bank men tended to go all girlish and shy the first time they saw a lifted lip or a clenched fist.

The man of the house didn't look dangerous. He looked, indeed, like Reverend Ike used to look, his hair touched with a tasteful silver. "Full Moon Madness," he said precisely, "is a corporation."

"It is also three-months delinquent on its payments," said Kearny, dropping the amiability from his face and putting the repossession agency into his voice. "I will have to get the money now or store the unit."

Like-Ike got a very sad look on his face. "Unfortunately, brother, the car is not here now. My son, the Archangel Gabriel, is driving it. In astrology, the angel of the moon is Gabriel—"

"The car is in the garage," grated Kearny. "I have to store it *now*. No exceptions."

The ministerial-looking gentleman leaned closer and made a completely impossible three-word suggestion to Kearny, and then added, "No exceptions."

Kearny was about to remonstrate in kind when the door behind Like-Ike burst open and the Archangel Gabriel arrived. He was the size of a Forty-Niner front four, he had green hair cut in a mohawk, he was dressed like a Hell's Angel. He said nothing. He merely swung the tire iron he was carrying at Dan Kearny's head.

Kearny ducked. The tire iron made a coarse round dent in one of the wooden porch pillars. Kearny left with an alacrity perhaps not remarkable under the circumstances. The tire iron made a round hole surprisingly like that a .45-caliber slug might have made in Kearny's window just after he had slammed his car door.

"Sorehead," he muttered to himself as he drove away.

With the Maserati locked in the garage, nothing could be done right now—except remember to warn Larry Ballard that Full Moon Madness was indeed a little salty, just as the Cal-Cit field man had suggested.

× × ×

It had been a good eighteen hours for Larry Ballard. Now, at 1:48 in the morning, he had worked all twenty-three cases he knew he had open, had repossessed three more cars after Bev's, had finished typing his last report, and had found Full Moon Madness sandwiched between a couple of other files in his Hold folder. He would work that one first thing in the morning.

Oddly, he found himself strutting, leaping up and clicking his heels, as he crossed Lincoln Way to his car, his files under his arm. The moon was full, that had to be it. If the moon could cause a tide in a teacup, what could it do in the human body? But, then, as he started down Lincoln Way in a direction definitely not toward the office, he realized that he was going to try to talk Bev into going out with him after she closed up the bar. Could *that* have had something to do with his capering around under the big glowing moon?

× × ×

"No, you may not drive me home," said Bev in an offended voice. "You took my car away from me just this morning!"

"Then how about I walk you home?"

"Well-l-l." He was really a very foxy-looking gent. "How about you take me out for pizza?"

But as they pulled away from the curb, Ballard's radio suddenly crackled with released static energy.

"SF-3 calling SF-6. Come in, Larry."

Bart Heslip, another field agent and Ballard's best friend, with a detachable ghetto accent he could use at will. Ballard unclipped his mike from the dash and depressed the red SEND button.

"Who dat?" he demanded.

"Who dat say who dat?" said Heslip in return.

"Who dat say who dat when I say who dat?"

Heslip said, "Full Moon Madness. Dan Kearny says don't work it alone. They ran him off with a tire iron today."

Dan Kearny in the field? Working Larry Ballard's cases?

"Ten-four," said Ballard in a tight-stretched voice. He hung up the mike again. Beverly was staring at him.

"You wouldn't," she said.

"I would," he said.

"*Now?* With me along? Right *now?*"

"Right now," he said.

× × ×

"There it is," she said twenty minutes later. Excitement danced in her voice.

Lights and decibels now poured from the garage at 24 Urbano Drive. Full Moon Madness was hard at work, rehearsing. Bev was up on her knees, facing backward on the seat like a little kid as they drove by, gaping out the rearview window at the little red sports car parked almost in front of the driveway. As Ballard drove a little bit farther on and parked, Full Moon Madness took a break. They spilled out onto the driveway, beers in hand: the Archangel himself, two other black young men, a young white man, and a white woman vocalist in her twenties.

Ballard opened his door, the Maserati key palmed in one hand.

"They're right in the driveway," said Bev hollowly. "What do we do now?"

"You keep the motor running, you slide into the driver's side, you watch the Maserati in the rearview mirror. When you see it take off from the curb, you follow me."

"But wait a minute! This isn't what—"

He had slid out of the car and was gone with appalling suddenness into the night. She couldn't even hear his footfalls. Icy with fear, she played with the mirror until the little red car was centered in it. How did he think he could take it right out from under their noses this way?

Never taking her eyes from the little red car for even a moment, she sought inner tranquility from recalling great moments in literature from her college days. All that came to mind was Raskalnikov's ax descending on the old woman's head in *Crime and Punishment.* Even when a car pulled up alongside and thrummed its engine, she refused to move her eyes from the little red sports car for even an instant.

× × ×

Ballard had run bent-over to crouch in the shadow beside the Maserati, shielded from them by the car itself, which they luckily had parked over here across the street. The key worked perfectly. One smooth flow of movement had the door open, him into the car, and the door closed again to douse the interior light after only a brief gleam.

He wormed over under the wheel. The throaty growl of 330 horses through the four Twin Weber carbs was almost sexual. What a car! He pulled out abruptly, stopped beside his own car, thrummed the engine twice. The gleaming blonde head did not turn.

What was she doing—transcendental meditation? He had told her to watch the car in her rearview mirror. He slammed his hand against the horn and all hell broke loose.

× × ×

A horn blared and Bev jerked her head around and there was Ballard. In *another* little red car. *She'd been watching the wrong car!*

She yelped in terror and killed her engine when the Archangel Gabriel, like a giant black bat in his black leathers, landed on the trunk-lid of the Maserati. Two others were jumping into the wrong red little car. Ballard goosed the Maserati and the Archangel fell off. Two more were leaping and jumping around Bev's car like feral hounds. Gabriel had whirled and was tearing at her hood-latch now. She got the car started and started moving. He leaped on the hood to block her vision.

She screamed and slammed on the brakes. The red Porsche rocketed by in futile pursuit of Ballard as the Archangel shot off her hood, hit the street running, got ahead of his feet, and furrowed a lawn with his chin.

Her off-side door was jerked open and the woman vocalist's face came across the seat at her as if disembodied, hate-filled, mouth gaping, teeth gleaming vampire-like. Bev hit the face with her handbag as she gathered speed, and it went away again. Her rearview mirror showed her the woman bouncing around in the street, screaming curses.

Hitting 50, 60, 70, Bev went up this street and down that. Around this corner, around that, up hills and down, tires screaming, brakes smoking. Finally she pulled in at a curb, panting as if she had been running instead of driving.

She was parked on the top of a hill on a broad paved street without any houses. She'd never been so scared in her life. Or so lost. Or so alone. Only the red pinpoint eye of the intercom radio told her anything lived outside this menacing street.

× × ×

Ballard dashed up the stairs to the deserted second-floor clerical offices where DKA's big central radio transmitter was. He grabbed the stand-up mike and flipped the TRANSMIT lever.

"KDM 366 Control calling SF-6. Beverly, unclip the mike from the dash, hold it up to your mouth, push the little red button on the side, and talk into it! Then let go of the button so I can talk to you! Go!"

After a silence, there was a sudden answering blare of static which resolved itself into hysteria-tinged words.

"What kind of crummy date is this?" Bev shrieked.

× × ×

Dan Kearny stared at the tremendous pile of reports on his blondewood desk. Twenty-three of them, all signed Ballard, four of them repos. But *no* Full Moon Madness. What was the matter, was Ballard losing his guts for the rough stuff these days?

He slid open his little soundproofed cubbyhole door and yelled down the length of the garage to the field agents' cubicles. *"Ballard!"*

Ballard sauntered in shortly, the picture of male animal health, no pieces missing, none of those perfect teeth loose, no black eyes to spoil the deep tan of his manly features. Kearny's hand described a parabola over the reports.

"There's nothing about Full Moon Madness here," he said.

Ballard dropped a three-page report on the desk. Stapled to the original was a condition report. Signed. A signed condition report meant a repo had been effected, and that the vehicle already had been returned to the dealer who had sold it. Ballard had even attached an executed police report. Nothing left for Kearny to do except Close and Bill.

"Any, ah, trouble?" he asked very casually.

Ballard frowned. "Trouble, Dan? Laying right on the address with two flat tires and cobwebs on the steering wheel. They gave me the keys and a cold beer and waved me goodbye." Then he added breezily, "I'd love to sit around and shoot the bull with you, Dan, but you know how it is—busy busy busy."

Kearny made a small strangled sound in his throat.

× × ×

Bev unlocked the front door from inside at noon sharp. At 12:01, the door creaked open a crack and a tire iron with a handkerchief knotted around the end was waggling back and forth in the opening. The door opened wider to admit Ballard's blond head.

"Truce?" he asked.

"If you take me to supper tonight," she said. "And no pizza. A *good* place. Something fancy . . ."

That's when she spilled the glass of draft beer she'd begun drawing for him down the front of the new dress she'd worn to work in case he came by to apologize.

FILE #10: THE MAIMED AND THE HALT

Preface

When I came to work for L.A. Walker Company in 1955, they were already taking Cadillacs away on a sort of regular basis from the retired full-bird Army Colonel I call Colonel Buford Sanders in "The Maimed and the Halt." About once a year, Colonel Sanders would buy a new Caddy, balloon as much of the down-payments as possible, drive it out of the dealer's lot, and not be heard from again. Quite easy to do in that pre-computer age.

In due course we would get the assignment, Vi Ramezzano (Walker's premier skip-tracer, she was deadly) would dig him out of the woodwork, and some field man, usually O'B, would go find the car and snatch it back. If it was in some other state, we would assign it to a local agency. There was very little enmity on either part. It was a series of small skirmishes where both sides knew the rules of engagement. We all loved the game.

Once, Vi, posing as a previous employer with a W-2 to mail Colonel Sanders, called the colonel's brother's wife's parents in Vero Beach, Florida, hoping to con information out of them. But the colonel himself, there on a visit, answered the phone. When she started her pitch, he recognized her voice from previous encounters and said, "Oh, Vi, who do you think you're kidding?"

It was the only time I ever saw her blush.

When we broke away from L.A. Walker to found DKA, we sort of took the colonel with us. He kept grifting Cadillacs, we kept snatching them back. I even grabbed a Caddy or two from him myself. But I never got around to using him in a File Story.

Then at lunch with a couple of insurance investigators, I was told about a guy they had paid $250,000 to on what they were convinced—but couldn't prove—was a fraudulent personal-injury claim. The story about what happened during their last-ditch attempt to prove it was fraud after the money was paid was just too good to pass up.

And I had just the subject to give it to: our Colonel Sanders of Cadillac fame. And his adversary? Well, wily old battle-scarred O'B seemed the perfect field agent to square off against the larcenous colonel.

Let the games begin.

FILE #10: THE MAIMED AND THE HALT

The silver-haired man paused at the head of the wide steps of San Francisco City Hall. He stuck his silver-headed black walking stick under one arm while lighting a thin cheroot. With his ramrod posture and his ascetic face he looked like an old-time riverboat gambler.

Then he started down the steps.

A grimace of pain contorted his features. Only the cane, thumping heavily on each step, kept him from falling. His crabwise downward progress was agonizingly slow; it was like watching a film depicting torture.

"You say *he* drives his own car?" demanded Dan Kearny unbelievingly. Kearny was pushing 50 but didn't look it, a hard-jawed man with a graying mane of hair and a nose bent and flattened by a lifetime of not backing away from trouble.

"Special controls so he can operate everything with the use of only one leg." Meyer Edmunds was pudgy and perspiring, with thinning sandy hair and an insistent cologne. "That man has just finished ripping off Fiduciary Trust Insurance for two-hundred-and-seventy-five thousand bucks. Don't quote me, of course."

"This special car of his—a Cadillac, I suppose?"

Edmunds nodded glumly. "Colonel Sanders always goes first cabin."

"The Colonel Sanders of chicken fame?"

Patrick Michael O'Bannon had thrust his flame-topped head into the crowded cubbyhole office. He pulled the door shut so that outside lights would not dim the moving images on the tacked-up screen.

"Colonel Buford Sanders, USAF Retired," said Kearny.

"*Buford* Sanders? You mean *my* Colonel Sanders?"

"Now you know why I wanted you in here."

Edmunds rewound the film as O'B sat down. Daniel Kearny Associates (Head Office in San Francisco, Branches Throughout California) seldom drew the VIP of a big insurance company as a possible client; it had to be something unusual if their own investigators couldn't handle it. Meyer Edmunds started the film over again.

"O'B, this is everything our boys have gotten on him over the past two years—since the car accident."

The clips, spliced end to end, showed twenty continuous minutes in the life of Colonel Buford Sanders. Some in black and white, some in color, some of theater excellence, others hand-held from moving cars or through fences, one from over a transom.

In all of them Sanders was doing the same thing. Limping.

"Are you *sure* he's faking it?" asked Kearny dubiously.

"No, I'm not, Dan, and that's the hell of it. I'm the only one who still thinks it's fraud. We've already paid off."

The lights went up. Willowy blonde Giselle Marc had delivered the ice Kearny had called upstairs to clerical for, had collected O'B's wink, and had departed. Drinks were in hand and cigarettes were alight. It was one of the few times, O'B thought, that Kearny's office in the basement of the old Victorian which housed DKA resembled the fictional private-eye's domain.

"Nine Caddys we've repossessed from that man," O'B mused. His seamed, freckle-spattered face blueprinted a middle-aged drinker's life, but next to Kearny he was the best field investigator DKA had. "Nine. Spread out over almost ten years. And this is the first time I've ever seen even a picture of the man."

"We haven't had a new assignment on him in thirty months," said Kearny as he consulted the Colonel's bulging file.

"Since the car accident," Edmunds said.

"We picked up four Caddys in California," said O'Bannon, "two in New York, one in New Orleans, one—no, two—in Florida. He plays games, that man does."

"With all the computerized credit checking there is today, how could he even *buy* nine Cadillacs, one after the other, and—"

"He looks so good on paper that the dealers just never bother to run him through a credit-reporting service," said O'B. "He's retired military, gets a fat government pension, has a hell of an expensive home in Seacliff—"

"Dealers are required by law to get a certain percentage of the sales price," Kearny explained, "but no law says they can't balloon six or seven hundred of that down payment and get it a couple of months after delivery. The Colonel never makes the balloon payment and it usually takes us about six months to drop a rock on the new Caddy. By then the bank's eaten the contract and it's on contingent."

"But you have *always* made recovery," Edmunds persisted.

"What's to recover?" said O'B. "Last one I picked up had tires you could read through, a cracked block, no transmission, and a crankshaft dragging on the ground. The client took a twelve-thousand-dollar bath when we sold it for junk in Tallahassee."

Edmunds sighed and stood up. "Ten days of additional surveillance is all I've been able to gouge out of the head office. After that we close the file— unless you turn up *proof* of fraud."

"Why us?" asked Kearny.

"By now he knows all my people by their first names."

"If he blows his nose, I'll be holding the handkerchief," promised O'Bannon.

× × ×

DKA seldom got to mount a concentrated surveillance on a single subject, expenses unlimited. O'B brought in two other DKA investigators, Larry Ballard and Bart Heslip. Heslip was a black ex-boxer who found the same excitement in manhunting that the ring had once given him; Ballard was a late-twenties blond man, just under six feet and conditioned like an athlete.

"Remember, gents, even more important than uninterrupted observation is the fact that he *must never know*, must never even *suspect*, that someone's staked out on him. If he's been disciplined enough to never give himself away once during two years—"

"But he's already been paid off," Heslip pointed out.

"That's what we're banking on," O'B said. "But remember, this guy can *smell* a setup. He's gun-shy. I've been after him for ten years."

"Unmarried, I take it?" asked Ballard.

"Widowed seven years ago."

"Why not get a woman next to him and—"

"Four insurance-company baggers tried in the last two years." Baggers are female investigators, who often carry tape-recorders in their handbags. "But part of the basis for the high settlement was his claim that the accident made him impotent. Nothing stirring."

"If we could catch him shacking up—" Heslip shook his head and chuckled. "Man, two *years*? That takes *some* sort of cool."

"He's got it," said O'Bannon.

Ballard was thoughtful. "How about—oh, sports? Catch him in a gymnasium? On a weekend hike? Horseback riding?"

"He does go to a gym five times a week—for whirlpool therapy. They haven't caught him taking a weekend anywhere since the accident. Church every Sunday—stands in back because he claims he can't kneel down. Until the accident he didn't go to church at all."

That briefing was on the first morning of surveillance, which was carried out essentially from the garret room of an elegant three-story red brick whose owner owed Edmunds a favor. It was directly across Scenic Way from the subject's distinctive colonial revival with its hipped roof and second-floor Palladian window.

"With a house like that, servants, a gardener—what's the cat on the hustle for?" mused Heslip.

"You've answered your own questions. He *likes* the hustle."

"There he is," said Ballard from the window.

The sandbagged 600mm lens brought Colonel Buford Sanders up close enough, as he laboriously descended his front steps, to count the hairs in his mustache. Click. Click. Click. But O'B knew, even as he took them, that the stills would only support Sanders' claim. He checked his watch and stood up. "Time for his hour with the Jacuzzi bath. See you gents later."

The therapist, Wednesday lunch at the Presidio officers' club, back home. O'B had the daily routine down pat. It was on the return trip, with Sanders' special Caddy two blocks ahead, that O'B became aware of a new element in the equation. On Thursday, when he popped into the office after business hours, he told Kearny about it.

"Edmunds must still have one of his people second-guessing us, Dan. There was a second tail on Sanders for five blocks yesterday afternoon, and this morning a TV repair truck from a company that isn't in the phone book was parked down the street for twenty minutes. Ballard thinks someone was tagging him, too."

Kearny was already at the phone, having Edmunds paged out of the steam room at the Elks Club. In a few minutes he hung up.

"Not Edmunds. But somebody else at Fiduciary must have had a bright idea. Edmunds will check around, make sure the field man gets yanked." He was on his feet. "Let's go get a drink."

"You'll find this hard to believe, but I can't. I'm due to relieve Bart in half an hour."

"His girlfriend's back east visiting her folks—so Bart's got nothing better to do. And this *might* be important. You know how good Larry is with women: well, day before yesterday he spotted that good-looking maid of Sanders drinking at a little bar on Lincoln Way and Twentieth Avenue where Larry hangs around."

They shouldered into their topcoats, then paused at the front of the garage to set the alarms and lock up before going out into the chill September evening. "Coincidence?"

"Can't see it being anything else," said Kearny. "She just likes to drink—with anybody who isn't her husband."

"That covers a lot of ground," said O'B. "And her with two kids at home. Tsk, tsk. We'd better go speak to the girl."

× × ×

Jacques Daniels' was not a fancy way of speaking about a sour-mash bourbon. It was a bar owned by two partners, one a small lively balding Frenchman from Algeria who had given his first name to the place, the other a pert little blonde named Beverly Daniels. She and Larry Ballard were talking across the bar when O'B and Kearny entered.

The place was warm and cosy and intimate, with mismatched hardwood tables, myriad hanging ferns, and handmade Tiffany-style lamps that cast a soft stained glow across the drinkers. Lying on the bar beside Ballard were two DKA report forms with typing on them. Ballard tapped them with a finger. Kearny scooped them up in passing.

Ballard murmured, apparently to Beverly, "Brunette by the jukebox. Tailed her last night."

The two detectives pulled out chairs on both sides of the generously endowed black-haired girl. She had a long upper lip that showed precise incisors. Those in the lower jaw had a habit of worrying the protruding lip as she talked.

Her voice was sullen. "I'm waiting for someone."

"You weren't yesterday when Frankie Gallaway stopped at your table." Kearny had scanned Ballard's report for a few moments.

"Your name is Rosario Renucci. You've been a maid for four years on Scenic Way." O'Bannon hadn't read Ballard's report, but he could follow Kearny's leads easily enough.

"*Married* name," said Kearny.

"What sort of scam is—" she began.

"Husband is Ermanno Renucci," said O'Bannon.

"Hard-working guy at a foundry on Brannon Street. Hot-tempered but a home-loving sort of person. Salt of the earth."

"If you think you can—"

"Two children, minors, ages four and two." O'B shook his head sadly. "Rosie, Rosie, what are we going to do with you? Ermanno finds out—" He shaped his lips in a *whew* position, shook one hand back and forth as if he'd caught it in a car door. "Comes home sometime, finds those two sweet little kids all alone—"

Her face seemed about to crumble, but she was still in there trying. "You guys don't beat it, I'll call the cops."

"And we'll call Ermanno." Kearny began reading in a low voice from Ballard's report. "Eight fifty-eight p.m., Wednesday, September twenty-ninth, subject met male Caucasian subsequently identified as Frankie Gallaway at Jacques Daniels', a bar at eighteen-forty-nine Lincoln Way."

He raised cold gray eyes to her defiant face, then read again.

"At twelve-o-seven a.m. subject and Gallaway left the bar and proceeded to the residence maintained by Gallaway at the rear of two-nine-eight Parnassus Street. This is a detached cottage reached by a passageway alongside the main building."

"Anybody who says Frankie and I—"

"Subject and Gallaway entered the bedroom at twelve forty-four a.m., switched out the lights at twelve fifty-eight. The lights remained off until two twenty-two a.m. Subject left Gallaway's residence at two forty a.m., after embracing with Gallaway in the open doorway."

She broke, abruptly, with a half-smothered sob.

"Damn you, you got any idea what it's like? The relatives drooling over the kids? Washing clothes? And dishes? And getting them up and off to school and—"

" 'Tis far better to have loved and lost than to do thirty pounds of dirty laundry a week," observed O'Bannon.

"Look, what can I offer you not to tell Ermanno—"

"Tell us about your boss," suggested Kearny.

She seemed dazed by the abrupt switch. "My boss?"

"He ever make a pass at you?"

"Have other girls in there?"

"He's faking it, isn't he? The limp?"

"Doesn't limp once the shades are drawn, does he, Rosie?"

"How does he get the girls in and out without being seen?"

"How much extra does he give you to cover for him?"

"C'mon, Rosie. Give, girl. Give."

Ashen-faced and shaken, Rosie gave.

× × ×

It was five a.m. on Saturday. O'Bannon stifled a vast yawn and shivered despite the car heater. He was on Seacliff Avenue, a block from the subject's house—where, surprise, surprise, he'd found the specially equipped Cadillac street-parked when he'd arrived two hours before. And Colonel Sanders with that spacious three-car garage under the house!

It fit with what Rosie had overheard Sanders saying on the phone while making motel reservations. He'd be leaving the city around five a.m. on Saturday and would be there by midday at the latest. The clandestine nature of the departure, the fact that the motel was six or seven hours away from San Francisco—a probably five-to-seven bet, O'B thought, that a woman was involved.

He stiffened, crushing the paper cup which had contained his third coffee of the day. His rearview mirror had seen a figure moving with the now-familiar crabwise shuffle. He used the radio.

"SF-2 to San F-3. Do you read me, Bart, over?"

"Loud and clear." Heslip was, by prearrangement, in his car a quarter block from the subject's house.

"He's just getting into the Caddy over here on Seacliff."

"He back-doored me! If he's tumbled to the stake—"

"Just being cautious. I've got him now. Out."

"10-4, cat. Good hunting. Over and out."

O'B already had his car in motion, backing and filling as the subject got the Caddy started. O'B was going to try a front tail, the most difficult but also the most difficult to spot. It meant making an educated guess in which direction Sanders would be going. O'B only knew for sure it wouldn't be west—not unless the Caddy came equipped with water wings.

He pulled away ten seconds before Sanders did, took a left into the Presidio off 25th Avenue when he saw Sanders' left blinker go on. That made it easy. Golden Gate Bridge. North.

It was gloriously clear, going to be hot, with the not-yet-risen sun reddening strata of clouds above the Oakland hills before it burst out to make crinkled lead foil of the Bay through the whizzing orange handrails of the bridge. O'B sang with the radio while beating time on the steering wheel. He felt it: this was the day, this was the trip on which he was going to nail Sanders.

And then he almost lost him. Sanders abruptly veered across all four lanes into the old Blackpoint Cut-off which led across the tidal marshes to Vallejo. It took O'B twenty minutes to get turned around, pick him up, pass him, and drop into line an eighth of a mile ahead of him.

Tricky cat. Start out north, then go east. Actually, O'B liked it. Sanders *really* didn't want anyone tagging along.

O'B had assumed it would be northeast from Vallejo on Interstate 80, toward Sacramento, Tahoe, Reno, places like that. But instead it was 680 through Benicia to Concord, then down to turn east on 580 to Livermore, a hot dusty suburban sprawl supported by the nuclear research facility of the University of California.

✕ ✕ ✕

"With *breakfast*?" exclaimed the dismayed waitress at the diner he'd chosen after Sanders had stopped at a more elaborate restaurant a block farther off the freeway.

"The sun is over the yardarm *somewhere* in this world, me lhove. So I'll be havin' a wee dram o' the Chablis wit' me eggs."

Stopping at Livermore for breakfast meant south on the new Interstate 5, which was unsullied by such namby-pamby things as restaurants, truck stops, gas stations, or roadside cafés. It was a freeway for the traveler in a rush. O'B was content to tag along behind now—Sanders surely would feel he'd shaken any possible tail by this time. Showed how wrong a man could be.

"Looks like it's Bakersfield," mused O'Bannon aloud.

Which again showed how wrong a man could be.

Fifty miles south on Interstate 5, Sanders turned west on California 152. *West?* Up through the Pacheco Pass? What the hell went on?

An hour later, when Sanders turned north on U.S. 101 at Gilroy, O'Bannon knew. Tricky, indeed! The subject had in effect made a giant circle down through the great interior depressed valley which formed the heart of California between the Sierras and the Coast Range. Now he was headed up toward the Bay area again; if he kept going far enough, he'd be back in San Francisco.

He didn't go that far. At San Jose, 50 miles from the city, he cut over to Interstate 280 and left the freeway at Winchester Boulevard—in plenty of time to honor his motel reservation.

× × ×

The Cozee-Up Motel was a U-shaped affair triple-tiered around a fiercely blue swimming pool masked from the street and the skyway by dense shrubbery. A motel designed for assignations. O'Bannon, his wrap-around dark glasses leaving little more than his teeth showing, was delving industriously in the trunk compartment of his Chevy Caprice when Sanders came from Registration in his crabwise shuffle. O'B watched him into the first-floor corner room farthest from the office, then went in himself.

"Something on the first floor," he told the iron-eyed woman behind the desk. "As far from the office as possible."

"The *very* end room was just rented, but—"

"How about the one next to it?"

"The maid hasn't gotten—"

"I'll have a cup of coffee while I wait."

A window booth in the coffee shop gave him an excellent view of the subject's dust-filmed Cadillac. The cups of coffee gave him heartburn in the two hours before the motel's senior-citizen maid had snailed her way in and out of his room. The temperature rose as the sun climbed a cloudless smoggy sky. O'B resisted the siren lure of a liquor store two blocks away; he didn't dare break surveillance that long. What the hell, his room would be air-conditioned. As O'B was fumbling open his door, Sanders emerged from the adjacent one without a glance at the perspiring red-haired man. This gave O'B a chance to see that Sanders' bed was obligingly headed up against the partition between their two rooms.

He watched Sanders take a booth in the coffee shop, then got the necessary equipment from his suitcase. Using a quarter-inch cordless battery-powered drill and a long bit, O'B holed the wainscoting to come out under Sanders' bed. Through this hole he inserted a delicate high-resolution pencil mike, which he patched into a sound-activated Uher recorder. Fortunately the hum of the subject's air conditioner was not loud enough to activate the mike.

Sanders returned half an hour later, looking very drawn as he limped across the heat-softened blacktop. Probably that coffee, O'B thought. But what if the guy really *was* crippled? No, couldn't be. Otherwise, what was he doing in San Jose, a mere 50 miles from the city but arrived at by over 200 circuitous miles? Why back-door his own house at five in the ayem? Why street-park his car a block away?

O'B put the monitor plug in his ear. He heard the door opening. Bedsprings. A sigh of relief. Phone. Asking for a number. O'B realized he was holding his breath. Would it be to a woman?

"Hello, Cassie? Just got in. That's right. Of *course* I made sure nobody saw me leave. Couldn't have anyone—what? Yes. What I thought, too. All right. Pick you up about six thirty. We'll eat early so nothing interferes with our night together."

Just what they had suspected! Sanders had a little thing going on the side down here in San Jose and had sneaked down to celebrate the end of his long charade with a shack-up in a motel. Well, kiss your two-seven-five thousand goodbye, baby. Say hello to them cold prison walls.

Cold. Shouldn't have thought of that. How good an icy beer would taste! Send out for a six-pack? No. Didn't want to pinpoint the fact that he was staying in his room.

Sanders was now in the shower, but O'B's, incredibly enough, didn't work. The opportunity had passed anyway, as Sanders was finished now. O'B couldn't chance being under the needle spray when the subject might suddenly decide to take off.

Pool, sparkling and inviting a few paces from his door? No. Same problem.

He tried again to make his air conditioner work. On the blink. Sweat was standing on O'B's face. At least he could get some ice. He found a pitcher and carried it down to the ice-making machine beside the office.

The machine was busted.

He drank tepid tapwater from a styrofoam cup—the maid had forgotten to leave any glasses in his room. The water smelled of chemicals and tasted of fluorine. He kept on sweating.

He was rapidly coming to hate the guts of the man in the next room.

Thanks to the overheard phone conversation O'B was pouring sweat onto the sun-hot vinyl seat of his Caprice when Sanders limped out to the Caddy at six fifteen. Cassie, the girl on the phone, turned out to be a stunning blonde who lived in a ticky-tacky house off South Bascom Avenue that she'd probably gotten in a divorce settlement.

They ate supper at a very fancy place on East San Carlos near the San Jose State campus. From across the street it looked like cracked crab cocktails, rare roast beef washed down with a vintage burgundy, and chocolate mousse for dessert. O'B watched them through the restaurant window while choking down a food-chain's Quarter-Pounder made of a glutinous mass of chopped cow and soya meal. He ached for them to get back to the motel.

But they didn't go back to the motel. Instead they went south on Market Street, right out of the congested areas of San Jose into, surprisingly, traffic which got fiercer the farther from the center of town they went. Abruptly O'B realized he was buried in a crush of almost stationary autos with no idea of where the Caddy was. Left turn into Umbarger Road.

Which meant the Santa Clara County fairgrounds.

The traffic turned again, O'B willy-nilly with it. Dirt road now, a boy with a flashlight waving the Caprice into one of countless rows of parked cars. O'B got out. The Caddy was nowhere in sight. If Sanders had chosen this way to lose any possible tail, he'd sure succeeded. All O'B could do now was hope that the subject and his blonde had been headed wherever everybody else was going.

He was afoot in a field of sun-yellowed grass which had been trampled flat by thousands of feet. The crowd made no sense. Young and old, middle-aged and senior citizen, babes in arms, long-hairs and straights. A shirt-sleeve crowd, dogs yipping in the dust, transistor radios blaring country music.

Country music? He'd been shucked for sure. Sanders wouldn't be caught dead in this sort of hick crowd.

The mass was funneling down into a sluggish river of elbow-to-elbow humanity which flowed toward a central destination—a massive canvas tent pitched near the racetrack.

Carnival? No trucks or wagons, no midway, no barkers. But the other possibilities were almost endless. Rodeo? Boxing card? Tent revival? Country-western music show? Old-fashioned barn dance? Cattle auction or livestock judging? He seemed to be the only one in ignorance of which it was. Ah. Posters. But the crush of people was so immense that O'B couldn't see what the posters said. Everyone except him was excited, up, hyper, full of anticipation.

Inside at last, and not even an admission charge collected. Nothing but a portable wooden stage set up at one end of the vast canvas structure and a sea of folding chairs rapidly filling with people. No trapezes slung high overhead. No center rings for performing dogs or horses. No pens, no judging blocks for cattle.

And no Colonel Sanders.

O'B prowled and looked. A group of youngsters in white gowns with gold collars took their place on the wooden risers to the rear of the stage. They started singing "That Old Time Religion." He remembered, vividly and abruptly, sneaking under the canvas of revival tent shows as a kid. The Holy Rollers one year.

One big roll and save your soul.

He'd clapped erasers for a week after school at Mission High for chanting *that* one in the hall.

Tonight it was a good old fundamentalist preacher all in black urging the sinful to save their souls, wash themselves free from all sin, find God, testify to the Power of The Word.

O'B turned to go. It had been a ploy on Colonel Sanders' part to throw off any possible tail. Carefully skirting the traffic going to the tent revival, leaving O'B hopelessly mired in the jam-up. O'B's only edge was the pencil mike. Sanders wouldn't know about that. Once he and his blonde got going in that motel room—

The preacher had begun exhorting now, cajoling, arms thrust wide to gather in the sinful, his sweat flying, his voice hoarsening as it began to draw its inevitable emotional response.

"He hath filled the hungry with good things. Am I right?"

"You are right!" answered some voices from the crowd.

"He hath sent the rich away empty. Am I right?"

"You are *right!*"

O'B was working his way toward the exit to the parking lots.

"And I say to you, brethren, that The Shepherd rejoices more in the return of one lost sheep than he does in maintaining the whole flock. *Am I right?*"

"You are right!" With him now, a massive chorus.

"Then bring me your poor, and your maimed, and your halt, and your blind. And I will make them whole again. So saith the Lord. Brethren, *am I right?*"

"YOU ARE RIGHT!"

Now O'Bannon was breasting a tide—the old and the crippled and the sinful, moving down the aisle to bear witness to the Lord. He paused, looked back, and was transfixed. There, among them, was the familiar silver hair, the pain-lined ascetic face, the bobbing crabwise movement. O'B gaped.

Colonel Buford Sanders, angle-player and game-player and insurance defrauder, going down the aisle of a tent preacher's—

That's when the images began to flick before O'Bannon's eyes, frame after frame like a slide show. Images created from a blazing, belated, but now total comprehension.

Sanders, hiring *his own* private eye. Not a second tail on Sanders that Wednesday—*a tail on O'B!* And, later, a tail on Ballard. Identifying them, clocking their movements, habits.

So Sanders could pay his maid to stage a seduction scene for Ballard, after she had hung around Jacques Daniels' to make sure he would notice her.

Sanders, street-parking his Caddy where he knew O'B would spot it, once O'B believed Sanders was sneaking out of town at five a.m.

Sanders deliberately being too difficult to tail for suspicions to be aroused, but never so difficult that the tail could be lost.

Sanders maybe even paying the management to gimmick the air conditioner and shower in the room whoever was tailing him would be sure to rent. Playing games, as usual.

And Sanders playing *more* games—the non-incriminating phone call to the blonde when he *knew* his room would be bugged.

And now Sanders, head bowed beneath the hands of the Healer in a revival tent at the Santa Clara County fairgrounds, under the watchful eyes of 20,000 people.

"Oh, God!" cried the Colonel in a loud voice. *"Oh, God, I am saved! Oh, God be praised! Oh, see me, a sinner, SAVED!"*

And he cavorted around on the stage, shouting the power of the Lord, and hurled up the aisle at a certain red-haired man the cane he would never need again—as 20,000 throats roared their hysterical approval.

Oh, yes, the cane he would never need again. Because Colonel Buford Sanders, USAF, Ret'd, was $275,000 richer with no possibility of ever being charged with fraud. Some 20,000 good souls, and a trained detective besides, had witnessed the miracle of his cure. A trained detective who, under oath, could only testify as to what he had seen and heard. Who, indeed, had been carefully lured there for that very purpose.

It was too much. It was all just too damned much.

The Colonel embraced the Healer with tears of joy running down his face. As O'B had no doubt, he soon would embrace his blonde—with no worries about what a pencil mike from the next room might pick up.

O'B started to curse. Aloud.

Then the king said to the attendants, Bind his hands and feet and cast him forth into the darkness outside . . .

Yes, O'B cursed. Loudly and bitterly and blasphemously, from the very core of his soul, at how thoroughly and totally he had been set up and taken in by the Colonel. O'Bannon, the Unbeliever, cursed.

. . . *where there shall be weeping and gnashing of teeth.*

And they threw O'B out. Bodily.

FILE #11: JUMP HER LIVELY, BOYS!

Preface

"Jump Her Lively, Boys!" is a cautionary tale showing what can happen when a local municipality doesn't pay for its shiny new red fire truck. Because they are a government body, they think they are exempt from retaliatory action by the institution that loaned them the money—using the truck itself as collateral—to buy the fire truck in the first place.

Published in July 1984, as File #11, it is the second strand of what was once "Double-Header"—that infamous DKA File story that Fred Dannay rejected for EQMM *because it dealt with two separate repos in the same story.*

Like the hearse in "The O'Bannon Blarney File," the fire truck in "Jump Her Lively, Boys!" was one of those assignments that afterwards always left Dave Kikkert shaking his head and chuckling over how I managed to close out the case. Afterwards. At the time—well, at the time, his reaction was just about as I have depicted it in the story. When it came time to write this one up, the fictional O'B, that perennial thorn in Dan Kearny's side, was the only possible field agent to give it to.

For more fun, I inserted as the local Fire Chief my Commanding Officer from my draftee army stint at South Post, Fort Meyer, just a brisk walk through a covered underpass from the Pentagon. Virtually everyone stationed at South Post had his duty assignment there (mine was in the Office of the Chief of Information, News Branch, writing biographies of generals for news releases).

Unfortunately for Stenger, a spit-and-polish officer, most of us were draftees and a little less than awed by military traditions. In truth, Stenger was the bane of our existence. So I was delighted at the chance to pay him back fictionally as the equally spit-and-polish Fire Chief of Tamalara Valley.

FILE #11: JUMP HER LIVELY, BOYS!

Patrick Michael O'Bannon was on his sixth cup of coffee in a coffee shop catchily titled The Coffee Shop, a phony rustic redwood affair ten minutes north of the Golden Gate Bridge. O'Bannon's eyes were sky-blue, his hair the color of carrot juice, his face a mass of freckles. He looked thirty-five and was ten years older, looked Irish and was, looked harmless and wasn't. Next to Kearny himself, O'B was the best investigator DKA had. Which was as good as there was.

When he wasn't hung over.

God, was he hung over. And despite his throbbing head and the heat building up outside, he had to *work* today. Case files unopened in several days. One especially.

The unincorporated area of Tamalara Valley was $2,455.80 delinquent on its new fire truck. What did you do with one like that . . . ?

Dan Kearny sneezed. His icy gray eyes were bloodshot. He went around the massive blondewood desk in his soundproofed basement cubbyhole at Daniel Kearny Associates to retrieve the cigarette from where his sneeze had hurled it. DKA investigated most breaches of the Ten Commandments except those strictly theological, with special emphasis on recovery of wandering people, chattels, or assets for banks, bonding agents, corporations, and insurance companies.

Kearny blew his bent and flattened nose into his handkerchief. The middle of the sort of heat wave San Francisco was never supposed to get, especially in the summer, half the office staff out and Kearny himself feeling miserable, and here was O'Bannon off on a toot or some damned thing. No reports in *four* days.

He jabbed Giselle Marc's intercom button, unconsciously thrusting out his battering-ram jaw when she answered from her office upstairs.

"I told you two hours ago I wanted O'Bannon."

"He doesn't answer his radio, Dan."

"At home sleeping it off?"

"He doesn't answer his phone, Dan."

Kearny cursed aloud. In mid-curse, he sneezed. His cigarette flew from his mouth to land on the far side of his desk.

× × ×

The sun boiled and burned and throbbed and snarled down on O'B's pounding head from the cloudless Marin sky. Most of Tamalara Valley's houses hung from steep wooded hillsides, but the firehouse, a shedlike building painted an off-white with a wood-framed siren tower, was on a sleepy flatland residential street.

O'B, however, had eyes for nothing but that glorious red fire engine. His grandfather had remembered, from *his* youth, San Francisco's great old volunteer departments with such names as the Lafayette Hook & Ladder, the Knickerbocker Hose Company, the Monumental Volunteers, and O'B as a child had chased such red gleaming trucks up and down the Mission District hills on his bike. Two reels of red hose—*red!*—a grandly disdainful red flasher above the seats, another hose under the ladder racks…

"What are you doing, trooper? Raising *spiders*?"

O'Bannon froze. That voice! Those very words! Though more than a quarter century had passed since he last had heard them, he knew it had to be then Lieutenant Robert Stenger, U.S. Army.

Through the station's side door he could see a small shed with two military-style bunks. Flanking the bunks were two strained-looking young men in dark-blue uniforms, standing at rigid attention. Another couple of steps showed him a third man—mid-fifties and slight and pinch-faced and pink-skinned, like something left too long in the sun. He was just brushing the cobweb he'd found behind the radiator from the fingertips of his white gloves. His uniform was complete with jacket and gold insignia despite the scorching heat. He dropped abruptly to one knee and swiped a hand under the radiator.

"Look at this!" he yelled, waggling his smudged fingers under the cowering fireman's nose. "*Look at it!* How do you explain this filth under your radiator?"

"There *is* no explanation!" roared O'Bannon in a fair imitation of Stenger's voice. "Gig this soldier!"

Stenger whirled, bristling with outrage at the red-headed detective lounging against the door frame.

"Who the devil are you?"

"Patrick Michael O'Bannon. *The* Patrick Michael O'Bannon." He unfolded his arms and stepped forward. "Fort Ord. C Company. You were Company Commander and I was the soldier who always—"

"I remember you," snapped Fire Chief Stenger. His voice became almost a sing-song. "Undisciplined. Poor soldier. A hater of authority—"

O'B, who had been none of these but had had his fun all the same, proffered a DKA business card. "And now representing an agency representing Freuden Truck/Trailer Sales."

"Well?" glared Stenger. He was blinking rapidly, a mannerism O'B remembered from whenever Stenger's superior officers had chanced to be about. "You people have already made your sale to the Fire District. What more do you expect?"

"M-o-n-e-y." O'B leaned slightly forward. "Two payments of twelve hundred and six dollars and sixty-seven cents each, plus late charges of forty-two forty-six, plus DKA charges of one hundred seventy-five point seventy-five for a total of two thousand six hundred thirty-one dollars and fifty-five cents."

Stenger was aquiver with civil-service outrage. "This is an inexcusable—"

"It certainly is," agreed O'B.

"Only the governing body of Tamalara Fire District can authorize such a payment—which means the Fire Commission." His eyes gleamed in fanatical triumph. "Since the Commission meets on the twenty-fifth of each month, and today is the twenty-seventh, you'll have to wait."

O'B thrust a red-thatched, horrendously freckled face into Stenger's. O'B wore his jewelry-collector's smile. Jewelry collectors are the toughest there are, because they're usually told to go take the no-longer beloved's finger along with the unpaid-for ring. "You'd better convene 'em right away, reverend," he said.

"I'll do no such thing," snapped Stenger.

"Then you'd better pray for rain. Because if I don't get the money by tonight, your boys'll be walking to their next fire."

He tipped a wink at the two gaping young firemen and sauntered off into the shimmering midday heat.

× × ×

Kearny felt his cold getting worse. Larry Ballard was taking off up the coast after abalone, leaving him a field man short over the last weekend of the month—always DKA's busiest time. Ken Harper, one of his best if not brightest car-hawks, was in Mission Emergency getting his head stitched up where an irate woman had beaned him with a three-pound can of coffee. And he still couldn't raise O'B on the radio.

He went up the interior stairs to the second floor of the old charcoal Victorian that had been a cathouse in its wayward youth and turned toward the front office which overlooked Golden Gate Avenue through grimy bay windows. Lanky, beautiful, brainy, and blonde Giselle Marc, who had taken over as office manager when Kathy Onoda had died at twenty-six of a CVA, was on the phone. She cast a guilty look at Kearny over her shoulder, so he quickly twitched the phone out of her hand and bawled into it, *"O'Bannon, where the hell are you and why the hell haven't you reported in?"*

"I am reporting in," said O'B's voice reasonably. "I'm in the field, working."

"In a gin mill, drinking."

"That, too. Listen, reverend, how tough am I getting on this fire engine over in Marin?"

Kearny, who was unfamiliar with the file but would never admit it, rasped like a nutmeg being grated, "You can read the instructions, can't you?"

" 'Collect full delinquency plus all charges or repossess.' "

"That's how tough you're getting. Now where—"

"Just asking, reverend," said O'B cheerfully and hung up.

One couldn't leave the area unprotected in case of fire, thought O'B as he slaked his thirst at the Fireside, a congenial place of assemblage beside Tamalara Valley's southbound freeway on-ramp. But Chief Stenger couldn't get away unscathed. O'B remembered too much excessive K.P., punitive grease-trap cleaning, weekend passes canceled without warning, endless company punishment under Article 19 of the Universal Military Code. It was twenty-five years ago, but honor demanded...

"Boss or Liar's?" demanded a familiar voice, and Deputy Sheriff Jock Mahoney's ham-sized hand clapped him on the shoulder as he took the next stool for a cooling brew before returning to duty.

The bartender slammed down the dice cups, rattling, in front of them. And O'B, who had begun to formulate a plan, remembered that the Sheriff's Department furnished Tam Valley with whatever law enforcement was needed. Lovely. Lovely indeed.

× × ×

O'Bannon left the Fireside feeling marvelous. Jock owed him twenty bucks, his hangover was gone, the calming hush of evening was descending, and the air was cooling delightfully. He turned off Shoreline to peer through the soft warm dusk at the brightly lit frame building. A man who would white-glove a radiator doubtless would demand, as the heat of the day abated, a polished fire truck and a hosed-down concrete apron.

The still-dripping red engine was parked in a large puddle on the dirt shoulder of Poplar Street. O'B parked beyond, under a weeping willow's trailing fingers, locked his car, and strolled back to the gleaming truck. From the firehouse came the sounds of frenzied cleaning. He climbed up onto the broad leather seat and pocketed the ignition key. He slid lower to cock his feet on the polished dash, lit a cigarette, and stared up at the stars through the foliage arching the narrow street. When they came out to bring in their truck, they would find him waiting.

× × ×

Chief Stenger bounced and yapped, stiff-legged, around the fire truck like a flea-plagued terrier. The sheriff's car cast a revolving red glow over the proceedings. O'B tried to tip Jock Mahoney a wink, but Mahoney would not meet his eye to avoid bursting out laughing.

"Arrest him for what?" Mahoney asked, not for the first time.

"For stealing government property!" exclaimed Stenger.

"The keys to a fire truck? Hey, Chief, c'mon."

O'B condescended from his leather throne. "I am the legal representative of this truck's legal owner. It was parked on a public thoroughfare and I have taken possession until such time as the entire delinquency plus all costs shall be paid in cash."

That's when the siren started. There was a frozen instant of everyone looking at everyone else, then O'B rammed the keys into the ignition and switched on. Lights came on here and there around the truck. It fired up. He clapped the fireman's hat on the seat beside him firmly on his head. He gave the air horn a couple of tweaks. The two young firemen came running out, hastily pulling on their gear and gaping at O'B in astonishment. He waved his arm at them and remembered what his grandfather had said the foreman of the volunteer fire departments always yelled at their men. "Jump her lively, boys!"

They jumped her lively. The kid with the spiderwebs under his radiator yelled at O'B, "One of those redwood duplexes on Garden Way!"

"Get off that fire truck!" bawled Chief Stenger. He was jumping up and down in the street in impotent rage.

O'B barely heard him. He was thinking, out Marin to Northern, Northern to Glenwood, Glenwood to Eucalyptus, Eucalyptus to Garden. Got it! In his business, you couldn't find people if you couldn't find where they lived. He stood up behind the wheel and yelled at Mahoney, "Lead the way, Jocko me bhoy!"

Siren keening, Mahoney fishtailed away. O'B slammed the fire truck into gear and roared after him. Stenger, belatedly realizing he was being left behind, leaped for the rear of the truck. He missed. He landed face down, resplendent uniform and all, right where the truck had been an instant before. Right in the only mud puddle in Marin County.

× × ×

Three hours later, O'B was seated at a table in the echoing Tamalara Valley Improvement Club hall just off Missouri Valley Road. It was one minute before two o'clock in the morning. His busy fingers were soot-smudged and ash was streaked down his freckled face under slightly singed red hair. He had burst into a ground-floor bedroom to find a three-year-old girl cowering, eyes like a terrified rabbit's . . . But there, he thought, faith and beJaysus, let the lads have the glory. We old veterans of many a roaring blaze take heroism as part of the job.

"Young man," broke in a heavy, authoritative, angry voice, "I demand to know how much longer this farce is—"

"Twenty-six hundred sixty-five," counted O'B loudly, "twenty-six hundred seventy-five, seventy-six, seventy-seven—you foul up my count and the charges go up again—seventy-eight, seventy-nine—they're already fifty bucks more than this morning—twenty-six hundred and eighty..."

He looked up at the ten stony eyes of the Tamalara Valley Fire Commission, met in emergency session an hour before.

"You come up a buck-fifty-five short," he told them.

The chairman, who happened to be president of First Marin Bank and Trust in his spare time, had a jaw even Kearny might have envied. But forty years of banking had taught him to control his temper. His hand went slowly into his pocket, brought out four pennies. His murderous eyes slid to the lady beside him. "Edna?"

Edna was rifling her purse. "I've got—um—sixty cents. Sixty-five—"

"Charles?"

"A quarter."

"Walter?"

"Ah, two quarters—"

"David?"

"Flat busted."

The gimlet eyes bored into O'B's. "We're eleven cents short. Perhaps you'll lower yourself to accept this."

"I bet the chief has it."

Stenger leaped as if bee-stung to grub in his mud-caked uniform pants for a dime and a penny. O'B signed the receipt with a flourish.

The banker's face was grim. "This does not end it, young man. Once I—"

"You're the president of a bank, aren't you, reverend?"

He went bone-white with rage, but managed to choke out, "That is correct."

O'B laid one of his DKA cards on the table in front of the chairman. "We do most of our work for banks. Give us a call."

× × ×

Dan Kearny parked on Golden Gate where the tow-away had ended sixty seconds earlier. The fog was in, the heat was broken, but his head was still stuffed and his throat still scratchy. Yet and all, there were going to be some good moments to the day. O'Bannon was going to be reamed out as O'Bannon had never been reamed out before in too long a career of airy manners, doing things his own way, ignoring proper procedure, showing up at the office only when he felt like it, and never answering his radio calls. All because of the radio call Kearny himself had received on his way to the office this morning.

He had just sat down in his cubbyhole behind the blondewood desk and lit up his seventh cigarette of the day—a Kool because of his scratchy throat— when O'B traipsed in with a steaming cup of coffee in each hand. One he set down beside Kearny's ashtray.

"The Giants are at home today, Dan," he said brightly.

Manufactured fury glinted in Kearny's eyes as he thought of all of O'B's years of transgressions, but before he could say anything O'B broke in again.

"But I produce, Dan'l," he said, as if having picked Kearny's bitter complaints right out of his mind.

Kearny found a voice like a rock polisher at work. "Like you produced over in Marin County last night? I don't have all the details yet, but the president of the First Marin Bank and Trust was on the horn at *eight o'clock* this morning trying to reach me."

His intercom rang. He picked up and it was Jane Goldson, the perky English receptionist who handled set-ups and field-agent assignments in the front clerical office upstairs.

"I've got that bank president again, Dan. He's also the chairman of the Tamalara Fire Commission and apparently O'B repossessed a fire truck in Marin last night and drove it to a blaze. He insulted the fire chief, and then the Fire Commissioners, and made them convene in the middle of the night to pay the delin—"

"That bad, huh?" grinned Kearny. "O'B is right here—"

"That *good*. He wants to give us a couple of dozen assignments to work for his bank. He says he's never seen such aggressive field work by any investigator, and he says O'B saved a little girl's life and is going to be awarded a medal for heroism, and—"

"Give the call to Giselle," said Kearny hollowly.

He hung up, feeling like a very old man. O'B was on his feet. "I'm going to catch a steam bath before the game, Dan'l."

"O'Bannon, damn you, come back here to—"

But O'Bannon was gone. Kearny picked up his cigarette and stuck it between his lips. Instantly, he sneezed. The cigarette shot halfway across the room to land against the old, dry, very flammable wood of the baseboard. Cursing wearily, Kearny got to his feet and went around the desk to retrieve it. His cold, he just knew, was going to get much, much worse.

FILE #12: DO NOT GO GENTLE

Preface

I wrote this story after hours at Universal Studio in 1988. At the time I was Story Editor on a series of two-hour network movies starring Burt Reynolds that was called, collectively, B. L. Stryker. *It was one spoke of the ABC Mystery Wheel—the other spokes were* Columbo *and* Gideon Oliver. *Overall producer of the* Wheel *was Bill Link, the surviving half of the famous Levinson-Link team that created, among many other shows,* Columbo *and* Mannix. *At* Stryker *we had to come up with one two-hour movie a month featuring Reynolds as a Florida private eye.*

I commuted weekly to L.A. for four days "at the office" as it were, staying at a local motel and flying home for the weekends. Since Dori could not break free to fly down there with me each week, there was nothing to do at the motel after dark except watch television. Most nights I stayed on the Universal lot until two or three in the morning.

On moonlit nights I would often walk around the back lot, drinking it all in: here was Andy Hardy's house; there the alley where Robert Redford and Paul Newman worked their scam on Robert Shaw in The Sting; *way up atop that hill the Bates Motel where Anthony Perkins did in Janet Leigh during* Psycho's *famous shower scene. That one was especially poignant because my little cubbyhole was in the Alfred Hitchcock building.*

But most of the time, my hours after the cleaning ladies left at seven p.m. were spent at the computer. During my year with B. L. Stryker *I always did my assigned work as Story Editor first. But with all those late hours, I also managed to complete a novel (*Wolf Time, *1989), a feature film script that was never produced, a TV movie that was ditto—and "Do Not Go Gentle."*

Writing this tale inspired me to write 32 Cadillacs, *14 years after the previous DKA File novel, and 22 years after I started these stories for EQMM. "Do Not Go Gentle" reminded me of how much I had come to love the series and the characters.*

Sister John the Divine is based on Sister John Bosco, a joyous Dominican nun Dori and I knew. Phil Canuli is based on old-time pulp writer Phil Richards, another dear departed friend, and is a salute to my Dad who had died a few years before. Villainous Johnstone is based on a rapacious developer, also now dead, whom Dori and I once faced off against.

R.I.P., all of you.

FILE #12: DO NOT GO GENTLE

Giselle Marc cast a quick glance from sharp blue eyes at the man in the adjoining bucket seat. Giselle was a rangy blonde, thirty-two years old, with a beautiful face, wickedly long and shapely legs, and the kind of mind usually found in a corporate boardroom. The man was shorter than her five-eight, broad and heavy-armed, perpetually undershaved, with black curly hair sprouting from his open shirt collar. He had the face of a thug.

"Left at the next corner." His guttural voice was not making a suggestion. Giselle turned left. She'd faced her share of tight situations during her years with Daniel Kearny Associates (Head Office in San Francisco, Branch Offices in All Major California Cities), even had her own private-investigator's license framed on the wall above her desk. But this was the scariest it had ever been. "Park here," commanded the thug.

Giselle maneuvered the Tercel into the parallel-parking slot, cut the engine, put it into park, and set the hand brake. Her burly tormentor, not satisfied, made an impatient gesture.

"Pull out again. Go down to the corner and turn left."

Giselle did, checking her rearview mirror and over her left shoulder, and making an arm signal before pulling out into the traffic of San Francisco's Oak Street. She made the left, then left again, then, as directed, turned into the driveway. Her heart was pounding. She wished she hadn't quit smoking.

"Stop here," the thug ordered. "Right here."

Giselle stopped beside the ugly gray building, squat as the man beside her. He stopped writing on his clipboard and raised his head to look at her from fine Italian eyes.

"Congratulations, Ms. Marc," he said, a suddenly beatific smile illuminating his suddenly beatific features. "You have just qualified for your California driver's license."

× × ×

"You drive. You got the right," said Bart Heslip when Giselle came back out of the DMV clutching that wondrous Temporary Permit. A huge grin split his plum-black face as he held the car door for her. "You got the *duty.*"

"I knew this was going to be a mistake," she said darkly.

But she got in under the wheel wanting to clench a fist and yell *"Yeah!"* Sixteen years after she started typing skip letters for DKA afternoons after high school, she had her driver's license. At last she could work field cases of her own.

No matter that since Kathy Onoda's death she had been DKA office manager and much more valuable behind a desk than she could ever be in the field. She was sick of managing a p.i. firm specializing in auto repos and being unable to drive. She needed to be, at least part of the time, out where the action was.

But as she threaded her way back to the office along city arteries bulging with rush-hour hypertension, Bart started cringing, grimacing, ducking, and, finally, sliding down under the dashboard at each intersection.

"You are *not* funny," she told him with great dignity.

"Man, your driving sure is," he said.

× × ×

For a little while longer, DKA was in a narrow charcoal-suited Victorian which once had rung with the bawdy laughter of ladies of the evening and their wing-collar clients. Over the years Dan Kearny had fought mightily with the city to have it given landmark status because of its scarlet youth, but last month the state had had its way with the old lady.

Soon, 760 Golden Gate would be part of a parking lot for the civil servants at the State Unemployment Office. DKA would be moving south of Market into the old 11th Street laundry Kearny had bought, where the boys already were storing their repos.

Giselle paused at the head of the narrow interior stairway to DKA's second-floor clerical offices.

"Bart—thanks. I don't know how you put up with me." Heslip just grinned. He and Larry Ballard had spent countless hours patiently prepping Giselle for her test. Dan Kearny had tried it just once, after hours in the parking lot of a supermarket. He had immediately changed places with her, driven back to the office, and gotten out swearing never to get into a car again with Giselle at the wheel.

Maybe getting her license was partly about that: making Kearny accept her on the same terms he accepted the field men.

She went up the hall into the front office where the clerical staff and skip-tracers worked, and stopped abruptly. The office was draped with twisted rolls of crepe paper. Jane Goldson's desk, where assignments were usually logged in and files set up, now bore a huge cake with pink and blue frosting and a single candle the size of a three-cell flashlight upright in the middle of it. Across bay windows looking down on Golden Gate through grimy glass hung a double banner of foil letters:

CONGRATULATIONS, GISELLE
TODAY YOU ARE A MAN

Flanking the cake was a beaming Dan Kearny. Despite flinty eyes and flattened nose and concrete jaw, he resembled a mongoose that had just discovered an unattended nest of snake eggs. On the other side was flame-topped O'Bannon, inevitable drink in hand and leathery freckled face wearing a funereal expression.

"You screwed up, sweetie. You passed. Now—"

"Now," said Kearny, as if creating a knight of the garter, "you have your first field assignment. Over in Oakland—right in your own back yard."

He handed her a DKA assignment sheet with the name and address of the subject, the type of car, the client's name, and the specific instructions typed in. Just as Giselle had done thousands of times herself. But now it was *her* assignment. Now it was *her* field responsibility.

Kearny added airily, "It's a Repo on Sight. You can knock it off tonight on your way home, toss it on a tow-bar and drag it over here to the office first thing in the ayem."

But Giselle was staring at the assignment sheet, appalled.

The subject, the registered owner from whom she was to take the old 1980 Ford Fairlane, was a Sister John the Divine. For her first field assignment, Dan Kearny had given her a repo order on a Catholic nun's car.

✕ ✕ ✕

"Assigning a nun's car to me is just Dan's way of putting me down," said Giselle almost bitterly.

"It could have been worse," said Larry Ballard. He was Giselle's age and 180 pounds, just under six feet, muscular and blond, verging on male beauty except for a hawk nose and blue eyes that could turn to cold slate under slight provocation. "Like that airplane you assigned to me to repossess last year."

"Or those tires you wanted me to grab off that mean mother's truck-trailer rig up around Arcata," said Heslip. "The one always left a pit bull with migraine in his cab-over."

Along with Patrick Michael O'Bannon, they were waiting out the rush hour in Harry's Bar on Van Ness, a bit of a stretch from Harry's Bar in Venice but equally successful. O'B was fifty, two years younger than Kearny, and gray was creeping into his russet hair. As usual, he was three knocks ahead of everyone else.

"Okay my expense account without Dan seeing it and I'll ride shotgun for you."

"For a *nun?*" Giselle spoke with a scorn she didn't feel. "What's she going to do if she catches me taking it—rap me on the knuckles with a ruler?"

"Listen, some of the nuns I had in grade school—"

Ballard interrupted. "What's the address on it?"

"On Fruitvale down in the flats, I'm not sure just—"

Heslip waved a hand as if in pain. "Whooee! In that neighborhood you need a gun to make it home from the Safeway."

"I'll get by." Giselle checked her watch and stood up. "The Bay Bridge ought to be unplugged by now."

So casual. But tension in the gut, too—her *first field assignment*. A Repo on Sight at that. But, hey, how tough could it be to talk a sixty-five-year-old Catholic nun out of her car keys?

× × ×

Repossess on Sight meant no talking was necessary. Spot it, grab it. But the car wasn't there to spot or grab when Giselle finished doing the standard nine-block cruise of the area around the given address, a modest one-story convent—muthah-house, maybe, in that part of the East Oakland slums?

So—check the area in the morning again before making personal contact? Or knock on the door and ask Sister John the Divine for the keys? But the street was ill-lit, devoid of all pedestrians. It was scary out there.

The CB radio blared. She adjusted the squelch. Larry Ballard's voice came through, weak from reaching across the bay but still audible.

"SF-6 to SF-10, do you read? Over."

Giselle unclipped the mike and depressed the SEND button. "This is SF-10, over."

"How you makin' it?" When she didn't quickly respond, he added, "Listen, I remember my first night's solo."

"Never better—now," said Giselle, suddenly feeling it was so. "SF-10 over and out." The radio fell silent.

But parking and locking the car and starting up the narrow shrubbery-shrouded walkway, Giselle felt warm and invulnerable. She wasn't alone in the night. What a difference between controlling a case from the office and working that same case in the field. In the field there were—

Uncurbed dogs. Ugh. She used a stick and some leaves, but still imagined that the nose poking out of the peephole in the convent's solid-core wood door was crinkled at the smell of doggy delight lingering on her shoe.

"May I help you?"

"I'm sorry to bother you after dark like this, but is Sister John the Divine here?"

The face was small, heart-shaped, concerned, the voice soft. "Oh, I'm sorry —Sister is in charge of Oakland's program of Christian Visitors to the Aged and Shut-In. Her office is at Our Lady of Perpetual Sorrows, Thirty-fourth and Salisbury. By the junior high. She often spends the night there."

Driving the empty streets to 34th Avenue, Giselle reflected that now the nun's automobile made sense. But if she needed a car, she also needed to learn to pay for it. Not that the delinquency was going to hurt the good sister very much tonight. Our Lady not only had Perpetual Sorrows, she had under-the-building parking. Locked.

✕ ✕ ✕

When the electric-eye gate rattled up to let a car out of Our Lady's garage the next morning at eight-thirty, Giselle was there. She walked through, looking for the sister's car. No 1980 Ford Fairlane. Upstairs, an administrator with a clipboard and a face like those made by painting eyes on dried apples told her that Sister John the Divine was at "that awful Phil person's house" over on East 16th off Fruitvale.

Followed to given address, cruised the area for the subject unit took on a whole new meaning when you had to edge through feeding-frenzy commute traffic just to find the address. Especially when you had to think through each separate movement—shifting gears, depressing the clutch, applying the brakes —because you just got your license yesterday.

Scorched earth. At East 16th, the entire city block had been leveled. No houses, no trees, no grass. No prisoners. After all these years as the best damned skip-tracer around, had she, Giselle Marc, been conned by a woman with a clipboard and a face made out of a wizzled apple?

In the next block were houses still standing. Deserted, lawns dry and brown, boards across the windows, but still standing. Facing the one still obviously occupied were three yellow bulldozers, their smokestack flutter-valves popping with discreet belches of fluorocarbon.

Giselle drove slowly by. Not her concern. No 1980 Ford Fairlane among the parked cars, two of which were black-and-whites with the uniformed blues leaning against the fenders, arms folded on their chests. A couple of dozen other people just standing about. Watching. Listening. Nobody who looked like a nun in the crowd—but in these days of relaxed dress code for the religious, what did a nun look like?

Still not her concern.

Strung on new metal fenceposts all the way around the shabby old frame house was a very heavy chain with a huge padlock on it. Standing in a wheel-barrow so he could straddle the chain, arms wide, haranguing those facing him, was a short fierce old man with silky white hair. That Phil person?

He reminded Giselle of her grandpa. A snatch of discourse through her window as she passed even *sounded* like her grandpa's.

"What is our crime? We want to refurbish these old but sound houses, with the help of city money and charity—and the donation of time and material by skilled builders!"

If she had learned anything studying for her M.A. in history from S.F. State —going to be a teacher then—it was that history repeats itself. Phil and his solitary defiance of change were doomed to failure. And were not her concern, anyway.

She circled the block. A new top-of-the-line Caddy had pulled up and a big, imposing man wearing a gray-wool suit worth the day's combined wages of the three 'dozer jockeys was getting out, waving a gold-headed walking stick.

Absolutely not her business. So Giselle parked and got out. Her grandfather was long dead, sure—but mightn't Phil know where Sister John the Divine could be found?

Gray-suit was brandishing his walking stick at the feisty old man. He was so much taller that he was just about face-to-face with the banty rooster in the wheelbarrow. Who was ignoring him, speaking around him.

"Each home will house a group of from six to eight elderly people, married and unmarried, both sexes together, shared chores and shopping, shared community rooms and activities. These houses will be integrated into the community at large, so the mixing of generations will be preserved."

"Shut up!" thundered gray-suit in frustration. "Get out of the way and let these men do their work!"

"Don't you mean let them rape, pillage, and burn?"

The big man's florid face congested with rage. Bristling brows and red jowls and Teddy Roosevelt teeth without Teddy's good nature. Tiger eyes without the nobility. A face without pity, without goodness, without hope. "The Oakland Housing Authority gave me a permit to—"

"Those bureaucrats? Those cowards? Those corrupt weasels? Because they gave you a permit doesn't make it right!"

"Excuse me," said Giselle.

Gray-suit whirled. "Who the hell are you?"

"Could you tell me—" She had been going to ask about Sister John the Divine. She really had. Instead, to her dismay she heard herself saying, "What's this all about?"

"Dignity," said Phil.

"Progress," said gray-suit. Then, so overcome by rage that spittle flew from his lips when he spoke, he whirled to the waiting policemen and yelled, *"Officers—do your duty!* Wheel this demented old bastard out of the way!"

The two cops moved forward—so did two of the 'dozer operators. The third held back, shaking his head. Gray-suit's face lost its satisfied look when Giselle got in their way.

"Lady," said the lead cop, "we're just here to keep the peace."

Giselle, who stood as tall as he, said, "Moving him is breaking the peace."

"They all left." He gestured at the leveled adjacent block. "Everybody else

in *this* block has left. The developer has a demolition order. He's got the right to—"

"He's got the *power* to. What about this old man's rights?"

"He's about exhausted them, lady."

Gray-suit butted in. "I've also got a contract to build high rise, low-income housing *for the elderly*. We're trying to help these people."

"By taking away their homes?"

"Better step aside, lady," said the cop.

For answer, Giselle turned and stepped lithely up into the wheelbarrow beside the old man. She linked arms with him.

"You remind me of my grandpa," she said.

"You remind me that beauty has not yet quite deserted this wicked old planet." The old man reached out his free hand across his body to shake. "Phil."

"Giselle."

Gray-suit had been rendered so apoplectic that he stepped forward with his walking stick half raised.

"My editor-in-chief would *love* you to do that," Giselle said.

"Press?" demanded the cop in a dismayed voice. "You're press?"

Looking over their heads, Giselle saw another cop car arriving, followed by two TV news vans bristling with antennas.

"And here come some more."

The cop car slid to a stop and the driver tumbled out. Well, not *exactly* a cop car. Black-and-white, all right, but no spotlight and no police-department decal on the door—just a faded spot where it used to be. And it was a 1980 Ford Fairlane.

And not exactly a cop driving it. As a matter of fact, a middle-aged nun in the knee-length habit and starched wimple of the Dominican. She bustled up to them and triumphantly slapped a sheaf of papers into gray-suit's hands. Her voice was cheery as a chickadee.

"There you are, Mr. Johnstone. A Temporary Restraining Order signed by good Judge Deiner himself. Nothing more is to be done until the Board of Supervisors' meeting next Monday." She looked up at Phil, limpid brown eyes dancing with delight. "You did it, Phil! You held them off until the cavalry got here!"

"With the help of my trusty scout," said Phil, intertwining blue-veined, knotty fingers with Giselle's.

Mr. *Johnstone*? Great. Just great. The guy she'd been mouthing off to was DKA's client.

The lead cop, leaning over Johnstone's shoulder to look at the legal papers, gave a shrug of resignation mixed with relief. In the background, the news anchor was positioned in front of the cameras to start her introductory spiel. Giselle clambered back down out of the wheelbarrow, unwittingly flashing a length of splendid thigh for the cameras as she did.

"Are you Sister John the Divine?" she asked as Johnstone moved away.

"Yes. And you're—?"

"Giselle Marc."

Sister beamed. "May I call you Giselle?"

"May I call you John?" Sister looked blank. Giselle added quickly, "I have a repossession order for your car."

"First, it's time for our elevenses," said Sister sensibly.

× × ×

The three of them had tea on the porch of Phil's embattled house. Johnstone had driven off in his gleaming Caddy in search of new blocks to level, the crowd had finally dispersed, and even the TV van and black-and-whites had departed.

"Death houses," said Sister John the Divine.

The respite, she had pointed out, was only for four days. The chain was still up and two out of the three bulldozers were still waiting there—the third, manned by the shame-faced youth who had hung back from the fray, had departed on its flatbed.

"When I heard about Phil's plight I looked into it," she went on. "Unlike Our Lady of Perpetual Sorrows, Johnstone's place will be run as a business, for a profit, with nursing wings and residence halls and paid attendants."

"Is that so bad?" asked Giselle. "If it doesn't want to go belly up, private enterprise has to make a profit."

Sister chuckled. She had a round, good-natured Italian face full of unexpected shrewd intelligence.

"By repossessing cars, for instance?"

"Something like that."

"Could you see me in one of those places?" demanded Phil, abruptly fierce over the rim of his glass. Their tea was a bottle of Seagram's Seven, a bottle of seltzer water, and a plastic bowl of ice cubes. Sister's was lemonade. "My Ellie died in this house fifteen years ago. I intend to do the same, because as long as I'm here I keep my personal identity."

"Phil is eighty-seven this year," said Sister with complacent pride, as if she had created him herself.

"I'm a congenital survivor—ninety-five out of every hundred persons born the year I was are dead. I've been a merchant seaman, a club fighter, a bartender, a pulp writer in the '30's—" Phil slammed his fist into his stomach. "I still feel the power of a sumo wrestler in my gut."

Sister John the Divine was leaning forward intently. "If the residents can't get to the community dining hall for supper a certain number of nights in a row, they're automatically transferred to the nursing wing and their room is given to the person on top of the waiting list. Being condemned to the nursing wing is like being condemned to die—most of them lose the will to live pretty quickly there."

"So in the non-nursing wing, most of their energies are spent on plots to help each other get to the dining room," said Phil. "And these are the joints people are *paying* to get into."

× × ×

"Damn it, your instructions were Repossess on Sight!"

Dan Kearny was in his cubbyhole office and Giselle was standing on the other side of his big blondewood desk like a schoolgirl called up before the principal. They'd had their share of arguments, even fights, over the years, but it had always been as equals. Giselle, after all, was office manager.

Now things were different. Now she was operating as a field agent. A repo man. Now Kearny's eighth cigarette of the morning was smoldering in an ashtray beside a cup of coffee long gone cold on top of a folder marked DIVINE, SISTER JOHN THE.

"Right there, see it? Repo on Sight. Those are the instructions on this file and I expect you to—"

"But she's not really delinquent."

" 'Not really delinquent.' " Kearny had started out as a repo man while still in knee britches, riding to his first repossession on a bicycle. He knew every trick in the book, and approved of almost none of them—unless he was pulling them himself. He shook his massive graying head in astonishment. "After all these years, Giselle, you fall for a line like that?"

"She's a Catholic nun, she's not going to—"

"I turn on the eleven-o'clock news last night, what do I see? The car you're supposed to be repossessing standing at the curb with the keys in the ignition and the motor running. Are you jumping into it and driving away? No. You're—"

"The motor wasn't running," said Giselle.

"You're standing in a wheelbarrow with some old guy you have to move from place to place with a shovel and—"

"Phil Canuli has the heart and lungs of an athlete." Giselle snatched up his cigarette and ground it to shreds in the ashtray. "He doesn't touch these filthy things."

"This from a former two-packs-a-day woman."

"Phil says senility is a lack of will power." Unbidden, she sat down and shook a cigarette from his pack. "He says—"

"I thought you quit again."

"I'm starting up again." She stuck the cigarette between her lips. "He says that exercising the mind with thought is like exercising a muscle with weight. He says—"

"What else do I see? My field agent *telling off* my client. When he calls for a progress report, do I tell him that the lanky blonde with the long legs is the field agent assigned to *repossess that screwy nun's car for him?*"

"It's all phony, Dan!" she blazed. "Her car is an old police car she calls Kojak 'cause all the sisters used to watch him on reruns. The guy at the corner gas station gave it to her to drive." Kearny leaned forward to fire up her cigarette. "But then Johnstone—this is a class-A bastard, Dan—offered him a lot of money for the pink slip. Once Johnstone had title to the car, he turned around and assigned it to us for repossession."

"Exactly!" Kearny slammed the flat of his hand on the desk, making the file jump. "Damn it, Giselle, we're hired to find people or chattels and bring 'em back alive—or at least in operating condition. You don't want to do that, you're in the wrong!" He slammed the desk again. "I can't believe I'm saying these things to you! To some green pea right off the pod, sure, okay, but to *you?*"

Giselle was on her feet, smearing out her cigarette. Kearny was still yelping.

"I *knew* I shouldn't let you out into the field. You're even starting to *sound* like Ballard."

Larry Ballard had a not entirely undeserved reputation for getting involved in the subjects' personal problems. Giselle had even reamed him out for it a few times herself. But this was different. She opened the sliding aluminum door with its one-way glass and started out into the garage proper.

"I need reports in this file," Kearny called threateningly after her. Then he yelled, *"And bring me down a cup of coffee!"*

Once she was gone, he stared moodily at DIVINE, SISTER JOHN THE. Sure, you could strike a match on his own conscience, but Giselle was different—she bled a lot. And now she'd gotten it into her head that the client was evil and the subject a saint.

Maybe the old guy and the nun *were* getting screwed—but that wasn't DKA's problem, right? With sudden decision, he tore the extra assignment sheet out of Sister John the Divine's file and punched a set of numbers on the intercom phone.

"Larry, get your butt in here. I've got a hot one for you."

× × ×

About thirty of the attendees at the informational meeting in the rec room of Our Lady of Perpetual Sorrows were Sister's Visitors—those who went around to help aged shut-ins. The rest were a mixed bag of the elderly—some in wheelchairs, some with canes, some as spry as people half their age.

One handsome boulevardier of ninety-three, who kept kissing Giselle's hand and patting her bottom, sang "O Sole Mio" in the flawless Italian of his youth. Twin sisters in their seventies did a tap-dance routine. Sister played the piano while the punch and cookies were served. By this time over a hundred people crowded the modest hall.

Sister opened the meeting.

"You all know there is a Board of Supervisors' meeting on Monday, during which the question of Phil Canuli's home and the other houses in that block on East 16th will be discussed and a decision made as to whether they will be torn down or not. We hope that as many of you as possible will attend the meeting and give moral support to our cause."

She stepped down. Phil took the mike.

"Why do I want to hang on to my home in a world of homicidal maniacs, where the midnight gunbutt on the door is a threat to every citizen? Because when you quit fighting back you're already dead. They just haven't buried you yet."

Larry Ballard came in. He looked around, saw Giselle in the back of the room, and went over to sit beside her.

"Some turnout," he said, low-voiced. What was he doing here? she wondered uneasily. What was Dan Kearny—?

Phil was saying, "Builders build. Developers destroy. The developers are the enemies. Once we get a builder behind us—"

Suddenly she saw it all. Kearny had realized she wasn't going to take Sister's car away from her, so he had called in Larry Ballard to do it.

"Sister's car is stashed in Phil's garage. Locked in with a big padlock. Try and get it and—"

"Hey, what are you talking about?" demanded Larry, too hurt to be really hurt. "Did I ask about the car?"

"You didn't have to. I know the way Dan's mind works."

The door opened again and Johnstone came in, accompanied by a handsome, whitely smiling priest in his thirties. He had crisp shining black hair with glinting blue highlights, that wash-and-wear smile, and the aggressive physique of a man who spent more time on the racquetball court than on the parish building fund.

Johnstone detoured to tower over Giselle as the priest went up between the ranks of folding chairs toward the front of the room. Johnstone began, "Now, you dumb broad, you'll see how—"

"Uh uh." Larry Ballard was up and between them. He gave Johnstone's necktie a little jerk, almost yanking the big developer's chin into his chest. "Nice tie."

Nice. Good word. It *was* kind of nice, Giselle thought, to have Larry around for the heavy breathing. She'd had her fill of *mano a mano* malarkey the day before. Ballard released the tie. Johnstone, livid, made little putting movements with his walking stick. Ballard shook his head.

"You want to end up sitting on the point of that thing?"

Up in the front of the room the priest was saying, smiling, "I'm sorry, Mr. Canuli, but I didn't authorized the use of this facility for this meeting tonight. I've already spoken with the bishop and with Sister's mother superior—"

Phil, not understanding they had already lost that round, was hanging on to the microphone. "How much did Johnstone promise the diocese for you to back him up?"

But Sister John the Divine had a stricken look on her face—she knew what Phil didn't. She said hurriedly, "If you would stay and hear what is being said, Father, I'm sure—"

The priest smiled. "I'm sorry, Sister, but you will be ordered not to testify at Monday's hearing."

From the mean triumph on Johnstone's face, Giselle realized this had all been planned. And from the absolute misery on Sister's, she knew it was working. Of course. Sister would have taken a vow of obedience. If her mother superior, with the bishop's concurrence, said she couldn't testify, she wouldn't.

But Phil had his jaw stuck out. "I'm a nobody who can say things a somebody wouldn't dare. You can't shut *me* up!"

The priest leaned down and twitched the microphone lead out of the wall socket. "I'm afraid I just did, Mr. Canuli." He turned to smile sadly at the people. "I'm sorry, folks, but we can't have Our Lady of Perpetual Sorrows facilities put to this sort of unChristian and disruptive use."

Phil raised his old voice to be heard without the mike.

"Everybody, come to the Supervisors' meeting on Monday—there they can't turn off the mike on me."

× × ×

That was Friday night. On Saturday morning, Giselle drove Sister around on her visiting schedule—with Ballard in the field, Sister's car stayed safely locked in Phil's garage—and then went in to the office because she knew Kearny always worked Saturdays. She stormed into his cubbyhole and told him off about assigning the car to Larry, then stormed back out again without giving him a chance to speak.

Then, paradoxically, she spent the rest of the day at her desk, catching up on neglected paperwork. There was a lot of it.

On Sunday, without avail, she tried to talk Sister into ignoring her vows of obedience. God, said Sister, unaware of any irony, would provide. Phil, of course, was undaunted.

"Well, damn it, Sister, *I'll* speak up! I won't let them treat *me* like a leper who's just crawled out of a manure pile! And if that worm Johnstone tries to stop me, I'll perform an autopsy on the living!"

Sister gave a little laugh that was almost a girlish giggle. "Phil, I'd rather you just stress that within each house, the residents will have private rooms for which they will be individually responsible. And that these houses of the elderly should, in turn, be integrated into the community at large."

Giselle asked, "Is the mixing of the generations so important, Sister?"

"Oh, very." She spoke with surprising heat. "Physical and mental deterioration quite often stems from old people being isolated from the stimulation of multi-generational contacts. They are rejected and cast off by their families—"

"And then they reject right back," said Phil. "Especially the young. Don't want 'em around. Scared of 'em. Too much life. So the old fools end up in deliberate self-isolation."

Sister looked at her watch. "My goodness, I have to get back to the convent for evening prayer!"

Phil was on his feet. "And I want to go down to the Eagle Inn for a buck-fifty braunschweiger sandwich and a draft."

"We'll drop you," said Giselle.

"I'd rather walk. Stir up the blood."

"Phil, in this neighborhood after dark—"

"Hell, woman, if I had a big nose I'd be Cyrano! 'I have ten hearts, I have a hundred arms, I feel too strong to war with mortals.' " He threw his arms wide and yelled at the top of his voice, " *'Bring me giants!' *"

Only Giselle noticed that the hand he brought out of his old Navy peacoat pocket was wrapped around a roll of nickels.

× × ×

"What can you do?" asked Kearny. "Two big guys just came up behind him and cold-cocked him right outside that skid-row honky-tonk where he had his sandwich and beer." He shook his head. "Damn! I didn't think he'd be in any—"

In any what? Giselle wondered. They were drinking coffee in her kitchen that overlooked Lake Merritt from West Grand Ave.

"But didn't anybody try to stop it?" she asked.

"A couple of months ago in L.A. fifty-three people saw a murder in a parking lot." Kearny's blunt features were disdainful. "Last week the case was dismissed for lack of evidence."

"That poor little old man."

"Vertebra in the neck looks collapsed, fracture over the left temporal bone, possible basal skull fracture."

"I don't know why, but that vermin Johnstone had it done."

"Yeah. You got any proof?"

"No, but—"

"Yeah." Kearny sighed and got to his feet.

She said thoughtfully, "If he *did* go after Phil, why didn't he go after me?"

"Ballard," said Kearny.

Then he was gone. For once she was speechless, feeling like every sort of rank creep for thinking that Larry Ballard was just there to repossess Sister's car. Phil had been beaten up because Kearny hadn't thought he was in any danger. Otherwise he would have put someone—probably Bart Heslip—on him the way he had put Ballard on her. That was why he had been disgusted with himself. That was why he had stopped by for coffee.

× × ×

The Oakland City Hall was on Washington Street downtown, and the Supervisors' Chambers was more like a sideshow than a hearing room. All that was missing were a troop of performing dogs and a marching band. Giselle arrived half an hour early but still was able to fight her way into the hearing room itself only because she was tall and had a sheaf of legal-looking papers in her hand. Sister John the Divine had saved her a seat.

"Did you hear about poor Phil, God save him?"

"Yes, I did, Sister. Is he—"

"They're worried about cerebral hemorrhage, which could kill him. I've been praying ever since I heard."

"And you still aren't going to speak?"

Sister's silence, miserable with conflicting loyalties and beliefs, spoke for her.

Giselle sighed and looked around. "What *is* all this?"

As expected, lots of old people. But also well-dressed matrons with beauty-parlor coifs, several priests, business types, contractor types—even the fresh-faced kid who had removed his bulldozer from the East 16th Street scene the previous week. And in the back of the room, the other two 'dozer jockeys.

"Interested parties."

When Sister added nothing further, Giselle waggled her fingers under the nun's quite memorable nose. "C'mon, give."

"Well, Father Frederick—he was at the meeting last—"

"Yes. The toothpaste ad."

Sister smiled, but acid tinged her voice. "Father Frederick pointed out to the conservative elements in the local hierarchy that unmarried old people of both sexes living together in the same house, as we envision our community idea, is shameless and immoral."

Giselle suddenly understood the blued-haired matrons. They would love Father Frederick—probably Father Freddie to that part of his flock. "And the business types?"

"If the houses should be saved, they want to turn them into commercially viable properties—boutiques, tea rooms, and the like."

"With Johnstone Construction doing the renovating, I bet," said Giselle. "He hasn't missed a trick, has he? The only thing he *won't* do is help old people live in their own homes."

The Speaker called the meeting to order. Johnstone appeared with an attorney whose head was skull-like and whose black tie was so narrow it looked like a line of ink running down the front of his shirt. The doors were left open to the hall so the overflow could hear the proceedings.

"We will first hear the Planning Commission report."

"Pursuant to the court's Temporary Restraining Order, we re-examined the legalities of the construction permit issued to Johnstone Construction for the razing of the existing structures at East 16th and Fruitvale, and for the subsequent construction of twin high rise structures for the housing of the elderly."

One of the two black women supervisors asked, "What is your *personal* opinion on the matter, Commissioner?"

The Planning Commission's man was in his thirties, slightly stooped. With his glasses and slicked-back hair, he would have looked the same at twenty and would look the same at fifty. He looked up at the members of the Board above him behind their long hardwood table and clutched the microphone more tightly. He swallowed visibly. He was about to give an Opinion. An Opinion was dangerous as a snake—no telling *where* it might turn up.

"The elderly are—um—*old*. They are—um—a problem for—um—Oakland. We—um—seek a final solution but—um—"

With an almost audible sigh of relief, he returned to his prepared text.

"But—um—the problem of the elderly has been handled in the past with the construction of professionally administered high rise buildings which do not cost the taxpayers any money. The Planning Commission can see no obstacle to demolition and construction as stated in Mr. Johnstone's permits."

Johnstone's attorney started to rise, but, surprisingly, the fresh-faced 'dozer driver was on his feet first and got recognized. He was in his mid-twenties, with the chunky, muscular body of many construction workers before junk food and beer take their toll. He clutched the stand-up microphone nervously and wasn't a very good speaker, but his sincerity came through.

"I was out there last week. When they were gonna tear down that old man's house. It was pretty sad. So I was glad when this lady helped him. Then the Sister come—came—with the restraining order and I got thinking about all the builders that I done work for. So I went around and got three of 'em to promise they'd donate time and men and materials to see those houses got fixed up right so groups of old people could live in 'em."

The black supervisor used her mike again. "Do these builders know that the City of Oakland has condemned these structures, so they are now city property?"

"Yes, ma'am."

"And they're still willing to go ahead with renovation?"

"As long as it's actually old people who get put in the houses when they're fixed up again—yes, ma'am."

She looked around at the other supervisors. "I believe this plan has merit. I believe we should explore it."

Johnstone's attorney tried again, but this time Johnstone clapped a big hand on the lawyer's bony shoulder and jammed him back into the seat. Then Johnstone strode to the mike instead.

"Mr. Chairman, distinguished members of the Board, concerned citizens."

He had an urgent, unpleasant voice that, however, carried plenty of punch. Giselle realized that she would be nowhere near as effective. If only Sister— Or if only Phil, with that fury in his gut that would melt steel—

"I object to this blatant favoritism of my competitors," said Johnstone. "My high rises are the only solution that makes sense. In today's violent society, the aged are helpless prey unless they are safely housed in high-security buildings."

Isolated, you mean, thought Giselle. As he proceeded, there was a slight commotion at the door, but she couldn't see what it was from where she was seated.

"Just last night, outside a brightly lit restaurant with dozens of people about, Mr. Phil Canuli, the fine, misguided old gentleman who has been opposing my building permit, was senselessly struck down by unknown assailants."

Giselle was on her feet. "You *bastard!*" she exclaimed under her breath. He had engineered the attack on Phil so he could use it to make his point *against* Phil!

Sister dragged her back down. "God will provide," she said almost tranquilly.

Giselle stared at her with amazement. The people were listening to Johnstone, mesmerized, but for her this was God's plan, this was the way the world worked. Or at least this was the way she was able to convince herself the world worked.

Johnstone said, "If we permit those houses to be renovated for habitation by groups of defenseless old people, this will continue to happen—"

"As long as *you're* around it'll keep happenin'!"

Giselle was on her feet. So was Sister. With interference being run by Bart Heslip and Larry Ballard, a wan and haggard Phil Canuli was there. They supported him across to the mike.

Johnstone said quickly, "Mr. Speaker, this man is obviously in no condition to—"

Heslip shouldered him aside and Phil grabbed the mike with both hands to keep himself upright. "Mr. Speaker—" his voice was surprisingly strong "—I demand to be recognized."

Giselle exclaimed loudly, "This is Phil Canuli, the man who was attacked last night!"

"Mr. Canuli, is this wise? You—"

"Not wise, but necessary, sonny," said Phil to the Speaker. He was deathly pale. He gestured at Johnstone. "This weasel is being so sweet about me you'd think we'd been sleepin' together."

Johnstone, face sheened with sweat, said, "I demand—"

"But he must be all colicky and fretful because here he thought I was out of the way so he could make out that the victim was the criminal, like his sort always do."

Giselle had grabbed Heslip's arm. "Bart, what in God's name possessed you to let him come here?"

"Let him? Dan put me on the hospital this ayem, just in case, and here comes old Phil staggerin' out the side door. Said he was going either here or to hell, so here is where we came."

Phil was saying, "He sent his mini-Mafia around to casually give me a touch of switchblade surgery, but they messed up."

Bart and Larry started working their way back to the door. Once there, they stood on either side of it with their backs against the wall.

"Are you charging, Mr. Canuli, that Mr. Johnstone was one of those who attacked you?" asked the Speaker.

"No." Phil clung fiercely to the podium. "I'm saying that he hired it done." He let go with one hand, and even though reeling managed to stay erect as he pointed. "It was those two bozos did it—and they drive 'dozer for Johnstone!"

Except for Sister John the Divine's, all eyes followed his pointing finger. The two heavy-set workmen were on their feet, panicked, plunging for the door. Which was suddenly filled by Ballard and Heslip.

Bart Heslip had won 39 out of 40 pro fights before realizing he was never going to be middleweight champ of the world and turning to private detection for his on-the-edge kicks. His man went down with a broken jaw and a bruised abdominal aorta from a lovely hook-jab-uppercut combination.

Ballard's sport was scuba diving, but four years before he had started adding three nights a week at a karate dojo out in the Sunset District where he lived. As his opponent started his first—and last—punch, Ballard delivered a truly stunning kick to his groin. The man fell on the floor and threw up.

Sister, ignoring all this, was at Phil's side, trying to support him until Giselle arrived, but he went down, taking both women with him. Somehow he found a raspy chuckle and enough breath to gasp out, " 'An hour or so before dinner, Monsieur de Bergerac died, foully murdered.' "

× × ×

Because he wasn't Catholic and had no cemetery plot, Phil was cremated. Because there wasn't much money, the service was held in his living room. Giselle brought over her Electrolux to get the place cleaned up for it—the Visitors from Sister's program furnished the food.

Several people gave eulogies and Sister did the reading—though not from Catholic liturgy. Instead, she chose that drunken Welsh poet whose thirst for booze had been exceeded only by his thirst for beauty. She read dry-eyed because of her total assurance that she would be seeing Phil Canuli again.

" 'And you, my father, there on the sad height,
Curse, bless, me now with your fierce tears, I pray.
Do not go gentle into that good night.
Rage, rage against the dying of the light.' "

Giselle turned away, blindly, to find Dan Kearny waiting for her just inside the front door.

"Oh, Dan'l," she wailed.

Kearny said, "Yeah, I know," and with an arm around her shoulders shepherded her out and across the lawn toward his company car. The chain and padlock were gone. So were the bulldozers. In their place were stacks of two-by-fours and a pile of plaster board under a tarp. And a new sign that had been put up just that morning after the Supervisors' decision had been posted.

"PHIL'S PLACE"
A PILOT PROGRAM FOR THE AGED
UNDER THE DIRECTION OF
THE RIGHT REVEREND SISTER JOHN THE DIVINE

"It isn't worth the cost," said Giselle bitterly.

"Maybe not," said Kearny, then added with grim satisfaction, "but Johnstone's going down for it. Once his two pigeons started to sing, not even his high-priced attorney could do much for him."

They had arrived at Kearny's car. He paused for a moment, then tossed Giselle the keys.

"Here," he said. "You drive."

JOE GORES: A CHECKLIST

BOOKS

MYSTERY NOVELS:

A Time of Predators. Random House, 1969.
Interface. M. Evans, 1974
Hammett. G.P. Putnam's, 1975.
Come Morning. Mysterious Press, 1986.
Wolf Time. G.P. Putnam's, 1989.
Dead Man. Mysterious Press, 1993.
Menaced Assassin. Mysterious Press, 1994.
Cases. Mysterious Press, 1999.

DKA FILE NOVELS:

Dead Skip. Random House, 1972.
Final Notice. Random House, 1973.
Gone, No Forwarding. Random House, 1978.
32 Cadillacs. Mysterious Press, 1992.
Contract Null & Void. Mysterious Press, 1996.
Cons, Scams & Grifts. Mysterious Press, forthcoming, 2001.

COLLECTIONS:

Mostly Murder. Mystery Scene Press, Pulphouse Publishing, 1992.
Speak of the Devil, 14 Tales of Crimes and Their Punishments. Five-Star, 1999.
Stakeout on Page Street and Other DKA Files. Crippen & Landru, 2000.

ANTHOLOGY EDITED BY JOE GORES:

Tricks and Treats (with Bill Pronzini). Doubleday, 1976.

MYSTERY SHORT STORIES

DKA FILE STORIES:

"File #1: Find the Girl," *Ellery Queen's Mystery Magazine* under the title "The Mayfield Case," December 1967.

"File #2: Stakeout on Page Street," *Ellery Queen's Mystery Magazine*, January 1968.

"File #3: The Three Halves," *Ellery Queen's Mystery Magazine* under the title "The Pedretti Case," July 1968.

"File #4: Lincoln Sedan Deadline," *Ellery Queen's Mystery Magazine*, September 1968.

"File #5: Be Nice To Me," *Ellery Queen's Mystery Magazine* under the title "The Maria Navarro Case," June 1969.

"File #6: Beyond the Shadow," *Ellery Queen's Mystery Magazine*, January 1972

"File #7: O Black and Unknown Bard," *Ellery Queen's Mystery Magazine*, April 1972.

"File #8: The O'Bannon Blarney File," *Men and Malice*, edited by Dean Dickensheet, Doubleday, 1973.

"File #9: Full Moon Madness," *Ellery Queen's Mystery Magazine*, February 1984.

"File #10: The Maimed and the Halt," *Ellery Queen's Mystery Magazine*, January 1976.

"File #11: Jump Her Lively, Boys!," *Ellery Queen's Mystery Magazine*, July 1984.

"File #12: Do Not Go Gentle," *Ellery Queen's Mystery Magazine*, March 1989.

OTHER MYSTERY SHORT STORIES:

"Chain Gang," *Manhunt*, December 1957.

"Pro," *Manhunt*, June 1958.

"Down and Out," *Manhunt*, June 1959.

"You Aren't Yellow," *Mike Shayne's Mystery Magazine*, January 1960.

"Sailor's Girl," *Man's World*, August 1961.

"Night Out," *Manhunt*, October 1961.

"The Mob," *Negro Digest*, December 1961.

"Muscle Beach," *Rogue*, March 1962.

"The Main Chance," *Gent*, April 1962.

"Trouble in Papeete," *Rake*, April 1962.

"Darl I Luv U," *Ellery Queen's Mystery Magazine*, February 1963.

"The Price of Lust," *Manhunt*, April 1963.

"Sweet Vengeance," *Manhunt*, July 1964.

"My Buddy," in a Camera-Arts Publication, 1965. The story sold (for $40.00) and was published, but I never got a copy of the magazine. I have no idea of when or where it appeared.

"A Sad and Bloody Hour, *Ellery Queen's Mystery Magazine*, April 1965.

"The Seeker of Ultimates," *Ellery Queen's Mystery Magazine*, November 1965.

"Kanaka," *Adam 10, No. 11*, 1966.

"The Second Coming," *Adam's Best Fiction*, 1966.

"Odendahl," *Argosy*, December 1967.

"Olmurani," *Argosy*, February 1968.

"The Golden Tiki," *Argosy*, June 1968.

"South of the Moon," *Argosy*, January 1969.

"Goodbye, Pops," *Ellery Queen's Mystery Magazine*, December 1969.

"Gunman in Town," *Zane Grey's Western Magazine*, October 1969.

"Quit Screaming," *Adam's Reader 41*, November 1969.

"The Criminal," *Adam 14, No. 12*, 1970.

"The Bear's Paw," *Argosy*, April 1970.

"The Andrech Samples," *Swank*, September 1970.

"Force Twelve," *Argosy*, January 1971.

"Trouble at 81 Fathoms," *Argosy*, June 1971.

"You're Putting Me On—Aren't You?" *Adam's 1971 Reader*, 1971.

"The War Club," *Argosy*, May 1972.

"Faulty Register," *Two Views of Wonder*, edited by Thomas N. Scortia and Chelsea Quin Yarbro, Doubleday, 1973.

"Watch for It," *Mirror, Mirror, Fatal Mirror*, edited by Hans S. Santesson, Doubleday, 1973.

"Kirinyaga," *Ellery Queen's Mystery Magazine*, March 1975.

"Rope Enough," *Tricks and Treats*, edited by Joe Gores and Bill Pronzini, Doubleday, 1976.

"Raptor," *Ellery Queen's Mystery Magazine*, October 1983.

"Smart Guys Don't Snore," *A Matter of Crime 2*, edited by Matthew J. Bruccoli and Richard Layman, Harcourt, Brace Jovanovich, 1987.

"Detectivitis, Anyone?" *Ellery Queen's Mystery Magazine*, January 1988.

"Dance of the Dead," *The Armchair Detective*, Spring 1991.

"Ishmael," *The New Mystery*, edited by Jerome Charyn, Dutton, 1993.

"Summer Fog," *Flesh and Blood*, edited by Max Allan Collins and Jeff Gelb, Mysterious Press, scheduled for 2001.
"Inscrutable," *The Collection*, Mysterious Press 25th Anniversary Anthology, scheduled for 2001.

MYSTERY SCREENPLAYS

Interface. 1974.
Hammett. 1977-1979.
Paper Crimes. 1978.
Paradise Road. 1978.
Fallen Angel. 1980.
Cover Story (with Kevin Wade) 1984-1985.
Come Morning. 1986.
Run Cunning. 1987.
Gangbusters. 1989-1990.
32 Cadillacs. 1996.

MYSTERY TELEPLAYS

High Risk (with Brian Garfield). 1985.
"Blind Chess" (*B.L. Stryker*). 1989.

EPISODIC TV MYSTERY SCRIPTS (1974-86)

Scripts for the following programs:
Columbo
Eischied
Eye to Eye
The Gangster Chronicles
Helltown
Kate Loves a Mystery
Kojak
Magnum, P.I.
Mike Hammer
Remington Steele
Scene of the Crime
Strike Force
T.J. Hooker

STAKEOUT ON PAGE STREET

Stakeout on Page Street and Other DKA Files by Joe Gores is printed on 60-pound Glatfelter Supple Opaque Natural (a recycled acid-free stock) from 11-point Times New Roman, a computer-generated version of a typeface designed by Stanley Morison and Victor Lardent in 1932 for *The Times* of London. The cover painting is by Carol Heyer and the design by Deborah Miller. The first printing comprises two hundred fifty copies sewn in cloth, signed and numbered by the author, and approximately one thousand two hundred softcover copies. Each of the cloth-bound copies includes a separate pamphlet, *File #9: Double-Header*, by Joe Gores. The book was printed and bound by Thomson-Shore, Inc., Dexter, Michigan, and published in December 2000 by Crippen & Landru Publishers, Norfolk, Virginia.

CRIPPEN & LANDRU, PUBLISHERS

P. O. Box 9315
Norfolk, VA 23505
E-mail: CrippenL@Pilot.Infi.Net
Web: www.crippenlandru.com

Crippen & Landru publishes first edition short-story collections by important detective and mystery writers. Currently (December 2000) available are:

The McCone Files by Marcia Muller. Trade softcover, $15.00.

Diagnosis: Impossible, The Problems of Dr. Sam Hawthorne by Edward D. Hoch. $15.00.

Spadework: A Collection of "Nameless Detective" Stories by Bill Pronzini. Trade softcover, $16.00.

Who Killed Father Christmas? And Other Unseasonable Demises by Patricia Moyes. Signed, numbered clothbound, $40.00; trade softcover, $16.00.

My Mother, The Detective: The Complete "Mom" Short Stories, by James Yaffe. Trade softcover, $15.00.

In Kensington Gardens Once . . . by H.R.F. Keating. Trade softcover, $12.00.

Shoveling Smoke by Margaret Maron. Trade softcover, $16.00.

The Man Who Hated Banks by Michael Gilbert. Trade softcover, $16.00.

The Ripper of Storyville and Other Ben Snow Tales by Edward D. Hoch. Trade softcover, $16.00.

Do Not Exceed the Stated Dose by Peter Lovesey. Trade softcover, $16.00.

Renowned Be Thy Grave by P. M. Carlson. Trade softcover, $16.00.

Carpenter and Quincannon, Professional Detective Services by Bill Pronzini. Trade softcover, $16.00.

Not Safe After Dark by Peter Robinson. Trade softcover, $16.00.

The Concise Cuddy by Jeremiah Healy. Trade softcover, $17.00.

All Creatures Dark and Dangerous by Doug Allyn. Trade softcover, $16.00.

Famous Blue Raincoat by Ed Gorman. Signed, unnumbered overrun clothbound, $30.00; trade softcover, $17.00.

The Tragedy of Errors and Others by Ellery Queen. Trade softcover, $16.00.

McCone and Friends by Marcia Muller. Trade softcover, $16.00.

Challenge the Widow Maker by Clark Howard. Trade softcover, $16.00.

The Velvet Touch by Edward D. Hoch. Trade softcover, $16.00.

Fortune's World by Michael Collins. Signed, unnumbered overrun clothbound, $30.00; trade softcover, $16.00.

Long Live the Dead: Tales from Black Mask by Hugh B. Cave. Signed, numbered clothbound, $40.00; trade softcover, $16.00.

Tales Out of School by Carolyn Wheat. Signed, numbered clothbound, $40.00; trade softcover, $16.00.

Stakeout on Page Street by Joe Gores. Signed, numbered clothbound, $40.00; trade softcover, $16.00.